A SERIOUS PERSON

A SERIOUS PERSON
ORLAND OUTLAND

alyson books
los angeles

© 2004 BY ORLAND OUTLAND. ALL RIGHTS RESERVED.

MANUFACTURED IN THE UNITED STATES OF AMERICA.

THIS HARDCOVER ORIGINAL IS PUBLISHED BY ALYSON PUBLICATIONS,
P.O. BOX 4371, LOS ANGELES, CALIFORNIA 90078-4371.
DISTRIBUTION IN THE UNITED KINGDOM BY TURNAROUND PUBLISHER SERVICES LTD.,
UNIT 3, OLYMPIA TRADING ESTATE, COBURG ROAD, WOOD GREEN,
LONDON N22 6TZ ENGLAND.

FIRST EDITION: OCTOBER 2004

04 05 06 07 08 **a** 10 9 8 7 6 5 4 3 2 1

ISBN 1-55583-864-2

CREDITS
FRONT JACKET PHOTOGRAPHY BY DAVID JENSEN.
JACKET DESIGN BY MATT SAMS.

ONE

This party is taking place at a venue so of-the-moment that it'll be out of business before you finish reading this sentence. It's a bar, but also a restaurant, but also a scene—the kind of place so hot that people go there to stand around waiting for a table they know they'll never get. Seeing, being seen—it's a way of life for a huge percentage of Manhattan's population. Me, I like being invisible, and I live in Brooklyn, which makes that easy. Or used to.

Is a party really such a treat? Why, honestly, do you spend hours planning and enacting your outfit, get the nervous jitters, check your hair and face and clothes before you walk in...sounds like a job interview, doesn't it? Your turn to shine, to grab the golden ring, the glittering prize. How is it everybody sees a party as a joyous occasion and a job interview as a thing to dread? They feel the same to me.

I don't hate people, just too many of them at once. Or music—I love it, it's my job, my love, and my life. God knows I don't hate good food and great booze. But to me, four people in a quiet restaurant is the apex of social encounters. My idea of hell, on the other hand, is a room filled with more people than any fire department would knowingly allow, music so loud you have to shout into the ear of the person next to you, and treacherous shoals of people whipping around, shouting "*Dah*-ling!"

This party is being thrown by a producer at CNN to celebrate, I don't know, twenty years of milestones or some such. Why am I here if I hate parties? Well, my significant other does regular cameos on CNN, and I was told I might get to meet Anderson Cooper, with whom I am not-so-secretly in love.

I shouldn't say "regular cameos"; it makes what Lyle does sound so…light. And believe me, I don't make light of what he does. Lyle is bright—okay, brilliant—and he's one of CNN's semi-resident experts on foreign policy. When the minister of transport of Bozinagovinastan is exiled to some former apparatchik resort town, Lyle's the one they call on to tell America and the world what that means to us. He hates it when I say that, Bozinetcetera; he always tells me America's greatest danger is its citizens' lack of interest in nations we don't visit recreationally and aren't at war with. So I told him that was a succinct and pithy explanation and next time he was on CNN he should use it. He did, it got a chuckle, and everyone was happy. Lyle's much more of a Serious Person than I am, but we get along pretty well anyway.

He goes to a lot more of these things than I do. We sit down every week or so with a list of all the invitations he's gotten and we grade them. "A" parties mean not necessarily A-list guests or A-level publicity, but events we should really both go to, either because it's a small gathering where I like the people, it's an art exhibit I'm curious enough about to brave the masses, or because it's just one of those damn things you have to go to with your hubby because people he works with expect it. "And where's _____?" they ask the hapless half of a couple who comes stag, the implication being that the other half should be here as a matter of course, save for some personal tragedy or pressing career demand.

"B" parties are the ones I might go to if I ever went into a "people-seeking" mode, which was rare for me even before I got on the omega-3s. Then we skip straight to the "F" events, things I wouldn't go to for all the tea in Dean & DeLuca. This includes pretty much anything with a red carpet, paparazzi, and/or a velvet rope. Luckily, Lyle doesn't go to many of these—senior fellows at the National Institute for International Policy Management are rarely called up to hobnob with Tara Reid or the Hilton sisters.

This being an "A" party, here I am. I've done my spousal duty by meeting and greeting and have retreated to a corner to drink a bottle of spring water while Lyle does what Serious People do: network. We had an interesting discussion about that one night—how much *work* it is to stay visible, especially in the media. If you really, truly want to drop off the radar, it only takes a few weeks of quiet time before your phone stops ringing, your e-mail contains only teen sluts on Viagra, your snail mail returns to bills and catalogs, and messengers stop dropping off goody bags full of Kiehl's products, Jamaica Blue Mountain coffee beans, and four-color pop-up invitations printed by the same Japanese concerns that do art books and museum catalogs. Especially in the great churning cauldron of New York media, every important person is constantly being introduced to fresh new faces eager for exposure. Stop reimprinting your face on Anna Wintour's memory and the new boys and girls will move into her head, remove your nameplate from the door to her memory of you, and put theirs up in its stead. I guess that's what I hate about these things—some people look at this kind of event and see excitement, glamour, fun. Me, I just see warfare.

But the good news is, when you're not anyone and you're not trying to be, it's easy to be left alone at this kind of thing. The only person who comes over to say hello is Craig, a make-up guy at CNN I know from when I've accompanied Lyle to the studio so he could weigh in on something before we went to dinner. Craig is probably the only person here who wants anything from me.

"So when's Christie's next video? Who's directing? Did you give him my name?" These are the first words out of Craig's mouth, and I have to laugh. He knows how these things work, and he knows I hate it, so he goes straight to the point. I've seen how most people do it, so subtle they're obvious—they sidle up to you while you're having a conversation with someone else, look thoughtful and nod at whatever you're saying, laugh at just the right moment, follow up your witty line with a slightly and deferentially less witty line of their own to get you to notice but not resent them, then wait until everyone else has drifted away, open a casual conversation in which they agree with pretty much anything you say, until eventually they get to their goal all along: the casual drop of a name, or talent—courtiers hoping you, the Sun King, will drop your garter so they can pick it up as the rest of the court looks on in envy. I hate it, I hate it when I see them doing this at these parties, and I hate it most of all when I turn out to be their Sun King, their gravy train, their golden ticket.

There's one nice thing about CNN parties: Nobody knows who I am. Unfortunately, when they find out who I am they almost always have an opinion, and the opinion of most Serious People other than Lyle (and, I like to imagine, Anderson Cooper) is that what I do is Not Good for The Culture.

"So what do you do?" It's the formal conversational opening of New York, the way people in the Midwest might ask about the wife and kids, or the way people in the South might ask about a mutual great aunt's complicated health.

"I'm in the music business," I used to say, to try and deflect interest. But it's not like saying I'm an actuary or a performance artist or something else that nobody wants to hear about.

"Oh, really!" Amazing how many people light up when they hear the most tangential reference to show business. "What do you *do*?" they ask again, but whereas the first time it's a general feeling-out, now they want details.

"I'm a lyricist."

"How marvelous!" If it's an old queen, she'll regale you with stale gossip about "Lenny" and "Stephen" that she thinks is fresh and interesting. Even if it's not, they'll still think you mean the *theatah*. And so when I'm squeezed through the third press, I have to either lie or tell the truth and watch The Change.

"I write songs for Christie Squires."

Suddenly you are not part of The Culture at all. Suddenly you are the Enemy of The Culture. There's a split second where I can see it in their faces, their eyes—the scorn, the loathing. Then on comes the mask.

There's a *Simpsons* episode where Lisa goes to the house of a friend—a friend even more brainy than Lisa. The girl's family has a game where they make anagrams out of famous names without a second's hesitation, and when Lisa fails to keep up the other girl's father looks at her, offers her a ball, and asks if she'd like to bounce it. That's pretty much what it's like when these people find out what I do. As far as they're concerned, treating you like a child at this point is as much politeness as you deserve.

"Oh, really? How nice," they manage. At best, they may ask another patronizing question, then nod encouragingly to your answer, as if you're Samuel Johnson's proverbial talking dog and the wonder is that it's done at all.

But I don't always have to pass under the Arch of Disdain when I meet Serious Persons. Not if the SP in question is Collecting me. See, people who go to parties in Manhattan are not expected to bring great wine, or complicated flowers, or anything that costs a lot of money; there will be many "struggling" artists, writers, or whatnots at any good party, and it's not good form to insult them by bringing some material object they couldn't possibly rival. Instead your hostess gift of choice for such parties is what you've Collected, which comes in the form of conversational fuel. Items for this grown-up version of show and tell are ranked in the following order of desirability (which, in turn, affects your ranking on the IS, or invitability scale, for future soirees): well-turned anecdotes; amusing celebrity sightings (before, it must be emphasized, they appear on Gawker.com); reliable gossip; unreliable gossip people want to believe (such as which incredibly hot baseball player is "definitely" gay); and unprintable slander about people everybody hates, delivered in a ring-of-truth tone that would pass any lie detector test.

I've found myself the target of Collectors, because if you're not aflame with loathing at the Decline of Our Culture it's amusing to meet one of the people responsible for it, and the IS potential, so to speak, of any horse's-mouth Christie gossip is just too much for them to resist. I was too old to claim innocence the first time I was suckered into this by a pretty face— whose interest in me I took for granted as genuine—but I was young enough in the world of celebrity to be ignorant of the value of my secondary fame as kindling for the bonfires of "great parties." There's nothing more mortifying than going home with someone so hot you know there's been a mistake, only to discover that like Mata Hari they've only given you a great toss so they can pump you afterward for inside dish.

The second response I get is a parental avidity far easier to manage. "Oh, my daughter *loves* her! Can you get us front row seats/an autographed T-shirt/a lock of her hair?" This one's easy; I say of course, take their card, and give it to our PR department, who sends the poor thing, say, a limited-edition Christie lunch box, which will promptly turn up on eBay for a Buy It Now price of $400.

Lyle succeeds in this environment not because of some sharklike ability to play the game, but because…he actually *likes* parties. He likes people. He loves the free exchange of ideas. He honest-to-God comes to these things to see people he respects and admires and to hone the edge of his latest theories against their whetstones. And in the process it just so happens that important people hear him speaking intelligently and passionately, and they say to themselves, *This guy would make great television.*

I can talk about a lot of things with Lyle, but there's one thing he can't stand to hear me say. See, Serious People have certain ideas they share, ideas about how The Culture should be shaped, how The Conversation should be managed. Lyle is on television because he is quick on the draw, he has encyclopedic political and historical knowledge, and he thinks deep and hard about pretty much any foreign event of note. Lyle is also on television because he's gorgeous. But he hates it when I say that. He wants to believe, needs to believe, that serious news organizations choose their commentators solely on those qualities noted above. Serious People are often genuinely appalled to discover that it's their beauty that that gives them the fame and fortune that so many other equally talented but more rumpled, disarrayed-looking types deserve as much as they do. I tell Lyle that rumpled, disarrayed-looking types can always find work as straw men on Fox News, which seems to have a never-ending need for liberal, humanist, absentminded professor types with flyaway hair and an inability to look directly into the camera, whom Sean Hannity can then dismiss with a withering "Thank you, *professor.*"

Once I asked Lyle if he really thought—regardless of how good *A Perfect Storm* was—that Sebastian Junger would have become such a media superstar if he hadn't been so fucking hot? I'd seen Lyle furious, but I'd never before been the object

7

of his anger; he didn't speak to me for a whole day. At first I thought he was mad because I called another guy "so fucking hot," but eventually I figured out that I'd called into question Lyle's own accomplishments—would he be taken as seriously as he was if he didn't look like a young Warren Beatty? (That is, if it's possible to imagine a young Warren Beatty ever walking around completely oblivious to his own hotness.) I managed to assure him that the editors of *Foreign Affairs* would never care how he looked since there were no pictures in it anyway, and since *Economist* articles are unsigned they'll never have an "Our Hot Contributors" page à la *Vanity Fair*. He looked at me for a minute, laughed, and that was that. (I met Sebastian Junger at one of these parties; I have the feeling he'd be equally appalled at being celebrated for his looks—he struck me as another Serious Person for whom The Work was everything, all else mere frippery and folly. And yeah, he was even hotter in person.)

Anderson Cooper is another Serious Person who also happens to be hot, and if you've ever seen him on CNN you know he's also got a great sense of humor. Lyle has grown used to me squealing like a teenage girl when Anderson comes on—he smiles indulgently and threatens to introduce me to him one day. I think he sees it as a respectable crush, a sign of good taste. Anderson's a prime-time anchor now, but I'd first seen him as an anchor on…well, it wasn't exactly morning television; he was always too sexy for morning television, whose male anchors are required to display an oatmealishly bland attractiveness that doesn't angry up the blood too early in the day. Anderson was on ABC's *World News Now,* which is really more for people who haven't gone to bed by 4 A.M. than it is for early risers.

Lyle will bring Anderson to me in my corner should he show up tonight. Meanwhile, Craig—who rather genially loathes Christie—is still pressing me. Because although at a party like this one he'd surely rather admit to distressing the Strokes's jeans for a living than confess that he does Christie Squires's makeup, at most gay and/or hipster scene events Christie has a certain camp cachet. And of course everyone involved with the care and maintenance of a major pop tart makes a good living and gets a great résumé credit.

"Craig, I'm just the lyrics guy. They keep me in a dark room and water me now and then, and that's the way I like it. Any suggestion I might have as to who should do makeup on Christie's next video would be greeted with shock and horror."

Craig laughed and ran his fingers through his stylin' hair. "Right, and the pope's favorite duty is to wash the feet of the poor. Listen," he said confidentially, "you wanna smoke a joint?"

"No, thanks," I said. "It makes me crazy."

Which is not literally true. I'm already crazy—but the kind of crazy you can put in a box with the proper chemistry. Bipolar II, according to the *DSM-IV*, which you'd think would be worse than Bipolar I, like a civil service promotion to a higher level of craziness, but it's not. Go figure. I take ten grams of fish oil a day, because omega-3 fatty acids have been proved by eminent clinicians in rigorous trials to do just as good a job as lithium in controlling manic-depressive illness. A better job, in my book, since lithium often has a stultifying effect on the creative brain, and while it's nice not to be crazy, it doesn't do you much good if you can't make a living.

New York City is a great place to be crazy. First of all, because your grade on the crazy curve is going to be deflated here thanks to the large percentage of residents either receiving signals from outer space, hiding from the Trilateral Commission, or simply, as Philip Larkin put it, fucked up by Mum and Dad. Before SSRIs, it was a status symbol in certain circles if you saw a shrink every day; a novel was even written about how a vast swath of the city fell apart when their shrinks went to the beach in August. So a little inflated self-esteem, a little sexual compulsion, a little shopping addiction, a tendency to stop in the middle of a busy street to announce your latest dictation from heaven—all of these fall under the radar here.

I was undiagnosed when I moved here seven years ago, still in my twenties. In fact, I had a pretty bad case of what the textbook calls "delusions of affect." That's when you see yourself as the All-Conquering One, armed with awesome talents and secret knowledge that, when revealed to the world at large, will change everything, especially your own level of fame and fortune. Fortunately, delusions of affect are a necessity for a young and ambitious Manhattanite, so nobody around you thinks you're crazy because they're all under the same delusion. Hell, without it, ninety-nine percent of this town's would-be Apprentices would have moved back to Iowherever within months.

But the difference between the ones who make it and the ones who don't is that the former are able to set their delusions aside when they actually sit down to do the work. Me, I couldn't do that—because I didn't yet know that the reason I thought my every word was a bolt of lightning to illuminate lesser souls was not because I had such magnificent things to say but because I was crazy. All the same, I was focused, organized, disciplined, well-schooled in the rules of my craft, phenomenally productive—in short, I was in an extended state of hypomania, which is the part of bipolar that feels so fucking good. It's why so many bipolars won't take their meds. The pharmaceutical giant that comes up with a drug that sustains hypomania but keeps it from turning into mania—as it almost always does— will make a mint. Mania is what happens when hypomania pushes the envelope, when the boosters push the rocket too hard and too fast and the rocket's structural integrity breaks down. Somehow I managed to stay hypomanic throughout the production of my first album. I didn't have a record contract, but who needs one when you've got ProTools, a CD burner, a photo-quality printer for your slip-ins, connections with distributors, and the greatest record ever made?

I shipped copies to important reviewers and waited for its arrival in the stores. I exercised more, because I knew I'd need to look my best when I was called to appear on the *Today* show. I spent my nights awake in bed, rehearsing snappy interview answers. I thought about which of my fellow famous people I'd like to date. (Lyle was then just a cute face I saw on TV sometimes.) I prepared myself for my annunciation, my assumption of the throne of Emperor of Pop. I raged and frothed over the delay: *The record was ready weeks ago, why the* fuck *are they taking so long to get it in the stores?*

And the album tanks. You cannot imagine my shock, my genuine disbelief, when the first reviews came out. (Never mind the fact that I was lucky to get reviewed at all.) "Overwritten." "Overwrought." "Melodramatic." Songs I'd thought would toll like bells out of radio stations across the land, songs that were supposed to make me the Bob Dylan—hell, the Joan of Arc—of our time...all destined for an early date with the Nice Price.

There's another reason the album failed, and that's because I don't go to parties. Seriously. See, if you go to parties, you meet people, at least a few of whom might like you, enough sometimes to champion you even if they don't think so much of your work. If I went to parties, I'd meet other musicians, music writers, promoters, ardent fans. But I didn't. And so when the album came out it could only triumph on its own merits, which weren't outstanding enough to overcome the general indifference most new products encounter. In short, I'd forgotten that to conquer the world you need an army.

The reason they call it "bipolar," besides the dramatic mood swings, is because in its worst manifestations, everything is all or nothing—there's triumph or tragedy, the attainment of eternal perfect love or the loss of the ability to feel, your head carved in stone the size of Constantine the Great's or an unmarked grave. Your well-adjusted optimistic person with reasonable self-esteem can take their failure on the chin, buck up, retool it into a learning experience, and move on. But your average bipolar artistic type, upon finding that adulation is not only not imminent but absurdly impossible, swings pretty immediately to the other pole. For us, one failure isn't anything other than the end of the world, Johnny Rotten shouting "no future" at you all the rest of your days.

The album came out in the fall, so as the days grew shorter and the reviews grew more dismissive it was easy to sleep more, eat more, cry more, die a little in so many little ways. The world I thought I was conquering had conquered me. I was afraid to go out, afraid people who'd seen me only weeks before strutting giddily down the street, people I'd imagined thinking *He's just received wonderful news, He's a success, He's golden* would now recognize me from my album cover, as seen in a withering review, and would whisper, "There he is, they tore him a new asshole." I retreated from the world, and the world made no effort to lure me back.

New York City is a great place to be alone, if that's what you want. You have only to reach out a little bit to be sucked into its maelstrom of socializing, but if you don't reach out, nobody will pull you in. People outside New York think it's because the natives are cold and heartless and don't ever want to be called upon to help a neighbor in need, but it's a more complex combination of things. First off, because many of the city's emigrants have escaped from small towns where everyone sticks their nose in your business, they often resist doing that unto others. Secondly, there's the aforementioned surplus of crazy people in New York—knock on your neighbor's door to introduce yourself and he may take it as license to knock on yours at 3 A.M. to show you his book of clippings on the links between the assassinations of John Paul I and John Lennon. And then there's the common state every New Yorker will claim: that they're "so busy these days," even if (especially if) they're not. People make a show of checking their date books to see when—or if—they're free, even when they know their books are sparsely dotted with haircut and shrink appointments. Busyness is a sign of success, which breeds success, and if New Yorkers were to allow other people to do such Midwestern things as come over unannounced and sit a spell, word might get out that they're really not as busy as they claim to be.

When you consider how many people run away from failure like it's catching, I was lucky to have a few friends whose own bruisings at the hands of the industry compelled them to call and check on me now and then. And I had Calliope, my best friend in the whole world and the music to my words. She looks like a scary insect—black hair in a Betty Page cut, long bony praying-mantis limbs, and a snarl that makes her teeth look twice as sharp as they are. We bonded in school over the fact that overeducated people gave us the same ration of shit—her for being a musician named Calliope and me for being named Adam Bede. "Ah, the Fair Muse," they sail off at the discovery of her name and occupation, sounding like Dan Aykroyd in *Trading Places* when he meets Ophelia. As for myself, I'm now familiar with one of George Eliot's minor works because I got sick of saying no when they said, "You *have* read the book, of course."

Callie (as only I and her mom are allowed to call her) wouldn't leave me alone when I was in my black hole. She brought me weird wheat grass–laden drinks and forced them down my throat, dug up terrible reviews of works that went on to change musical history, and generally just wouldn't let me die.

13

"You," she would announce darkly and selfishly, "are the only lyricist I have worked with in all my professional life whom I do not despise, whom I could not write circles around were I so inclined, and with whom I intend to someday split enormous royalties. You are not allowed to die."

"Such perfect grammar," I mumbled. "Obviously the only reason you're not writing lyrics is because you're a cold, heartless bitch, and since Grace Jones isn't recording any more there's no market for you."

"You should be proud of yourself," she said. "You had the balls to dump me to do a solo album, and you did said album. I congratulate you, since you won't congratulate yourself. And when you're ready to get up and work again, I will guarantee you one thing."

"What's that?"

"On your next album, if you fail, you won't fail alone."

"You know, I love your pep talks. You're like a goth cheerleader. Black pleated skirt, black turtleneck."

"Black lipstick."

"Thigh-high black leather boots."

"Black pom-poms made entirely out of black crepe."

"Rah, rah, will the other team score, quoth the raven—nevermore."

"Not your best effort, but I'll accept it as a first sign of life. Drink up."

For the most part, though, I was able to sit in my apartment unmolested. I lived on the good graces of the only great remaining patron of the arts in these decadent days—revolving credit. I'd go to Barnes & Noble to load up on books and to the local liquor emporium to load up on Cointreau and Absolut and Veuve Clicquot, then I'd drink and read until I couldn't read for the drink, then I'd scream and shout and cry (all into my pillow, for fear someone might hear and call the landlord). Until one day the trigger was pulled by a book I'd picked up out of curiosity.

"The trigger" is that mysterious whatever, the external event that grabs the wheel of my mood and turns it in the direction of the other pole. The crash and burn of the album had been the trigger to send me down, but *Touched With Fire* was the trigger that turned me back up again.

Kay Redfield Jamison's book is about crazy artists. More to the point, how many people with the "artistic temperament" have been bipolar. As I read it, I found myself nodding, gasping, even underlining, which I've always associated with people who leave their unsolicited opinions in library books to be inflicted on the next reader. And when I got to the section of the *DSM-IV* (the official *Encyclopedia Insanica*) that she'd reproduced, which diagnosed bipolar in a nutshell, I said out loud, "That's me."

Productive hypomania ensued. I became a mighty wind, sucking in every bit of information on my condition from the Internet, Barnes & Noble, the New York Public Library. The depression started to lift as shame was replaced by symptom— I wasn't a goddamn fool for thinking my record would win every prize, I was merely suffering "delusions of affect." My failure wasn't being whispered about on the street, that was only "ideas of reference," the paranoia that comes with the illness. The world wasn't a grandfather clock determined to tick my life away at its own dreary pace; my pace of thought was distorting my sense of time. This might sound craziest of all, but I was so blessedly relieved to discover there was something wrong with me, something with a name, something that would explain to myself and everyone else why I'd been such an arrogant asshole, why I'd curled up in a ball in my apartment for a whole winter, even why the discovery of what was wrong with me was bringing me such pleasure.

So I was all ready to go on lithium when Callie put a stop to that idea. "You'll be a zombie," she said assertively, having done her own research. "A Stepford wife. A handmaid. A Republican."

"So you got any better ideas?"

Sure enough, Wheat Grass Girl had a study in hand by a Dr. Andrew Stoll that said that high doses of omega-3 fatty acids, easily accessible in fish-oil capsules, were as effective a mood stabilizer as lithium in mild to moderate bipolar illness. "That's you," Callie added. I read it, and it made sense; plus, the idea of taking a pill that would rob me of my creativity was like...well, death. Sure, I'd no longer be a crazy person, but what would total sanity do to my income? Callie and I had sold a few songs here and there, but we'd hardly made a huge splash in the music world; she wasn't crazy, but she was as melodramatic as I was when it came to songwriting. Our songs full of bitter humor, wry self-deprecation, romantic loneliness, and political screeds might have gone over if we'd been charismatic performers; unfortunately, while Callie could thump a guitar to beat any band, she couldn't sing a lick, and though I had a fair voice, well, there was no way I was getting in front of an audience. Still, we *were* in show business, and it *was* a living, however precarious at times. I wasn't ready to take the chance that lithium would leave me suitable only for employment transcribing depositions for lawyers or making endless copies of securities filings. Plus I wanted Callie to stop dropping casual references to Frances Farmer and Sylvia Plath into our conversations (no, they weren't bipolar, but she hung their fates over my head just the same).

I'd like to tell you that there followed a great golden explosion of joy, my own personal Hosanna in Excelsis, salvation with bells on. Because that's the kind of burst of emotion I'd gotten used to having all my life, the only kind that counted, the signal the depression was over. Instead, the fish oil crept up on me. I wasn't depressed anymore, but I didn't come out of it like the phoenix from the ashes either. I was...stabilized. Which was kind of demoralizing in itself. I *missed* being crazy. I missed feeling like I was walking down the streets faster than anyone else, hyperaware of openings in the stream of pedestrians, exploiting them just as they occurred, agilely skating through the blundering orbits of tourists walking forward while looking up. I missed sitting down and writing a song in thirty minutes or less.

More than anything I missed the certainty that comes with bipolar—you think so fast and make so many intuitive leaps that you can skip all the boring step-by-step problem-solving they made us do in math class and go right to the solution. Some part of you just *knows* you're right without being able to diagram the steps that took you there—and yet that self-same certainty had recently been responsible for the most crushing depression I'd ever experienced, because I'd been so *sure* I was about to become an international superstar. I haven't come across it in the literature, but I'll tell you something else we creative bipolars are good at: I call it "projection," the process by which your creativity and your certainty hijack your reason—you're so sure you're on the cusp of something great, you can *see* yourself projected into a future as real as today, only with you sitting as pretty as you like. There is simply *no way* things could turn out otherwise. And then they do. I don't miss that, or the blind fury of frustration I'd feel on sidewalks when the openings didn't come, when I didn't see the tourist who blindsided me, the grief I'd feel when the song didn't write itself.

On the fish oil, I could keep working. I didn't become a zombie. Callie and I still wrote songs, though they were a bit more muted in tone and ambition than before. As a result, I've got to admit, we sold more songs. Professional performers who rely on others to write their material don't want you to be "too" anything—after all, it wouldn't do if they were to sing a song full of biting satire and were then unable to think of a single funny thing to say in an interview. You can't hire someone else to make you look brilliant, but you can hire someone to make you look clever. Callie and I were learning to be less "By" and more "As Told To," and I suppose I might have felt worse about that if it wasn't for the fact that we no longer had to rob Visa to pay MasterCard.

Then one night, we got together with some people we knew from the industry. Robin was one of the only PR people in the world I respected; he didn't make a very good living because he had what he called a "lie cap." Basically that was the level to which Robin was prepared to lie for his clients. He'd say you were sick if you were spun-out or hungover, but he wouldn't say you were "addicted to painkillers" when you went into rehab for heroin. He'd say you and your latest romantic linkage in the 'bloids are "just good friends," but if your closeted gay self were to announce you're "madly in love" with some B-list actress, he wouldn't cover your ass. In short, Robin wasn't any better off than we were.

Aquanetta was the world's greatest personal manager. She's legendary for not having gotten a computer until about 1998, since her head held her entire Rolodex as well as every tour date every client of hers had ever played, the names of every Grammy winner since the award's inception, and not only a perfect map of the interstate highway system but also the names of side roads to take during rush hour in forty-three metropolitan areas. However, most of her clients counted on her most to remember where they left their underwear last night and what clubs not to go back to on their next tour because they'd danced naked on the bar. Aquanetta made a *lot* of money.

And then there was Gordon the accountant, a perfectly nice individual. Really nice. That's the best I could say at the time. (Little did I know how many nice things we'd have to say about him soon enough.) He was Aquanetta's husband, so we were "nice" to him, when we remembered he was there.

We were all sitting there bitching about the industry. Well, Callie and I were. The recording industry operates under accounting methods so byzantine they make Enron's look transparent, but since the recording industry only screws one person at a time for a dollar here and a dollar there, they get away with it. Callie and I had recently scored a moderate success, getting three songs onto a pop diva wanna-be's breakthrough album, and we'd been eagerly counting the royalties to come for too long. Our ride, Kelly August, had already been named Fresh Face of the Year, dated a rap star, been involved in an incident involving said rap star and a gun in a nightclub, battled rumors of crack addiction, walked off the stage after her second number at her Vegas debut, disappeared into a Buddhist nunnery, and reemerged with a second album of chants and ragas that according to SoundScan had sold 2,147 copies to date. And we still hadn't gotten paid.

Here's a greatest-hits package of how the record industry manages not to pay what it owes. Their big favorite is the "reserve on return." This is an amount they hold back from you on the presumption that a certain number of albums are going to be returned unsold. If you're dumb enough to sign a contract that specifies a "reasonable reserve on return," be prepared for the company to hold fifty percent of your royalties, and good luck suing them to prove that's not reasonable. (Ideally you get a contract that presumes a fifteen percent hold-back.) The sleaziest companies also still use a concept called "breakage." This has been in contracts since the good old days, when records were stiff things in thin sleeves that broke easily and companies kept back ten percent of net sales to cover for that. Even though CDs now come in sturdy plastic cases and don't break during shipment unless you drop a tank on a pallet of them, you still have to watch out for that "breakage" clause. And even though thanks to SoundScan your record company knows every day exactly how many units have been sold (as opposed to merely shipped), you're lucky if you get your royalties paid twice a year. And that's for the six months ending six months before the statement date—another hangover from the old days, when royalties had to be tabulated by men in green visors pulling levers on adding machines, but since, like breakage, it's to the company's advantage, it remains in the boilerplate of contracts. Then that money has to go from the record company to your publishing company before it gets to you. And so songwriting is one of those jobs where you never know if you'll actually get paid until the check comes, you never know how much the check will be, and at best you only get paid a couple times a year.

Gordon, as an accountant for the likes of us, wasn't any happier with this inefficient and unjust system. Robin found himself billing clients who might or might not be able to pay his bill. Aquanetta found herself in the position of telling her clients no, they couldn't have a case of Cristal for lunch because they'd blown their advance and the arrival of the next check was a long, long time away.

Bitterly apropos, one of our songs for Kelly came on the jukebox, one of the bluesy numbers she'd bought because she needed at least one to prove she was "keepin' it real":

It's harder every day to find nice things to say
Has this world become less rich? Am I just more of a
*   bitch?*

"No comment," Callie and I said on cue.

I know I'm sick of life, and I guess life's sick of me
Should I pick up a drug habit, pose buck-naked, or turn
*   gay?*

"It's a pity you two aren't recording artists," Gordon said.

"You kidding?" Callie said. Gordon had just explained to us how the companies screw the recording artists with things like "packaging fees" (the cost of producing a CD deducted even when the album is sold as a download and the packaging cost is essentially zero), or subtracting from sales for "free goods" (the reason it's so easy to get swag in the form of free CDs from your friendly neighborhood radio station—we don't see a penny on those).

"If you were recording your own songs, you wouldn't have to deal with any of this." He leaned forward intently. "I could set you up as your own publishing company, you could do your albums' P&D…"

"Say what?" I interjected.

"Pressing and distribution. You record the masters and pay someone to press the CDs, and then all you have to do is to get a major distributor to carry it. Which, since you were on Kelly August's album—her *first* album, that is—shouldn't be hard."

Callie and I looked at each other. I wasn't so hot on the idea—I still felt like I'd made a fool of myself with my solo attempt. Aquanetta cleared her throat. "I'd be delighted to manage you two. Why, you could be the next White Stripes!"

We laughed. "More like the next Raveonettes," Callie offered.

"The next Junior Senior," I cracked.

Robin added his two cents. "What you need is a front man."

"Or woman," Callie said. "I'm not being correct, I'm just thinking… How many acts are really just producer-songwriters who find some chick to wail it out for them, and all of a sudden they have a monster hit?"

"Black Box and Loleatta Holloway."

"Delerium and Sarah McLachlan."

"Oakenfold and Jan Johnston."

Then we were all silent for a minute. Something big was sitting on the table and we all knew it. But could we write synthesizer anthems? I'm not degrading electronic music—I mean, if you'd ever heard This Mortal Coil do "Song to the Siren," neither would you—but I didn't know if it was for us.

"I think we should think even bigger," Gordon said, surprising us all. We looked at him. "I think we should think Kelly August. I think we should create our own pop diva."

"Our own *teen* pop diva," Aquanetta corrected. "Not some bitch who's gonna go off and find Krishna or some damn thing. A girl who wants *shoes,* not illumination."

"And if she does go off and find God while on crack," Robin added, "we can just replace her on the next album. Like our own one-girl Menudo. My God, it's a publicist's dream."

"A manager's dream," Aquanetta chimed in. "Bitch gets uppity? Out the door. With my connections, I could find a girl who's just right."

"I could structure the whole thing as a partnership," Gordon said. "You'd be the record company, the songwriters, the artist. You'd get the royalties, the merchandising, and there'd be no breakage, no inflated reserve on return, no creative accounting jacking up producer and video costs—you'd control it all."

"We'd need you guys," Callie added. "All of you, to run the thing."

They looked at us. Callie looked at me. "I guess all we have to do is write the songs."

I laughed. "What the hell. Let's do it."

TWO

And so it began, a legend was born, et cetera. Callie and I lived in Brooklyn, and we liked it. This was before the grooveoisie stormed out of BAM and conquered the rest of our fair borough, back in the halcyon days when Manhattan sophistos cracked wise about wastelands. And you know what? It *was* kind of a wasteland, culturally and economically, and that's why we could afford to live there. Never mind the fact that there are neighborhoods in Brooklyn as exquisitely leafy and charming as Gramercy Park; without anything in the borough remotely resembling an Angelika Film Center, my God, the horror. Those jokes on *Will & Grace* about Karen wanting to visit Grace in Brooklyn but she couldn't get a flight? Classic Manhattan humor. But fashion is fickle, of course, and the same zip code that got us snickered at back then now produces the knowing nod of the insider, even as the wheel turns again and natives (and Original Hipstas) rebel against the influx and the snarkiest sneer at us as if we too were arrivistes.

We went to Starbucks the next morning to eat pastry and drink coffee, notepads in hand. Yeah, I know I'm supposed to hate Starbucks, but once you've been to enough funky cafés staffed by surly still-stoned English majors, a chain staffed by cheerful young people who always get your order right is a welcome change. And hey—a huge chain that gives part-time workers health insurance is not *my* enemy.

Caffeine stimulated plenty of pen- and toe-tapping, a big headline on the top of the pad (*** The Svengali Project***), but nothing further. "We need to do research," Callie decided.

"How do you mean?"

"We need teeny-bop pop slop, and lots of it." That was the kind of research I was up for—we hopped on the subway to HMV and the Virgin Megastore in order to immerse ourselves in the oeuvre of Stock/Aitken/Waterman, Maurice Starr, Lou Perlman, and all the other Svengalis of the boy band world. We bought CDs, DVDs, used Kazaa to download obscure songs we couldn't find to buy (yes, songwriters using Kazaa, but we only drove it on Sundays), and hauled them back to my place.

Callie produced a joint. Now, as noted, this makes me crazy, and she knew it. "I think we *have* to get a little crazy to do this. It's not exactly our style, you know."

I sighed. "No shit." Our previous works had been far more Billy Bragg than Backstreet Boys, and something was needed to help us handle the unreality of the whole thing. Weed, alcohol, speed—pretty much anything that makes other people jolly makes me manic. I took a single hit off the joint and thereby guaranteed my inability to leave the house for the rest of the day, my capacity to eat everything in sight, and the probability that I would come up with lots of long strings of rhyming nonsense.

Four hours later, we had our first songs. At first we'd giggled at the absurdity of the first verses I'd cranked out, but then we dug in to do the serious work of catchy choruses and memorable melodies. By the time we'd finished, we were a little bit in awe of how "just so" they were—just so perfect for radio, for the market. "Writing for the market" was something we'd always despised, believing that you should do what's in your heart and wait for the fucking market to get a clue. But there was no doubt that if the Svengali Project didn't fly, we could strike our own coins off these tunes.

Okay, here's the awful truth, the absolute final nail in the coffin of any ambition I might have of one day being taken seriously: That day, I discovered my niche. All the terrible flaws in my art that bipolar illness had created, all the "overwritten/overwrought" emotions so real to me and so fake to everyone else, all the things, in short, that had doomed my solo album made me the perfect person to write music for teenagers. See, since this whole thing took off I've developed this theory: Medical professionals should be very careful about diagnosing and treating teenagers for bipolar illness because, essentially, all teenagers are bipolar. Think about it: the frenzied emotions and penchant for displays thereof (be it teenage girls shrieking up at the boy on the stage or the boy on the stage Emo-ting and screaming); the reckless driving; the quick and easy transition from love to hate and vice versa; the flaming impatience; the appetite for drugs, sex, and shopping; that absolute *certainty* about everything…hell, medicating teenagers for that is like trying to give them a pill to cure adolescence. I think they're almost all bipolar, only most of them grow out of it, and some of us never do. And of those of us who never do, well, who better to speak their language?

And teenagers are hardly the only ones rapidly cycling from one emotional extreme to the other. Think about it: We already live in a world where emotions are only allowed life spans measured in minutes. Movies careen you between delight and tears, and there's almost no tragedy on the nightly news that can foreclose on the fuzzy puppy story at the end of the half hour. What other world was better made for pop songs than our cyclothymic society, in which you can feel wonderful or terrible for three minutes and then, guilt-free, move back to the other pole? God help me, I'd found my calling.

Gordon drew up the contracts, Aquanetta screened the girls who'd audition for us, Robin studied boy-band PR as if his dissertation depended on it. Soon we had a short list of girls to see. "I get to be Simon," I said.

"No," Callie said firmly. "You get to be Paula. *I* get to be Simon. I'm far crueler than you."

"We'll see about that. We'll have a competition to see which of us can make more teenage girls burst into tears."

"God will reward us for the kindness we'll do them by shattering their dreams early."

There was no need to Simonize anybody. Aquanetta had ensured that only viable candidates had made it this far. We'd been through nearly the whole dozen—a smeary blur of perky hairdos, creepy child-beauty-pageant photos, renditions of "Tomorrow" and "And I Am Telling You I Am Not Going"—one girl even got as far as "Isn't it rich…" before Callie clamped her hands on her ears and said, "Thank you! Next!"

Nobody believes it now, it sounds like such perfect PR bullshit. But it's true. We were down to one girl and wondering which of the previous potentially adequate candidates we'd have to settle for when Christie walked in, her mother in tow. That in itself was a change; pushy stage moms eager to live through their children had been the order of the day. Instead here was a preternaturally blasé and beautiful young woman—well, "girl," as we'd have to remind ourselves more than once in the future—with a frazzled, bemused woman clearly only along to sign papers. Christie was blond and buxom, with a Monroe-esque curviness we'd soon discover men liked a whole lot more than the skinny fish-stick bodies of so many other performers. She handed us a set of glossies and sat down in the folding metal chair in front of us and lit a cigarette without asking. We looked from the pictures to her and back again, disbelieving—the girl in the pictures was sitting on a bed full of rag dolls, holding a puppy, eyes as wide and innocent as the eyes regarding us were narrow and knowing. But she had the same ample chest, the same hourglass figure, the same honey-gold hair.

"Your twin sister is adorable," Callie said. "Perhaps she'd like to come in and audition."

Christie cracked up. Her laugh was Julia Roberts infectious, you wanted to laugh at and with her at the same time. "What can I say, I'm a girl of many moods."

"And your real age?" Callie pressed. The contact sheet in front of us said she was sixteen, with acting credits from a smattering of second-tier teen angst drama series, singing credits on several Kidz Bop records, and a solo on one of those "your body is changing in wonderful ways" educational videos. It was possible she was only sixteen, considering the growth hormones saturating most fast food these days, but hard to believe from the look on her face.

"My mom is here," she sighed. "If I could sign my own contracts, do you think I'd bring *her*?" The withering scorn in her voice was apparent. We looked over to Mom, whose only response was to smile and wave feebly.

"What are you going to sing for us today?" I asked.

Instead of answering, she stood up, and we watched her face change. She went from bored and disdainful to pursed and concentrated to dreamy and abstracted as she began to sing the old standard "Summertime."

It was unreal. She caressed every note, some as a child would a kitten and some as a woman would her lover. Her ability to switch back and forth between both personae—the one in the photos and the one who'd sat and smoked and dissed her mother—was uncanny. Callie and I didn't look at each other once, afraid to betray anything to this girl.

When she finished, she sat down and lit another cigarette. "Thank you," I said. "That was wonderful."

Christie smiled. "Thanks. I love that old shit."

Callie leaned forward. "Listen. You're quite something. But I'm not sure you're what we're looking for. We're looking for...an employee. Someone who's going to sing what we write, dance the moves we create for her, say what we want her to say in interviews. You don't strike me as the kind of girl who's willing to be posed and manipulated."

Callie's honesty clearly took Christie by surprise, enough so that she answered in kind. "And I'm looking for a job. And this sounds like it beats the fuck out of joining Hooray for Everything and riding around the country in a fucking *van* where the highlight of my *career* will be playing the *Mall of Fucking America.*" I snuck a look at her mother, who looked pained—clearly that had been her dream job for Christie. As for me, a girl who makes a *Simpsons* reference has my heart. "Have you got the songs written?" she asked us.

I thought about it for a second and handed her a copy of "Boyfriend in a Band" to see what she'd do with it. She read it and laughed, but not unkindly, read it again, stood up, and knocked it out:

I want a boyfriend in a band
After the show he'll hold my hand
'Cause that way all the girls will see
The cutest boy in the band belongs to me!

She sung it with such innocence, such yearning, such...perfect *teenageness.* When Callie and I wrote it we laughed, thinking about every *Teen Cream* magazine pullout poster we'd ever seen. But when Christie sang it, she *meant* it, she honestly believed that she'd soon be making all the other girls jealous with her cute guitar-strumming boyfriend, and that having the boyfriend and inciting jealousy were equally important.

We'd tried to sneak one adult-appeal verse into each song, something the kiddies could sing along with but that would make their parents hold back from changing the station at what we called the PIP, or Parental Irritability Point, that point where the song the kids just *love* is so irritating they'd rather hear the kids scream in rage as they change the channel than hear the damn thing again. Christie tackled this verse with equally adult aplomb:

> His arms make you think he plays the drums
> But his hands tell you that he plays guitar
> He strums my body till my skin starts to hum
> And his voice turns asphalt back to tar

"He sounds hot," she said, as if "he" was a real person. (Well, I *was* thinking of Gavin Rossdale when I wrote it.) You could see her thinking, *If I were a pop star, I could have a boyfriend like that instead of the nicey-nices that Mom keeps introducing me to.*

"Would you excuse us for a moment?" Callie said. When they left the room she said, "We have to have her, and we're going to regret it."

"Why?" I said, wondering what on earth there could be to regret about signing a contract with the next musical icon of a generation.

"We're looking for a girl we can mold. This girl is already set in her mold."

"Yeah, but she's set in liquid, not stone. She's a chameleon, Callie, she can pour herself into anything we give her. We have to have her," I reiterated her first statement, and that was that.

"You're hired," we told her when she came back in, sans Mom this time. "Our attorney will call your agent and your mother with the details."

"Fifty thousand for the first six months," she said flatly. "I have final approval on wardrobe for stage performances and videos, and I get to keep the clothes." At last, I thought, a flash of a normal teenage desire! "A hundred thousand for the second six months, and we renegotiate in a year depending on sales. You *will* have an album out by then, won't you?"

"We start recording next week," I said.

I felt it coming on, a manic surge only generous lubrication of fish oil over neurons could tamp down. This girl was going to make us all richer than our wildest dreams.

Anderson never showed up at the party that night, so Lyle and I were able to make our excuses and head home. The trip from Midtown to our house in Brooklyn takes about forty-five minutes, long enough to make most Manhattan residents consider you an out-of-towner, the advantage of which is that you can leave almost any party with the excuse that you have a long commute home.

Neither of us minded the commute; Lyle usually spent the ride catching up on his reading, and I usually listened to music. But tonight it was just nice "together time."

"I'm sorry you came out tonight for nothing."

"Oh, it was fine. It's never for nothing when I'm with you." This sounds gushy, but I have a matter-of-fact way of saying it that keeps down the sugar.

Lyle smiled. "Did Craig have any better success tonight?"

I laughed. "Well, I didn't tell *him,* but I did give his name to Aquanetta, who's going to pass it on to the video guy."

"That was nice of you."

"I like him. He's pushy and ambitious, you know, but he's so blunt about it. It's refreshing."

"What song's the video for?"

"'Our Own Sweet Time.'"

Lyle broke into a wide grin. "I love that song." He sung a verse under his breath.

> For everything there is a season
> God made me love you for a reason
> I must believe one day you'll find
> I'm one of your kind

And he meant it. Lyle saw something in my songs that was not apparent to most people over the age of seventeen. As I mentioned, Callie and I tried to put something into each song that kept soccer moms from going insane in a minivan full of Christie fans, but so far Lyle was the only adult I'd met who'd actually noticed and enjoyed our tidbits of mature humor or emotion.

If you saw us on the subway, there wouldn't be anything to tell you we were an odd couple. Two urban gentlemen in their mid thirties, well-groomed and well-dressed and at ease with themselves and each other. You'd never dream our romance had elements of Montague v. Capulet.

The fact of the matter was, we moved in pretty much entirely separate circles, neither of which had much interest in the other. Lyle's friends were Serious People, holders forth on matters of weight in magazines that begin with *The*. They were the novelists you hear on NPR, reading from their work in that Russell Banks–Garrison Keillor voice, *roll*ing their *syll*ables like *bowl*ing balls, to*ward* the *hap*less *list*ener. The people who called poems "*po*-ems," who wore bow ties without irony and scowled over their cocktails at parties while saying things like "I'm working on a piece about laughter." They claimed a fascination with the literary subject of "failure" even though they'd been on the Golden Path since their first day of college. They were editors at *Twee,* which informally billed itself as "the magazine *The New*

Yorker used to be" and prided itself on the sort of articles Tina Brown once dismissed as "fifty thousand words about zinc."

My friends, namely my partners in the great Christie *keiretsu*, tapped their feet impatiently at newsstands waiting for the new issues of *NME* and *Q* to reach our shores, reading *In Touch* and *Us Weekly* while they waited. The burning cultural issue among our circle was the question of how rabidly you could reasonably denounce Kazaa in an age when most performers issued singles that made you race out and buy an album that otherwise sucked, and whether Bonnie Fuller really deserved it when her employees spit in her lunch. Each year the SPs made their pilgrimage to the G8 summit; my friends made theirs to Glastonbury. Passionate argument broke out in our office as to whether the Mercury Music Prize meant a tinker's damn anymore. We speculated whether someone as blandly pleasant as Ricky Martin could possibly be a good lay.

As I said, Lyle's friends considered me to be a temporary aberration, a flirtation he'd developed due to his sudden prominence in the national spotlight. Fame had gone to his head, it was reasoned, and once he saw through the glitter and glitz of mere celebrity, he'd return to the fold and marry a nice assistant professor at NYU. My friends thought I was looking for an Arthur to my Marilyn and waited for the day I'd settle down with a nice hot baseball player. All of them continued to think this way even after Lyle and I had been together for three years, living together for two. His friends were right about one thing: Celebrity *had* brought us together.

It did so one fine morning at Rockefeller Plaza. Christie had proved a dream to work with. She could turn on a dime from naughty to nice, both in her vocal inflections and, crucial for MTV, on camera. It didn't hurt that she spent nearly her entire first video in a bikini that became so popular it brought neon back from its '80s grave (neon-green bottom, neon-yellow top—horrible to behold but impossible to forget, and that's what counted). What happened next was amazing, fantastic, unbelievable. Even well-medicated on omega-3, I continued to feel a general impatience with time and people who didn't move through it as quickly as I did, but even I had a hard time keeping up with the pace of Christie's success. Six months after we hired her, the first single was shipped to radio programmers around the country, who test-marketed it and promptly went apeshit.

"Sunny Sunshine" was the first single off the album, which floored Callie and me—it was the song we'd written at our most stoned, the one we thought of as practice, something to get us in the mood for the "real" songs. Aquanetta, with infallible instinct as to what would sell, insisted on it being the first single, which Callie and I were so sure meant the end of our little experiment that we started reading the classifieds, looking for work writing jingles.

The video went into heavy rotation on MTV, the song tore through the top 40 like an armor-piercing bullet—if you can imagine an armor-piercing bullet made of buxom girl-flesh and coated with honey. There were only five of us, and we were totally unequipped for success on this scale. One day Aquanetta called me and said, "You've got to take Christie to her *Today* show thing tomorrow."

"You're kidding."

"I have to fly to Taiwan right away to meet with the merchandise people." This was, Aquanetta promised, the jewel in the crown—Christie albums could produce a plush income, but it was Christie™ T-shirts, posters, lunch boxes, dolls, watches, hair extensions, navel rings, et cetera that would bring in the obscene CEO-salary-level buckets of cash. "You don't have to do anything, just get her there and sit there while she does her little concert in the plaza, and get her home."

"Can't we just *pay* someone else to do it?" I pleaded.

"*No!* She's a minor, Adam, and ChrisCo is liable should anything happen to her." She scared me when she suddenly dropped her accent and used phrases like "liable should."

"If we farm out our responsibility and she falls off their stage like Lisa Marie Presley did, or gets abducted by some stalker, we couldn't prove we'd at least acted in good faith to keep an eye on her."

"The law is an ass," I said, and steeled myself for the worst by calling my shrink and getting an emergency refill on my Xanax. Fact was, pretty much everyone but Callie and I were working like dogs on this thing, and I knew that I'd been pretty much getting a free ride. So I bit the bullet, then tried to keep myself from choking on it.

If you've ever seen the *Today* show on a concert day, you have a picture of what I was about to face. A lot of people—a lot of hopped-up, hyped-up, screaming, jostling, jumping, sign-waving people. The horror! And I didn't just have to *be* there, I had to get Christie in and out of this mob, and I had no idea how I was supposed to do that.

I love music, but I rarely hear it live. I know, *live music is where it's at, man*—shoot me, denounce me, burn me at the stake. See, what I consider a god-awful press of people, jostling me back and forth, in a hot and smoky and confusing and noisy room, is what your average hipster would call "a really great turnout." Overstimulation tends to bring out the crazy in me, and on the *Today* show they *pay* people to come outside and overstimulate the audience into a frenzy of idolatry before the advent of Al Roker makes their lives complete. And now I had to get America's Sweetheart through this madding crowd and into the safety of the green room.

The car service picked us up at 6:30 in the morning and skillfully if hair-raisingly zipped us to our destination. Christie smoked and chatted on her cell phone in a low undertone, her Mona Lisa smile giving away nothing save that it was a boy on the other end. I eyed the liquor and wondered how early was too early.

Then we were at Rockefeller Plaza, alone and defenseless. The outdoor stage was all set up, the technicians having been at work for hours in a light drizzle. I couldn't *believe* the people! Could they really all be here to see Christie?

"Hell is other people," I sighed as I stepped out of the car, preparing to take her hand and begin our descent into the first circle.

"What fresh hell is this?" a voice next to me replied, and I turned to see a gently smiling fashion model next to me. Now, in New York you get used to this kind of thing. The town's just overpopulated with men who are handsome, clever, and rich, and though the first time you find yourself engaged in witty banter with one of them you think you've found your prince, the fact of the matter is that such men are so happy, so confident, so verbally facile that they just talk that way whenever they think they're around someone who can keep up. That's another bipolar curse I'd had to get over—one of the great leaps forward I used to make on a daily basis was planning the wedding the moment a hottie was nice to me. It took me a while to learn to enjoy this kind of thing for what it is: a New York moment, your role as prompter in someone else's rehearsals for greatness.

"Do you have any idea how I can get in there without getting through *that*?" I asked him, nodding toward the crowd.

"As a matter of fact, I'm headed in there myself, I'll show you the secret garden path."

"Bless you." We followed him around the corner, past the Pokémon store, through the service entrance, and into the green room. I'd never been in one before and was surprised what an odd mix of people were in there, though I shouldn't have been; it was a typical morning-show guest roster—a hapless older couple and their attorney, victims of some bizarre medical malpractice; NBC's in-house TV lawyer, to weigh in on the Morning Show Murder of the Month; a wedding expert from *Us Weekly*; a bunch of fashion models; Christie's backup dancers (forced inside by the rain); this charming man who escorted us in; and us. Christie had kept up her phone conversation throughout, and I assumed it was getting hot and heavy as she was now in a far corner of the room with her back to us all.

Our escort was chatting it up with one of the male models, so of course I assumed he was one of them. Then I saw the scandal lawyer tap him on the shoulder; they greeted each other warmly and discussed something. I'd like to say I stared at him because there really wasn't much else to do, but who would I be kidding: I watched this guy because he was beautiful and because, well, he had this *light* in him. He had the long, lean body, the black hair and pale skin, the earnest cheekbones and deep, brown "do tell" eyes, the lips patiently poised to say "really!" at just the right moment…he was one of those guys you could tell just by look- ing was a good listener. He was so clearly interested in what the other guy had to say. It wasn't the look that bored people get when someone finally breaks their malaise; this was the look of someone so engaged with the world that just being alive in it is an endless supply of worthwhile input.

He noticed me looking at him. I looked away, pretending to be absorbed in watching Al Roker warm up the crowd on the monitor. Next thing I knew he was sitting down next to me with two cups in his hands. "I thought a nice cup of tea might help you recover."

I laughed. "Thanks, a cuppa would be loverly."

"I'm Lyle," he introduced himself.

"Adam," I replied, shaking his free hand.

"So you're here with Christie Squires," he said, and although

I'd already learned to be defensive on this subject I nodded. "What do you do for her?"

"I write her songs."

My God, if I'd thought his face had been lit up before, it went supernova now. "You're kidding! I love 'Boyfriend in a Band.' You wrote that?"

"Well, the lyrics."

"Well, it's the lyrics I'm talking about. 'And his voice turns asphalt back to tar.' That's so clever, so...sexy."

This was not happening. One of the Golden was casting his rays on me, clearly starstruck. "It's just pop music," I shrugged.

"You're Adam Bede," he startled me. "I have your album. I *love* your album. Oh, wow, this is amazing."

I laughed. "You mock me, sir." It's a fact that no matter how awful any artist, one day he will find he has at least one ardent, obsessed fan who thinks he's the greatest thing since sliced bread. If you're truly awful, chances are said fan usually looks like Stephen Root's character in *Office Space,* and nothing like Lyle.

That was the first time I ever saw the Furrow, and I'll never forget it. If I'd thought he was beautiful when he was bright and sunny and open, well, I wasn't prepared for how magnificent he looked when the brows lowered like dark clouds to shadow the bright eyes, the open mouth closed firmly, and the Furrow appeared on his forehead like a line written in fire by God. He started singing the song that was supposed to have been my big hit off the album:

What you don't get you'll get away with
If the door's locked you'll blow the lock...smith
Truth doesn't pay and it's strenuous
The smart money's on disingenuous

"I've never been so enraged as I was by the damn fool critics who panned your record. And to…step sideways the way you did after that, to take your sense of humor and put it in the mouth of a teenage girl. My God, genius."

I didn't know what to say. Self-esteem was not exactly my stock in trade; all I could do was mutter a thank you. "Mr. Kent," announced a headset with a clipboard, the stroke of midnight calling him away from me.

"That's my call, will you stay after the show?" Lyle asked. "I'd love to…" he stopped, blushed. "I'd love to talk to you some more."

"Well, yeah. I mean, yeah." And he was gone.

Next thing I knew I was looking at the monitor, half listening as Katie Couric started in on whether the United States should invade Columbia. Leftist and rightist gangs had brought total chaos, and the discovery of massive oil reserves had suddenly turned a country with a bothersome habit of supplying Americans with drugs into a most glittering prize. Then on split screen I was seeing some old leftist on one side and Lyle on the other. The leftist was rattling on about imperialism, colonialism, all the words that were supposed to trigger righteously indignant salivation. But then the screen had only Lyle on it, with his daunting title of SENIOR FELLOW, NATIONAL INSTITUTE FOR INTERNATIONAL POLICY MANAGEMENT.

"Sure, it's colonialism. Sure, it's imperialism. But what those terms meant a hundred and fifty years ago to some passel of pious, bigoted Colonel Blimps isn't what they have to mean now. We have to face reality"—and there was that Furrow again—"and accept that American foreign policy *will* be dictated by oil companies, that the United States military is going to go into Columbia and not some other lawless nation because there's money to be made. But think of the people of Columbia—who's a worse tyrant, an oil company or a drug lord? Which standard of living is worse: a job that doesn't pay much or a job you never get to because you're one of the innocent bystanders killed by a car bomb?"

"So to hell with democracy," the other man shouted via satellite hookup. "Democracy is chaos, so let's make the trains run on time!"

"There's no democracy in Columbia," Lyle spat contemptuously. "There's no democracy when there's no rule of law."

And that was it. I was in love. No, it wasn't his closely reasoned positions on international matters of moment (with which I was relatively unfamiliar—I kept up on world headlines but didn't have a whole lot of deep philosophical positions on manifest destiny or the like). It was his *passion* about those positions. These weren't just things to be blandly commented on; they were matters of life and death to be discussed heatedly. And who hasn't heard the phrase, "You're beautiful when you're angry"? Well, the way Lyle looked just then was the reason that phrase will never leave the vocabulary.

There was one more reason I was in love—the idea that a person like that took *me* seriously. I was used to clever types talking to me so as to add me to their ironic collection of charm bracelets, to be jangled at parties to the amusement of all. Lyle's passion for my work was no less ardent, albeit in a different key, than his opinion about how much better off the Columbian people would be under American occupation.

But as the first half hour of the show wound to a close, suddenly Mr. Headphones Clipboard was there to collect Christie and I had no choice but to accompany her, with the full intention of racing back to the green room to reunite with Lyle.

It always gave me the creeps to watch Christie go through the transformation from bored, sullen teen into Girly Rah Rah. I always thought about that piece Truman Capote wrote about walking down the street with Marilyn Monroe as she sardonically talked about "It," the public creature, something to be turned on and off. But you knew when Marilyn did it that she was bringing her old true self back up to the surface, that happy innocence that had made her famous in the first place, that still lived if only as a memory somewhere under all the disappointment and hurt, however deeply it stayed out of sight in her later life as a matter of self-defense. When I watched Christie do it, I knew I was watching a mask being put on. Suddenly young Fran Lebowitz turned into a sunny little girl puppy, waving at the crowd like Serena Williams after a victory on the tennis court. She got up on the stage and took the mike and started into "Sunny Sunshine," working through it without a wink or a nod or any indication it was anything but a song about innocent fun.

> It's nightie-night time for the sunny sunshine
> Spent the day at the beach and I'm feeling so fine
> Took a walk with a boy down the coastline
> And he filled me full of sunny sunshine

Callie and I had been smoking a joint when we thought of that one, on the beach at Fire Island, watching the men disappear into the Pines. We'd written it as a joke, but Aquanetta had insisted on having Christie record it. She'd come into the studio, read it, burst into laughter, then sung it as wide-eyed and innocent as any 1920s chorus girl.

> Sunny sunshine makes me feel so fine
> Take me back above the timberline
> Nothing sends shivers up my spine
> Like monkeyshines in the sunny sunshine

I mean, you never know, do you? Malcolm McLaren entertained himself after the Sex Pistols imploded by creating Bow Wow Wow, and who would have dreamed that twenty years later some blond teenage boy would make him rich sixty times over by turning "I Want Candy" into an international hit? Or that whoever wrote Billy Idol's songs would suddenly find his mailbox overflowing with royalty checks again after the advent of "classic alternative" radio?

Girls were going apeshit, screaming their heads off for Christie, while their brothers and boyfriends watched her naturally ample bosom dance to the music. Their bemused parents stood by, most of them never having really listened to a single word of the song.

The concert was going fine, I wasn't needed, so I tried to make my way back to the green room. Suddenly my cell rang; it was Aquanetta. "Bitch, I'm in the airport and I can see you on TV sneaking away, where the hell do you think you're going?"

"I've got to get back inside. It's a matter of life and death."

"You leave that stage and something happens to her, you're not there to say you were at least a material witness, we are all fucked. Get back there!"

I wanted to just hang up on her and go back in anyway, but knowing the gimlet eye of any one of a dozen shoulder-mounted cameras could have caught me in the act, I had to console myself that maybe Lyle would wait for me. Back in my full-on manic days, I would have left Christie to her own devices and plunged headlong towards The Only Thing That Mattered, which at that point would have been Lyle. But in addition to no longer being at the mercy of the rising and falling tides in my brain, there was now the nagging fear that I was being ridiculous in thinking that Lyle wanted anything more than to have a pleasant conversation with an artist he admired. Which, to be honest, would have killed me—to shake his hand and smile and thank him for the compliments and watch him walk away. It didn't take much time to convince myself it had been nothing but another of those pleasant moments, and that dwelling on it

41

or allowing my wishes to have free rein would only make me sore with longing.

So I watched Christie gyrate and twist, watched her flirt with Matt Lauer with a subtlety that would have impressed a Frenchman, and then went back to the green room, where I found Lyle had been called away but had left me his card. One of the worst things about bipolar is, well, the poles—all or nothing is the order of the day; either he's the man you're going to marry or he's just another encounter you fucked up. And fish oil or no fish oil, a lifetime spent living with such absolutes had predisposed me to fatalism. He was gone, a business card in his place, let's do lunch, call me. The rest of the morning is a dull smear in my memory. Christie and I got back in the car, where she promptly got back on the phone. I stared out the window at the wet gray streets, dumped her off at her hotel, and had the car let me off at our offices in the Flatiron Building.

Everyone was there, and they burst into applause when I came in, as if I'd done something other than stand around feeling sorry for myself. "That was unreal," Robin said. "Did you see the turnout? Do you have any idea what the SoundScan numbers are going to look like after that?"

"Aquanetta wanted me to make sure you got Miss Scarlett home in one piece," Gordon said, and I nodded glumly.

Callie pulled me aside, seeing my funk. "So what gives?"

"Oh, the usual. Handsome prince approaches, a favor is thrown, the glittering retinue marches on."

"Uh-oh. Sounds serious."

I tried to pull myself together. "No, no. You know. I'll be fine." I saw a box of Krispy Kremes and resolved to drown my sorrows in a deep-fried bath.

This was Friday, the morning of our weekly summary meeting and the only time Callie and I really had to come into the office. This was the Friday of the month Callie and I secretly called the Golden Calving, a ceremony that involved a litany by Gordon of all the treasure pouring into our coffers, with refrains by Aquanetta detailing upcoming concerts and appearances (Robin was her stand-in this morning), followed by communion with Mammon in the form of monthly paycheck distribution. At that time, my paycheck from ChrisCo was about twenty thousand dollars a month—yeah, a lot, but nothing compared to what Gordon promised us was coming down the pipeline. All the same, this morning I took my check and stuck it in my shirt pocket without my usual anticipatory glee at the compulsive shopping to follow.

Then we were interrupted by a knock on the open door of the conference room. "I'm sorry, there was nobody in the lobby, I'm looking for…hi!"

It was Lyle. "It's you!" I said disbelievingly.

"I can't deny that. Is this a bad time?"

"Meeting's over," Callie declared firmly, giving me a wink.

The one thing I've learned about love—which is surprisingly little for someone who's written so many cream-filled, sugar-coated love songs—is this: Every now and then someone turns up in your life who has no business there. Someone who's better off, better looking, better adjusted, better at living. And there are two ways to respond to this. Naturally you immediately plunge into a deep sense of unworthiness when someone like this somehow gets their wires crossed and gets interested in you. Now, you can let them know they've made a terrible mistake, tell them over and over again what a mess you are and how fat and ugly and how many psychiatric medications you take and how your family hasn't spoken to you since that incident at Thanksgiving, 1998. Do this enough and sooner or later anyone worth having will accept your words at face value and book on out of there. The other way to respond is to fill like a balloon, even to bursting, holding back all the dire warnings about your screwed-up self till you look like Cassandra as played by Veruca Salt, and never once question the will of the gods (since, as we know, the gods have some mental health issues too, and it's best to take advantage of that when it goes your way). There's a song by Dead Can Dance called "Fortune Presents Gifts Not According to the Book"; I considered that what with all I'd been through with the bipolar and its attendant fractious miseries, if someone up there had mistakenly handed me a gift from column A instead of column B, I wasn't going to say a fucking word.

"How'd you find me so fast?" I asked him, as we stood out on the sidewalk.

"Research," he answered simply. "Didn't take much. I Googled you, got ChrisCo, looked up the address, ta da."

"You could have called the office," I said, more wondering than chastising.

He shrugged. "Yeah. But…" He blushed, I swear to God he did. "I didn't want to waste any time, and I was afraid you might say no on the phone."

And modest too. Now I was totally slain. "I'm crazy, but not stupid." Shit! Shit! Why did I say that! How fucking bright is that: *Nice to meet you, before this goes any farther you should know I'm mental as anything.* As I mentioned, being crazy in New York City hardly makes you a member of a minority, but for the most part I've found that when I drop the crazy bomb on guys, they nod earnestly with plenty of perfectly interspersed "mm-hmms," ask pertinent questions, and never call again.

"Right," he said absently, "the bipolar thing."

I looked at him, startled. "How'd you know?"

His eyebrows went up earnestly. "Oh, I haven't been prying, I don't mean to…well, Alex Mann is a friend of mine, and when we started talking about your album he told me about your condition. It didn't seem like he was breaking a confidence, I hope not, that is…"

I waved it away. Alex Mann had been Callie's and my manager before Christie happened. He'd believed in us, and in me as a solo act, and when I'd finally gotten diagnosed I'd told him so that he could understand why my album sank.

"Don't sweat it. So…you've known a lot about me for a while." I couldn't help but feel pleased, like a little girl who hears from another little girl, "Bobby likes you. Tee hee hee!"

"Well, not a lot, but I loved your album. I loved the intensity of it, the passion, I thought it was…grand, in every sense of the word."

"You're a pretty intense person yourself. I watched you debating that guy this morning."

He laughed. "I do get carried away sometimes."

"There's nothing wrong with getting carried away."

By the time we'd reached Central Park, the morning drizzle had ended and the clouds had split, letting in the hard Atlantic light. Every leaf shined doubly bright with its double glaze of water, a cool, mild breeze scrubbed us crisp and clean, and the leftover humidity served as a buffer against the city noises. We found a dry bench and he bought us ice creams from a vendor. When I dripped a bit on my shirt, he opened his briefcase to get me a handkerchief and I saw the portable *Simpsons* trivia game in the case.

"You play?" I asked, indicating the box.

He grinned wickedly. "I'm very good."

"Level five good?" I challenged.

We spent hours playing, not keeping score. I had some early stumbles (do *you* know how many Duff labels you have to send in to get Duff Man to show up?) but I kept up, for the most part. Lyle and I had found another thing in common: a deep and abiding belief that encyclopedic knowledge of *The Simpsons*

45

was an indication of a higher state of being, and that people who'd watched every episode twenty times over had a sensibility that bonded them together, and playing *Simpsons* trivia identified them to each other the way complicated handshakes had once signaled fellow secret society members.

Then we went and had lunch and told each other our life stories. Then we walked some more, went book and CD shopping, went to see *Avenue Q* for like the millionth time apiece, had dinner, and spent the night at his place. I never really went back to my old place after that except to pack.

I had lived in New York about seven years by then, and I'd been single almost the whole time. I'd once heard someone assert that you were only single in New York because you wanted to be—if you really wanted "a relationship," it was easy pickings. You could do like Grandma and Grandpa did and marry now and fall in love later. But the easy availability of "someone," anyone, somehow made it all the more important to find the glittering prize. That's one thing I had in common with the rest of the singletons: that burning desire to have it all, that motivational-seminar Total Quality Excellence thing about only everything being enough. Of course, being crazy, I met someone and either internally denounced and dismissed him on the spot or fell madly in love and lay abed planning the wedding, the years of faith and devotion, the trials that would try our souls, the co-interviews we'd do when we were both obscenely famous…all coalescing in my mad bad bipolar creative mind into the hardened gel of fact, far too often to the point where I'd assume he was spending as much of his free time confabulating the same future web, when instead he was starting to worry about a bunny in the cook pot. When I got interested in someone, really intently intensely— which was the only way to feel about another person—I got scary. Normal people don't fall in love in intuitive leaps, especially not in a city where there's always something better around the corner. Now and then I'd meet another fellow crazy person and we'd ring each other's bells, all right, and how surprised we'd both be when we found our ringing bells were deafening each other.

If you've gotten to a certain point in life without true love, one of two things usually happens. You put on the tall peaked princess cap with the veil streaming off the tip and swear that you'll never abandon your quest. Or you give your whole hat collection away, saying, okay, it didn't happen, the market is oversaturated with desirable mates and what with all my problems and my age and my luck, I just don't have the capital you have to invest to expect the high rate of return that is true love. And I don't mean that in the bitter "God damn all men to hell" way, which is really just the black witches' hat that's the flip side of the princess cap—and which can be magically transformed back into fairy tale pastels by the prince you still believe in even as you're swearing to make stew of his bones. No, I mean a surrender, a shrugging off of the whole burden of picking which fucking hat will make your face look thinner, younger, more interesting. You've got one good friend, you own property, you enjoy life alone because you have what Jane Austen characters called "internal resources." If you're lucky you pick up Anneli Rufus's *Party of One—A Loner's Manifesto,* the greatest book ever written for people like me, and realize that you're not the only one who would like to be in love but who just can't go to parties, to wine tastings, to classes at the fucking Learning Annex, to crowded bars—who just isn't going to swim deeply enough in the stream of life to lower those astronomical odds against your ever finding *him.*

And then I hit the Lotto. *If* we all hadn't had drinks that night and dreamed up that project, *if* Christie hadn't been the last and best candidate for the job and made us all rich, *if* Aquanetta hadn't whisked off to Taipei that morning, *if*

47

she'd been able to find anybody who wasn't me to take Christie, *if* there'd been a juicy white suburban murder to bump Colombia off the first half hour of the *Today* show, *if* Lyle hadn't just published an article in *Foreign Affairs* about the rule of law in the Roman Empire and its application to today's geopolitical realities, *if* he hadn't been so damn good-looking no morning-show booker could forget him…I mean, honestly, there was no way I could have engineered any of this. Sure, as I soon found out, Lyle knew or knew of most of the few people I knew because his voracious omnidirectional curiosity brought him into circles highbrow and low, but that was no guarantee *we'd* ever meet. Still, it happened. And you don't go back to the store with your Lotto ticket and say, there's been a mistake, I don't deserve ninety million dollars, I'm not worthy.

I don't know if it's a bipolar thing or a loner thing, after reading Anneli Rufus. She says loners are all-or-nothing too, passionately attaching to one mate, one best friend, with little use for acquaintances. (Maybe most loners are bipolar? I suggest these things to Lyle, who tells me it would be something interesting to research, meaning I should research it.) Call it cold, but I remember, during the worst days of AIDS, hearing people say that they'd crossed "hundreds of people" out of their address books, and thinking to myself, *How the hell did you get an address book with so many people in it that the dead alone could be counted in the hundreds?* Suddenly I had Lyle, and I had Callie, and my cup was full.

I still saw plenty of Callie; Lyle worked like a bee, and when his work didn't involve sitting in a library absorbed in books and journals and dissertations until the lights flashed closing time, it meant hitching rides on C5s to places where only military transports could land. He'd go off to sandblown deserts or bitterly cold and bleak steppes or smotheringly hot and humid jungles, then come back and make war with some administration official on CNN.

I remember once after a segment on Columbia, when some toady was parroting the line that basically whatever we did in Columbia was worth doing if it "fought drugs," I mentioned to Lyle my theory on why the drug war will never end, even though everyone knows it should be run as a relief effort (rehab, medication) and not a merciless conquest (jail time, then more jail time). "See, most every politician in America is a lawyer. And lawyers are trained that when you take on a client, you defend that client to the bitter end. Doesn't matter if you find out they're guilty, they're still your client. Same with lawyers-turned-politicians on an issue. An issue becomes their client, and it doesn't matter if it turns out to be a bad idea, it's *your client*, and you'll never admit it's guilty, never admit it's a bad idea." He'd look at me for a moment at times like that, tell me to repeat it, write it down, then disappear into libraries for weeks to verify my intuitive leap.

See, that's what I had that Lyle was missing. He could think, reason, proceed from step to step. He had the passion to defend his convictions and enough left over to attack other people's. He could read till his eyes fell out, make notes with bullets whistling past his ears, he could get the facts exact, he could come to conclusions, but he could not *make things up*. Some nights we'd sit on the couch, watching the news or some commercial, and I'd toss out a rhyme. Not even anything immortal, just some gibberish like:

Have you been injured in an accident, doo dah, doo dah?
Have you been injured in an accident, oh, doo dah day?
Clutch your neck in pain, in the name of gain,
Your suffering we'll misrepresent, oh, doo dah day!

And he'd just *look* at me and I'd know we were going to have

49

great sex, and soon. And that was part of what made Lyle so special to me: All my life I'd been told, and it had been proved true, that to be sexy as a gay man you had to have a flat tummy, keep your hair and glasses from getting outdated, wear shoes so uncomfortable no human being should have to endure them for a moment. Nobody had ever told me that there was even a slim possibility of getting a man with a woman's brain. By which I mean, you see a lot of ugly men with hot women. A *lot*. You don't see men, gay or straight, with someone much uglier than themselves. Men require hotness. A man will love you more for your external assets, but a woman will love you more for your internal ones. And not just love you emotionally but actually be *turned on sexually* by the person you are. Somehow, I'd been lucky enough to find a man with a woman's brain—anytime I spun out something clever, it made him warm for my form.

When he'd leave for a few days, it felt the way it does when you're a teenager and your parents go away without you, because you're finally old enough and trusted enough to be left to yourself. It's a one-man party, not because you're going to replace him with other people while he's gone but because there's a joy in just being *alone*. I loved him, I loved his company, I loved the conversation and the food and the sex and the sitting together separately—you know, when you're on the couch touching or even slumped together, but one of you is reading a book and the other is watching TV, and it's okay, you don't have to be doing the same thing, it's enough to be together. But creativity adores a vacuum; all the seeds planted quietly in your subconscious by the talking and the walking and the general living need the light of solitude to come back up in their new form. Well, for me, anyway.

Then, after a few days, I'd see something on the news and shout out a retort, only there wouldn't be anyone to hear it. It would be like the old days when I'd yell at the TV alone, partly because I couldn't stand to hear such things and keep silent and partly just to keep in practice, stay sharp, an intellectual apple a day to keep the Alzheimer's away. But what's the point of playing lightning *Jeopardy* when nobody can see you win? (That's how Lyle and I play along with the show; you yell the answer out as soon as you know it. You have to be a fast reader, you have to know a lot, you have to be able to flip through your internal database at supercomputing speeds, you need a short connection between your head and your mouth, and you have to want to beat or impress—or both—the other person really badly.) That's when I'd reach for the phone and spend a big chunk of the monthly calf trying to get connected to a satellite phone in a galaxy far far away, using the world's most advanced technology system to deliver such urgent messages as "I want you" and "I miss you" and "The teaching assistants at NYU are on strike again."

We'd bought a house in Brooklyn before it was trendy. Lyle wanted Brooklyn because he wanted a house and because the distractions of Manhattan were easier to resist, even if it was only a subway ride away. I wanted Brooklyn because I was used to Brooklyn, and I wanted a house too, and I didn't want Manhattan 24/7; the pace of it day after day is enough to trigger mania in and of itself. I wanted a place where we'd have an excuse not to go to parties because they were too far, a place where we wouldn't have to throw any because *we* were too far. Then Brooklyn had to go and get fashionable, damn it, and suddenly every acronym-crazed maniac wanted to come to our house for a party before seeing some hot band down in DUMBO or a performance at BAM.

Naturally it was parties that nearly queered the deal. Lyle and I together were a harmonic convergence, but as with so many relationships, things got a little hairy when it was time to meet the folks. Not his biological folks—who were Serious People themselves (his father a retired UNICEF official and his mother a Broadway wardrobe supervisor) but who still thought I was *such* a nice boy—but his extended urban family. When we met, Lyle had a big place on the Upper West Side with plenty of room to entertain. And it was my own fault, I suppose, that when he said he wanted me to have dinner with him and his friends, I visualized what that would have meant to *me,* namely, a nice little dinner with Callie, Aquanetta, Robin, Gordon, and Lyle. So imagine my shock when I arrived to find some twenty people mingling, arguing, laughing, shoveling catered hors d'oeuvres…I froze. Twenty people were going to pass judgment on me tonight, I thought—the typical panic response of the socially retarded individual. The problem was, as the evening passed I was proven right.

When you were a kid, did you ever have a teacher who reminded you of a bird of prey? Swooping over you, bright beady greedy eyes evaluating the best place to begin pecking a hole in you? And what could you do when this awful squawking animal had so much power over you? When you didn't dare answer the questions with "Piss off" or "What's it to you?" And the terrible shaming things they used to get away with saying back when it was thought good for your character for both teachers and bullies to knock you around.

"Christie Squires? You must love children, to write songs for them."

"I'd disagree, Charlotte; one could hardly *love* children and employ child labor."

"Roberts, I'm sure she's treated as well as any Mouseketeer, isn't that so?"

"I doubt many Mouseketeers will be able to retire in comfort by the time they're twenty-one," I replied.

"I doubt," a purse-lipped man in a bow tie chimed in, "that many Mouseketeers are asked to stick their finger in their exposed navel and then *lick it* on camera."

"Your improper plurals aside, didn't I just hear you declaiming loudly that you didn't *own* a television?" I asked coolly.

"I don't own a television. But one can hardly avoid your little protégé's presence on the public stage."

"So you go to a lot of concerts, then? Have a teenage daughter of your own?"

"No, I simply meant there are certain cultural *signifiers* one can't ignore, hard as one tries..." And with that he and his friends were off; nothing like a restorative drop of Barthes to refresh one for the task of Defending The Culture. I suppose it was possible he'd seen Christie's video for "Can I Have a Taste of Your Ice Cream" in HMV or Virgin, forced to crane his head up at a monitor for three and a half minutes by the demands of Christie's hypnotically abundant pair of signifiers while he was shopping for an obscure Astor Piazzolla CD. Not bloody likely, but there you go.

"I just adore what Jonathan Franzen said about museums, 'a genuine public space,' he said. I especially love, I think it was something like, 'a delicious absence of in-your-face consumerism.'"

Something like, I snorted to myself, knowing nobody in here would dare paraphrase. And what kind of nonsense was that, anyway? Half the museums I'd ever been in, the only way out was through the fucking gift shop, chockablock with opportunities to consume what you'd just seen.

The rest of the evening was like that—a roomful of George and Marthas and me doing my best not to sink back into Sandy Dennis mode. See, a lot of shy people are like frightened animals: avoiding strangers, afraid of attack, but once attacked, merciless in self-defense. The culture vultures had gotten a taste of that during the cocktail hour, while Lyle was busy talking to the people who'd greeted me politely and then ignored me, the politicos he worked with who simply didn't *care* about what Christie was doing to The Culture, who had their hands full of mass graves and show trials and border skirmishes and homicidal disputes over which religion owned some old pile of rocks. They weren't the problem—it was the other ones, whose hands made passes over one another in the form of such declarations as "I *was* a staff writer at *The New Yorker,* until, you know" or "Since *Joe* died the Public has gone to hell" or "She writes such *luminous* prose," the most overused adjective in the history of book reviewing.

I wasn't as educated as they were, but I was sharp and willing to use my tongue, as Bow Tie had found out earlier. So when we all sat down to dinner they started making little jokes, the punch lines of which were French homonyms. Now, I love France, but let me put it this way—left in a French restaurant by myself, I'm capable of ordering the chicken. It's hard to defend yourself against invisible weapons. So I sat there steaming, but not too visibly, because my old bipolar paranoia warned me—they're talking about you! But what if they aren't? What if nerves have just brought back your paranoia? And there's no fish on the table so you can't boost your omega-3s! And you didn't bring your Xanax because you expected, like, six people max! You're fucked! They're all going to tell him how awful you are, open his eyes to his folly, and it'll all be over. It's a test and you've failed. His friends hate you; do not pass Go.

Lyle had, with the best of intentions, seated me at the far end of the table, probably presuming I'd have more to talk about with the cultural types than the politicos. But as a mortified silence spread among his side of the table as they picked up on the French assault on my hapless castle, Lyle broke away from his conversation about the World Court and listened for about two seconds before breaking in just as Bow Tie suggested, *en français,* that I cover "Thank Heaven for Little Girls" on my next album, and the otters tittered agreeably.

"Roberts, can I see you in the kitchen, please?" Lyle was

clearly Furrowed, and my heart leaped. As much as I would have preferred sticking my steak knife into Bow Tie's throat, the rule of law clearly prevailed here and Lyle was about to exercise it by cutting Bow Tie's head off in a judicially restrained manner. He was on *my* side, I thought. When he returned the Furrow was gone, and so was Bow Tie. He smiled at me, filling me full of sunny sunshine and leaving me without a doubt in my mind that this was the man for me.

Of course I had to reciprocate, but introducing him to my friends wasn't nearly such a trial. We all went out for drinks, and Lyle surprised me with the breadth of his working knowledge of pop culture. Aquanetta and Callie disputed whether Julia Roberts had stolen her new husband or won him fair and square, and whether it was true all of her paramours had legendarily heavy equipment. Lyle said he'd met said new husband and considered him the sort to be fair game for any robber bride. He winked at me when he said it, already knowing that Margaret Atwood's book of that name was one of my favorite books ever, and I thought, *How does he do it? How can he be so smooth without being suave, so smart without being showy, and so goddamn sexy no matter what he does?*

Afterward I apologized. "I know they're not very serious people, but they're good friends, they're good people."

"What, you think they're not serious people?"

"Well, what do you think would have happened if you'd tried to open, say, a discussion about the Milosevic trial? They'd have thought you were talking about something they'd missed on the Murder Channel."

"Stop that," he laughed, "I have friends who work for Court TV. I think it says something about the condition of our empire that we can afford to have so many smart, driven, creative people who don't have to worry about foreign affairs. Some people would say it's decadence, a sign of a civilization in decline, but in empires in decline you don't see creativity flourishing, there's too much chaos, too much anxiety…" And away he went, and I just bathed in it, his knowledge, his thoughtfulness, his respect for my ability to follow if not always contribute.

That night, as we often did, we walked over the Brooklyn Bridge together. I walk the bridge often, for a lot of reasons. I started after 9/11 because it was the basic medieval way of getting from mainland to island, and for some undoubtedly irrational reason I always feel safe on it. I *know* Al Qilyual had plans to blow it up, but I guess I just refused to believe it because, well, I had to believe *something* was safe. Even though I watch *Modern Marvels* and I know them newfangled spider web–looking bridges are probably more sturdy, the Brooklyn Bridge *looks* indestructible, and that's what mattered to me. After the subways were running again, after the fear died down, I still took the bridge unless the cold or heat were especially fierce. I liked the feeling of being suspended over water, the illusion that it *was* a medieval bridge, built only to carry self-propelled traffic.

The morning after our first night together, the weather was lovely. We sat in a sidewalk café and ate a late breakfast, and then Lyle offered to walk me home. I laughed. "I live in Brooklyn," I told him, waiting for the standard "how nice for you" response. Instead he merely faced southeast, crooked his arm for me to slip mine through, and walked me home, through Manhattan, across the bridge, and down to the apartment I shared with Callie.

One particular night, after I'd met his closest friends (diminished in number after that evening, I discovered later) and he'd met mine, he was walking me home again. We stopped in the middle to rest on one of the few benches. The Brooklyn Bridge walkway is divided neatly into the pedestrian side and the bicycle side. More than one tourist has been nearly terrified off the walkway into the cars below by a whistle-blower on a mountain bike, unwilling to brake for pedestrians dumb enough to wander across the yellow line to the two-wheeled side. Unfortunately, some dummy gave the south side of the walkway to the pedestrians, meaning that the benches are all on that side and face most unromantically north toward the boring Manhattan Bridge and some dreary old buildings, rather than south as they ought to, toward the Statue of Liberty and the wide waters.

"I like Brooklyn," Lyle said. This was at the time an urban blasphemy, which explained the note of mild surprise in his voice.

"I do too. I feel...*safer* there. Not physically—I mean, I know a dirty bomb will get us all—but just calmer. Like my head has more room."

He nodded. "I'm about to start on a new book. And I think my head needs more room too. What do you think of making it official?"

"Huh?"

He shuffled on the bench. "I mean..." He sighed. For the first time, I saw him at a loss for words. He turned to me, eyes bright, hair blown by the salt wind, the sun accenting his every perfect feature. "I love you and I want to live with you. I want us to buy a house together."

That was the first of two times in my life that I've fainted. Lyle told me later how fainting works, something about the flow of oxygen to your brain, your blood pressure changing abruptly. It made sense. See, when he'd said he was starting a new book and his head needed more room, I was sure he was saying goodbye. When you're in love with someone, you don't have to be bipolar to jump to conclusions. So I guess right around then I stopped breathing. And then, when he suggested we move in together, I'm sure that did a number on my blood pressure. And when he went so far as to suggest we *own property together,* I went right out.

I came to as he was giving me mouth-to-mouth resuscitation. Trust me, it doesn't get much more romantic than that. "Are you okay?" he asked.

"Yes," I answered, delirious as Molly Bloom. "Yes."

And that was my life for two years. The Golden Calving went up to forty grand a month. Lyle and I threw parties sometimes, but I got used to it once he eliminated the ninnies and the twits. Callie and I had slumber parties when Lyle was out of town. Christie became the third most popular Google search after "MP3" and "free porn."

And at the end of two years, the Lotto officials knocked on the door. There had, after all, been a terrible mistake.

THREE

Not all at once. No spectacular disaster—at least then there would have been the satisfaction of a big show. Actually, it started kind of innocuously.

It was at the Golden Calving, and we were all abuzz over the latest show biz news. For ten years, Taquito had been an international boy band sensation, and I mean "boy" in the literal sense—Taquito was a group of five kids whose membership was highly fluid, each of them leaving the band at the advent of either puberty or the whiff of scandal. Most of us in the business knew about little Ramon, who had "left" the band at the age of 11 (about a year short of retirement age) because of his rapacious cocaine habit. Most people were also aware that Columbian organized crime was behind the band, which was how the news about Ramon had managed to escape the notice of pretty much every Central American news outlet. Most of the former band members went on to some sort of position in the cartel; occasionally there were the exceptions who went on to have full-blown adult singing careers, though with the exception of international sensations like Marty Ricon, most of them never made a name for themselves outside Latin America.

But this was the biggest scandal of all. Two Columbian cartels had blown each other sky high, a reform government had been swept into power under the threat of imminent American invasion if the nation didn't settle its own crises, and the boys in Taquito had filed suit in Columbian court declaring that they'd not been living the high life portrayed in *Hola!* magazine but rather had been spending their offstage existence in the sort of quarters Pol Pot had in mind for his enemies, eating gruel, whipped for making choreographic errors in rehearsals, sewing their own sequins onto their flared pants, and other gruesome conditions. Naturally the world wrung its hands at the thought that every Taquito album ever purchased had gone to enrich child exploiters, and similar lawsuits were filed in courts around the world against the band's Western distributors to recoup a share of the money for present and past members of Taquito, who dared speak out only now that the cartel that had owned them was no more.

"*J'accuse!*" Callie shouted, slapping the newspaper like an indignant old Frenchman.

"It's no joke," Aquanetta said. "Those kids were slave laborers. Not only that, they had to smile and pretend they *loved* it. And when these things get started…" she finished darkly.

"What do you mean?" I asked her, a thread of dread lacing through my guts.

"Kathie *Lee*, hon. International sweatshop crusades immediately following. Anyone who hires underage performers is going to be under the media microscope."

"C'mon," Robin snorted. "Christie's 18 now, and she's hardly sewn her own costumes."

Aquanetta said nothing as Gordon distributed what were to be our last checks. What would I have done with my forty grand had I known then that it would be the last money I'd see from ChrisCo? Put it in CDs? (Well, I did do that, just not the kind that earn interest.) I like to imagine I might have been a little tighter with it, wouldn't have bought an upgrade to ProTools or the more powerful computer it took to run it, wouldn't have bought nonrefundable first-class tickets for Lyle and me to go to New Zealand for our anniversary, or the top-of-the-line aluminum-core Burton snowboard and Vans Boa boots I'd gotten him so he could learn to ride while we where there, or…hell, who am I kidding? Saving is a habit ingrained in childhood, and I was way beyond my second one of those as far as my bank account was concerned.

Callie and I had a ritual after each Calving. We hired a car, drove around shopping, dumped all our purchases in the car, and spent two hours at lunch somewhere that wouldn't hurry us as long as we kept drinking. We were on our dessert wine at a little Greek restaurant on 21st Street when she sprang her news on me.

"Adam, how long have we been working together?"

"God, I don't know. Since college, I suppose. Why?"

She squirmed in her chair. "Well, don't you ever get sick of writing, you know…? You know."

"Songs like 'Sunny Sunshine'? Sure, but hey," I said, sweeping an expansive hand, "look what it buys. Honey, I tried art; it didn't pay. Not financially, not emotionally."

"Well, it's just that…you remember Ronny Wycoff?"

I laughed. "Ronny Wycoff! How could I forget?" Ronny was an international superstar who could walk any street in America unrecognized. He was huge in the U.K., the E.U., the PRC, everywhere but the USA. Of course, a lot of this had to do with the fact that the alleged "breakthrough" albums he kept putting out in the U.S. were full of songs about how hard it was to be obscenely famous, which didn't make a whole lot of sense to people who'd never heard of him. Ronny had tried to recruit me into his star-maker machinery just after my solo album had

come out, and I'd turned him down. Partly because of the delusions of affect—what did I need with Ronny Wycoff when I was
about to become far richer and more famous than he could ever
be, with a reputation as a Serious Artist to boot? But part of it
was also that Ronny was crazier than I was. Like many successful performers, Ronny wanted to be adored, but also, like an
unfortunate few, he *needed* it. And not just from the audience
but from his mates (in both the British and American meanings
of that word), his employees, his friends...hell, if the guy at
stage left with the clipboard and the headset didn't weep with
joy as Ronny bounded off the stage, Ronny would be certain the
show had been a dog. He just needed too much emotional
grooming from everyone around him.

"Well, you know, he's always looking for new talent..."

"Of course he is, since the old talent keeps ending up at
Hazelden. Or McLean Hospital."

She sighed. "He's offered me a job."

"Oh."

"Adam, c'mon, you know Christie's almost over. I mean, that
thing with the leather and the camel she did at the VMAs? She's
outgrown her audience. Aquanetta and Robin are trying to
remarket her as some kind of Madonna Jr., and I just don't think
it's going to fly. Even if it does, it's gonna be more about her
ever-increasing boobies than about the music."

"So you're jumping ship."

"I'm moving on, Adam." She took my hand. "Listen to me. I
told Ronny he could have me, but that I wanted you to come
with me. I'm sorry, I'm going no matter what, but I made sure
there'd be a job for you too."

"I can't work for him," I said flatly. "And I wish you luck."

The car took us and our purchases home, and we didn't say
much. It was so weird, it was like she'd asked for a divorce. Of
course she was still my best friend, even if she was moving to

London. She disparaged herself, said anyone could crank out Stock/Aitken/Waterman-style tunage, that I was the real brains behind Christie's success, et cetera. But I knew better. Yeah, what we were putting out was disposable music, the sort of stuff that rakes it in for a few years, disappears under a mountain of scorn as musical fashion moves on, then gets resurrected twenty years later by ironic hipsters who weren't even born when it was popular and therefore can enjoy it without being held responsible for it. Callie knew it, and I knew it, because in our own time we'd been the hipsters who'd resurrected Dusty Springfield, and Nancy Sinatra, and Julie London. She understood what we were doing, what would happen to this stuff. Her music was tongue ever so slightly in one cheek, and my lyrics were the knowing smile. Twenty years from now we might be resurrected and given our proper artistic due—hell, if Yoko-fucking-Ono's music could be dug up and turned into dance floor hits, anything was possible.

I sat at home, looking out our parlor window onto the well-manicured street, moping. Collaboration *is* like marriage; it's not something you usually find through a newspaper ad. How was I ever going to find a new partner? And even if I did, I was afraid I'd sit there staring at the new person the way a stepchild stares at the trophy wife, wishing she was Mom. But my greatest fear was that Aquanetta would hire someone *for* me—an arranged marriage, the worst kind—to make sure there was no burp in the orderly release schedule of Christie records.

I felt sad, and lonely, and scared. Impulsively, I decided to go back into town and see Lyle at his office at the Institute. I'd never showed up there unannounced, but I knew Lyle: Even buried forehead-deep in position papers, he was always glad to see me, and right now I very much needed to dump on someone.

Another of my crackpot theories: Some of the world's greatest thinking takes place on subways, especially in places like London, Paris, and New York, where the trips across town can take half an hour or more. The seasoned subway traveler tunes out the conductor and stops looking at the station names on the walls, much like an experienced typist never looks at the keyboard; your subconscious takes over and rings the bell in your head when it's time to get off. After a while you even tune out the raucous teenagers and the loud pleas for financial assistance, and since the art of riding public transportation consists of sitting across from people and not meeting their eyes, at a certain point you enter a trance, the hypnotic sound of the train's chuffing through the tunnels a helpful aide. In a trance, you have no obligation to do anything but sit and wait, or read, or think.

What I was thinking wasn't easy for me. See, the truth about why I wanted to write off Ronny Wycoff is a little more complicated than I made out. First off, I have a huge crush on him. I know, I've made such a *show* of my ardency for Anderson and Sebastian and the like, and what was Ronny but an ordinary punter made good, a geezer in need of excitement who'd provided so much of it to others, a member of that rarefied club consisting of the few who'd survived the death of their careers as *Nonthreatening Boys* cover models to transition to adult musical stardom? What was he but a blue-eyed, black-haired, hot-ass motherfucker who turned *my* asphalt back to tar every time he smiled at me? I mean, I knew he was a flirt, I knew he was trying to get in my head and not my pants, but still...I admit it. I burned with lust for Ronny, and I think I might have been more afraid that he *would* give me a toss one day than that he wouldn't.

Lyle and I had never formally discussed monogamy, never pledged not to sleep with other men. Probably because neither one of us had ever really thought it necessary. To me, the idea of sleeping with Ronny was anathema, because it would be cheating on Lyle, and cheating on him only out of raw lust.

There's a subtle ethics about Manhattan adultery: If you sleep with someone who might be a better version of your mate—tenured when he's assistant professor, editor when he's assistant editor, et cetera—well, it's a competitive world; at least the cuckold can grasp how and why it happened. But to cheat with someone who was just twisting your knobs on a primal level, how gauche, at least if you're past thirty.

And yet. If I could keep my throbbing thighs together around Ronny—er, I mean when I was in his vicinity—there was a lot to be said about taking the job. First, I wouldn't lose Callie. If I left ChrisCo to remain her partner, we could use our leverage to make Ronny let us stay here rather than move to London. Secondly, there'd be the enormous relief I'd feel at Lyle's parties—what a promotion in that world for me, to leave Christie behind as if she'd been my own teeny-pop stepping stone to mature artistry. I could go to parties and say I wrote songs for Ronny Wycoff and be met with, praise the Lord, blank stares!

And there was one more reason to take the job. Ronny Wycoff wasn't famous around the world just for his looks and charm. The bastard could *sing*. The clearest, smoothest, most golden honeyed voice you'd ever heard. He'd gotten this far singing okay songs—just think, I had to prompt myself, what he could do with Callie and I at our best behind him. It wouldn't elevate me to the rank of Serious Person, but a Q Award or two on my mantle would prevent me from dying a joke.

I got off the A at 42nd and took the crosstown bus toward the UN, feeling better every moment. I could handle Ronny! I felt a moment of dread at losing the monthly paycheck, at the idea of going back to being at the mercy of publishing companies for royalty checks that might or might not come, that might be big or small. I wasn't young enough anymore to live as perilously as that. But then a surge of certainty that had been building in me pushed the fish oil aside for its moment in the sun. So

I'd make Ronny give me a signing bonus! He could afford it. Enough to live on for...oh, six months, in the manner to which I'd become accustomed. I might not be a kid anymore, but six months still seemed a lifetime away.

I practically bounded into the Institute's offices. There was nobody at reception but I knew my way, so I nearly skipped down the hall, humming a new tune that would be perfect for Ronny, knowing Lyle would support me no matter what I decided to do.

I heard voices coming from his open office and slowed down, not wanting to disturb a meeting. As I got closer, I heard someone ardently discussing the plight of refugees in Britain, especially those who were trying to make it there on foot from the continent via the Chunnel, which had recently resulted in a series of gruesome incidents.

"It's sad," Lyle was saying, "and if we could..."

"It's *criminal!*" the other, younger voice shouted him down. "They're *dying* in the Chunnel, run down like roadkill trying to get to freedom."

"And we're working as hard as we can to change that."

"I know you are," the voice said, and my blood froze. "You're doing wonderful work. I know the Institute and you especially had a lot of influence on the home secretary."

Lyle laughed. "No, no, we don't 'influence' foreign governments."

"You know what I mean," the young man said flirtatiously. "You've got friends on the UNHCR, Human Rights Watch. I think you're very influential. Just from seeing you on TV, you've had a great influence on me."

Okay. Okay. Wanna know what I hate? Stories driven entirely by wacky misunderstandings. I don't care if it's some ABC shitcom or a Restoration comedy. I hate modernist tragedies and Henry James novels equally when they rotate around "the unsaid." I guess a lot of people would have run away and let this all turn into some painful drama, but I was like Eli Wallach in *The Good, the Bad, and the Ugly*. Some guy bursts in on him in the bathtub and starts telling him how he's been waiting for this vengeful moment for so long, and while he natters on, Wallach blows him away with the gun hidden in the soap suds, then says, "If you have to shoot, shoot—don't talk." It was time to shoot, so I walked into Lyle's offices to see who this flirty little shit was and what he was up to with my husband.

I was startled, I'll admit. I was expecting some fresh-faced little intern, straight outta Princeton, albeit in Ben Davis pants and thrift-store tie, because this wasn't exactly the Heritage Foundation, but I wasn't ready for this wisp of a thing in a fisherman's sweater that looked like it had survived the Perfect Storm. (I was right about the Ben Davis pants, anyway.) He was your typical East Village angel, with ratty hair and perfect skin, warm brown eyes behind nonprescription horn rims.

Lyle was looking at this young man with what I tried to convince myself was nothing more than his usual intent interest. Seriously: I was doing my best to look at the situation as Lyle would, objectively, dispassionately, critically. But come on—I'd heard the lust in the little bastard's tone, and Lyle was clearly flattered, clearly intrigued with *something* about him.

"Adam!" Lyle said, guilelessly smiling at me. "What a surprise!"

"I'm sorry, there was no one at the reception desk..." I got a little dizzy as I realized that was what he said to me the first time *he* came unannounced to *my* office.

"Come in! Adam, this is Sam Sparks. Sam, this is Adam Bede, my partner." God, I hated that word. It was sexless, a business relationship, a property agreement—too much like marriage for my taste. Why couldn't he just call me his boyfriend? Besides, I was terrified this young hottie would deliberately misinterpret the meaning of "partner."

"Sam's a songwriter too," Lyle offered, as if eager to see the two of us get on. Sam gave me a tight, patronizing smile that reassured me he wouldn't be asking me who I wrote songs for; clearly he'd done his research on me as well as on Lyle. "He's got a wonderful idea for a concert to benefit refugees in the U.K."

"And who better than a think tank to promote a rock concert?" I said, trying to match Sam's condescension.

Lyle laughed. "Sam's just…well, Sam, you tell him."

"I've been trying to get this off the ground for a while now, and it finally dawned on me after seeing Lyle on TV so many times that what I need is an in with the real policy makers, the people who'd be distributing the money we raise. I knew if Lyle took my idea seriously, well…" He gave Lyle one of those flattering cocktail party smiles I hate so much.

"Why aren't you out shopping with Callie?" Lyle asked, and I flinched. It was a perfectly reasonable question, just one I didn't want asked in front of this audience.

"Callie's leaving ChrisCo. To work for Ronny Wycoff. She's asked me to go with her." Was it petty? Was I rubbing my enormous current and future success in a struggling young artist's face? Hell, yes. I was jealous. And I was scared.

Lyle was suddenly at my side. "Oh, my God, I'm so sorry to hear that. I can't imagine Callie leaving you…" He could see the pain on my face, though not all the reasons for it, and suddenly turned to Sam. "Sam, I'm sorry, can we continue this some other time?"

"Of course, thanks so much for your time." He shook Lyle's hand and nodded to me before leaving.

Lyle got me to Starbucks, where I forswore coffee (I was already too agitated) in favor of hot chocolate. On autopilot, I gave him Callie's news, including her offer to me—leaving out, of course, the factor of my shameful lust for Ronny. Lyle was everything he'd ever been—attentive, considerate, thoughtful—

as he helped me weigh the pros and cons of leaving ChrisCo. We walked down the street, Lyle reaching to touch my hand, pat my shoulder, and I was overwhelmed with shame at the idea that he'd ever toss me over for some hot little cookie just because he happened to be so much younger, cuter, smarter, engaged with foreign affairs, *and* creative…

Fortunately we'd gotten to Broadway, so there was a bench for me to sit on. I had to do some research of my own, because if this kid was everything I was and so much more, so much more suitable to Lyle's life than I was…and why now? Why did he have to come along just as my career was suddenly so unsure, so unstable? This was more on my plate at one time than I could handle.

Lyle's phone rang and he answered it. "It's for you," he said, handing it to me.

"Where the fuck's your phone?" Aquanetta shouted at me. I'd seen her number pop up again and again but had ignored it, finally turning my phone off.

"I turned it off. I already know, hon."

"Well, you're mighty calm considering your paycheck just went bye-bye."

"Callie's leaving isn't the end of ChrisCo, she's…"

"Fuck Callie! You think I've been calling you about *her?* Hell, even CNN's got it on twice an hour. You'd best get down to the offices *now* if you want to take any personal belongings out before they seal the office. I gotta go." She hung up abruptly and I sat there staring at the phone.

"I need to get to the office. Aquanetta's yelling something about news on CNN and sealing the offices and…"

Lyle flagged down a cab and we headed downtown, arriving just a little too late. It looked like *Dog Day Afternoon* outside the Flatiron Building. There were crowds gathering in Madison Square Park, held back by pedestrian barricades being quickly put in place by NYPD, and squad cars with flashing lights blocking off the street. Men in suits were pouring out of our building with banker's boxes full of papers, with computers, with pretty much everything not nailed down.

"There goes my porn collection," Robin sighed as someone walked by with one of our Macs. I'd found him, Gordon, and Aquanetta glumly watching the procession.

"What the hell is going on?" I asked.

"Guess they think we're gonna be the Arthur Anderson of the music biz," Aquanetta sighed. "They're taking everything they're afraid we'll shred."

"Shred? Who are these people?"

Gordon answered. "Federal marshals. Our little girl is all grown up, and she's suing our asses off."

"What?"

"It's Christie, Adam," Robin clarified. "She's filing suit against us. Child labor law violations, child endangerment, child neglect, financial mis-, mal-, and nonfeasance…that's the criminal part. Never mind the civil suit."

"Humiliation, degradation, pain, suffering, whiplash…" Gordon said. "We're safe, individually. But the company's assets are frozen. There won't be any more distributions until all this is settled."

Aquanetta snorted. "Yeah, in about seven years. Sorry, hon, but as of right now we are all basically unemployed."

Gordon sighed. "Though I'll be busy enough, what with all the subpoenas we got today. None for you," he hastened to reassure me.

I walked away in a daze. Fuses—hell, transformers—were blowing all over my brain. I had no job. No, I had a job with Ronny Wycoff. A job I had to take, if I wasn't going to be totally broke. Which might or might not raise my status in Lyle's world enough to hold off whoever this punk kid was who was trying to seduce him.

"Don't worry," Lyle said, consoling me again. "We'll just have to economize, that's all."

And that's the second time I ever fainted.

Now let me explain. I like to shop. Part of it's the bipolar thing, that compulsion to do, to go, to have, and all of it now. But not irrationally. I'm not a totally compulsive shopper. Okay, I had hundreds of thousands of dollars a year to fuck away, and I did, but let me make one thing perfectly clear: *no bling.* I think bling is gross. All the suffering in the world, okay, maybe I'm not doing any more about it than the next person, but to have millions of dollars and spend it on…a rock? That's just gross.

Now, it's still very easy to spend all your money without any bling. Let's start small and see how it adds up. First, the music magazines. Sure, *Rolling Stone* and *Billboard* and *Spin* and *Hits,* but also *Q* and *NME,* because Britain has so much incredible music going on that just isn't ever going to make it to these shores. Do I subscribe? No, because, living in New York, I'm always going to get my copy at the newsstand faster than I'm going to get it in the mail, especially the Britmags. That's not such an expense, save that it's the gateway to all my CD shopping. Which of course I buy—I tried downloading music, really I did, but as a songwriter I felt like a cannibal. And when you've just got to have ten or twenty new import CDs each week, at thirty dollars a pop (or more, as the dollar falls), there's a nice chunk of change.

Books. I buy a lot of books. Hardbacks, usually list price. I could get them from Amazon.com for thirty percent less, but I don't. I could kid you and tell you I enjoy supporting my local independent bookseller, but the truth is Amazon.com can't beat NYC for immediate gratification—a phone call, a subway ride, and within an hour I can purchase anything in the world I might desire. And I never read library books. You have to wait for the

71

good ones, you can't read them on your own schedule, they're usually full of smudges of things that aren't ink.

Don't get me wrong, I love our libraries. I give them money. Lots of money, in fact. I give a lot to charity. That can empty your pockets in a hurry too. And I'd never gotten a receipt. I always figured, it's a gift, right? Do you give someone a gift and ask them for a receipt? Gordon wanted to kill me because I never got a fucking receipt that I could now oh-so-desperately use so I wouldn't have to pay taxes with cash I no longer have on money I've already given away. I don't wish I hadn't given it away, I just wish I'd been a little skinflintier and gotten the goddamn receipt. Now I have to go through all the canceled checks I shoved in a drawer and write to the nice people to get proof for the IRS that I didn't buy anything from them with the money.

Clothes. I like clothes. Not Prada or whatever the label du jour is, but really nice tailored stuff. Good quality. Cashmere. Merino wool. Egyptian cotton. Handmade shoes. Bye-bye right there to a shitload of money.

Personal care—the older you get, the more you need to spend on skin and hair care. And New York's full of people who can take better care of that for me than I can.

Dining out, ditto. For God's sake, it's New York City; unless you're Julia Child or poor you only cook for yourself for recreational purposes, or on romantic or social occasions.

Plays. Okay, sometimes I get free tickets. They come for Christie from flacks hoping she'll show up and turn their off-Broadway production into a Page Six item, and we all use them instead. But since I'm not greedy, I usually would let the office staff have my share and pay my own way. Since I could afford to. (I'm feeling stupider by the minute here.)

Travel. Did you know that for some time after becoming a billionaire, Bill Gates used to fly coach? Sick. Sick sick sick. I can't imagine flying to London or Paris without a big fat kick-ass kick-back seat, hot wet towels, warm chocolate-chip cookies, champagne before I have my seat belt fastened. It's just…wrong. I mean, once I'm there I don't need much in a hotel besides my own bathroom and prewar walls between me and the next room, but getting there's where the cash really flows out. Though I did start saving money on travel without even trying when they discontinued the Concorde.

So nothing seriously wasteful or spendthrift or evil. I've always just…enjoyed life. Money was for spending. If you had it, you spent it. Once I had it, it seemed clear, it seemed assured that there'd always be more. Now suddenly the tap was turned off and I was going to have to…*economize*. Mass-market paperbacks—used. Home-burned CDs (they don't ever sound as good as the real thing; you know it too). Traveling…*coach*. Making my own soup. Marie Antoinette playing shepherdess, only I could never set down the crook, because there was no more Versailles to frolic back to where squadrons of servants would exfoliate off any taint of sleep.

And that left the awful matter of time. Remember Hugh Grant in *About a Boy*? All the time he spent doing nothing? Where do you think Nick Hornby, already a successful novelist by the time he wrote the book, got that idea? It's like this: Creative people are creative maybe three to four hours a day, if they're supremely, intensely motivated and fertile. So what do you do with the rest of your day? Well, you could drink, or fight, or womanize. Or shop. Shopping doesn't give you as romantic a reputation, but it fills the time as well or better and you don't have anything worse the next day than a case of buyer's remorse. So I'd write songs in the morning, maybe, and then shop. Read a thirty-dollar book over a five-dollar mocha while noshing on an eight-dollar sandwich and maybe a four-dollar lemon tart to boot. Walk through HMV or Virgin Mega with a little basket like single people carry in the supermarket because I won't be able to juggle all the CDs I'm about to buy. Take them home and put them into the pricey Mac I had to buy back when I got my first iPod, and download them to my new, top-of-the-line iPod.

Anyway, you catch my drift. It takes a heroic effort for people like me to save a penny. We despise the nickel-skinners, the pathological misers, so afraid to let a penny out the door because they're afraid it'll hold the door open for all the other pennies to escape with it. Who wants to live like that? What good does it do to have all that lovely money if you don't convert it into real goods, happy memories, audio adventures, exquisite fabrics? Why bother to be rich if you're just going to lock it away and count it?

Which of course is why I'm now about to become as poor as a church mouse.

Fortunately nobody was paying any attention to our little group; you wouldn't have known our faces at that point any more than you knew Jeff Skilling's or Ken Lay's before Enron crumbled. So, cradled by Lyle and slapped by Aquanetta, I was able to come back to myself and get in a cab. Lyle got me home only to receive an urgent message of his own: Milosevic's war crimes trial had taken a surprising turn and CNN wanted Lyle on site. I reassured him all I needed was a few days in bed (and home-delivered champagne and lobster soup, though I didn't mention that, what with the "e" word still hovering in the air).

I watched *Entertainment Tonight* and *E! News Daily* with all the relish of someone whose problem this wasn't. It was a touching tableau, Christie's news conference; her confession of years of hard work with nothing to show for it but a paycheck—like most people in this country, I dare say, but she made you believe she was entitled to everything from the money coming in from the lunch boxes (which she didn't even pose for; they'd used the animé Christie from the Japanese TV series) to the songwriting royalties. Now, the lunch box I'd have conceded, but she'd never changed so much as a word in any song we'd ever given her to sing. Still, the whole Taquito thing was whipping people into a frenzy, and she was no dummy. When she bursting into tears, stuttering, "I just wanted to sing," I rolled my eyes, knowing she was faking it and wondering how her acting chops could have eluded Aquanetta.

I bet you think I'm a heartless bastard, feeling so little sympathy for the poor little girl. Fact of the matter was, we'd paid Christie about a million dollars over the past couple years, and unlike a lot of other pop diva wanna-bes, she'd had a complete package to step into—no muss, no fuss. No having to sleep with DJs to get your record played, no having to date loathsome famous people just to get your visibility raised, no having to worry about your costumes, no embarrassing yourself in interviews (she got her questions in advance, so Robin could write her answers)—it was a nice slice of cake for any young artist.

I had to hand it to her: Her "all this sleazy leather school-girl kink onstage is just playacting, really I'm a sweet virgin from Mississippi" schtick was paying off big now, especially since she was claiming to have been coerced into outfits and choreography counter to her innocent nature. I knew there were men in her life; long, whispered cell phone conversations were an art form with her. But she must have been careful to find men who appreciated discretion—not for her the sort to shoot up nightclubs with guns toted in their Escalade glove boxes, or go on *Howard Stern* the following morning to discuss her orgasmic nature or lack thereof. She'd built up a solid reputation as a goody-goody and—barring her own personal Paul Burrell coming forward to spill the beans—it would stand her in good stead in the upcoming trial in the courts, and in the court of public opinion.

Would you believe me if I told you the money was the least

of my concerns? It's true. I'm a short-sighted individual, so as long as there is enough money to pay the FreshDirect bill and keep the corner bodega coming around with the Mumm's Cuvée Napa (and Cointreau, and Hypnotiq, and Absolut Citron), tomorrow is another day. And I had excellent credit, which I could always start dipping into when the cash ran out. (After all, what was a line of credit but free money on demand?)

So, my earthly needs in no jeopardy as long as Shittybank could be fooled into thinking I was financially stable, I was free to dwell on the real crisis. And believe it or not, I plunged into some serious research, because if there was one topic important enough to me to force me into manual mental labor, that topic was Sam Sparks.

I knew what I saw, and more to the point I knew what I knew. Part of the bipolar gift-curse is that ability to make an intuitive leap—more widely known among normal people as "jumping to conclusions," especially by people who have to solve problems step by step. I'd heard his tone of voice, I'd seen the light in Lyle's eyes, and while I didn't think Lyle was the sort to trade in one boyfriend for a newer, shinier model, there was no underestimating the allure of someone who had everything I did and more.

Even though I hated all that "the unsaid" crap, I avoided asking Lyle about Sam. I questioned him as idly as I could about Sam's project and found out he was a big player in a group called Musicians Against Discrimination, or MAD. If I ever watched MTV instead of MTV2, which I didn't, I might've seen the inspiring documentary, which included shots of Sam walking thoughtfully and tattily through the East Village, supplying his own voice-over on how he wanted to make a difference in the world while some Cat Power song played winsomely in the background. (One of the laid-off staffers at ChrisCo, glad to have a paying gig as my research assistant, had dug up the tape.

You ask: Could I afford to hire someone? I answer: Could I afford not to?)

Like every young performer, Sam had a Web site, from which you could download his songs for free, since he wasn't signed to a label yet—though I imagined his good looks and MTV exposure were provoking more than nibbles. I spent an afternoon listening to the downloads and perusing the lyrics. There were a lot of typical indie artist themes, such as selling out, but I had to admit some of them were clever:

> You were Yahweh to a generation
> Till you said yeah to a corporation
> People marked their lives with your one hit single
> Now it's just another fucking jingle
>
> I sang along with that song when it hit
> It attached itself to my fondest memories
> Now they're used against me to sell me useless shit
> The past can't be remade in a factory
>
> Were you so short of cash?
> Was the mansion so run-down
> That you had to sell your stash
> Of our love for you?

One of the most important things to me in a song is that it's performed in a good voice. There are a lot of hipster bands out there reviving some great old sounds, sounds of bands like Gang of Four and the Cure, bands I loved and still love. But one of today's musical fashions is yelping lead singers. These things come and go, but once they've come it seems everyone jumps on the bandwagon. Back in the days of grunge, you needed a deep, guttural groan; just after that, in the age of the Sensitive

Solo Guitar Chick, you needed a plaintively squeaky voice; and after that, Emo required you to shout yourself hoarse almost to the point of vomiting, just to prove how much anger you had bottled up inside. Now there were some great bands, musically, like Stellastarr and the Rapture, but I couldn't listen to them because, well, the lead singers yelped. I guess they were trying to sound like Robert Smith, but see, he could carry a yelp, and in the end his yelps only accented his singing.

In my nonscientific opinion, bipolar is more tangled up with the brain's auditory system than with any other sense. In its psychotic manifestation it more often results in auditory hallucinations than any other kind, and another of my crackpot theories is that my kind's brains are just keyed into our ears more than other people's. I think the reason you see more bipolar writers and poets is because language is, well, aural. How many bipolar painters have you ever heard of? Kay Jamison's *Touched With Fire* is full of writers and poets and...hey! Composers.

So being doubly keen-eared, and a professional lyricist, is it any wonder the vocal aspect of a song is the most important to me? Sam's voice seemed to be all over the place on this record—a typical young person trying on other people's personae to see which one fit best. There were his growly Tom Waits/Dylan moments, his smooth adult contemporary love songs (I had to hand it to him for writing non-gender-specific songs; I fucking hate homo singers singing "ooh girl this" and "ooh girl that"), and of course the obligatory yelping du jour. No doubt about it, his voice had passion, and there were one or two songs in which you could hear him literally finding his voice: a bit high, a bit nasal, but with a distinct ring to it, an undoubtable charm.

Having separated my critical faculties from my anxieties long enough to give him a fair listen, I was now free to stare at his pictures on the Web site and hate him again. He had black shiny hair, unkempt just so, skin I knew from my personal encounter was as good as it looked on camera, and a peculiarly compelling combination of cold, thin, pursed Puritan lips and wide, warm, dark, come-hither eyes. They suggested that should you break through his Heathcliff™ brand ice mask, tempestuous storms of passionate ecstasy awaited you.

Now, Lyle and I had pretty good sex, as far as I was concerned, but I wasn't dumb to the fact that we'd been together three years and, well, unless you're Paul Newman and Joanne Woodward, it's not bloody likely you're as hot for each other after years together as you once were. I knew that for Lyle, sex was something that nestled inside his other desires (that woman brain thing again), which was exactly why I so dreaded someone like Sam, who could so ably fulfill each of them until the last one seemed like such a natural next step.

I (okay, my research assistant) culled press clips on him— not much in mainstream media, but fortunately most groovy publications have Web sites, where I could at least track down which issue he'd been interviewed in, and if I couldn't find it online, my research guy would go snag the print copy somewhere. My office started to look like Lyle's, what with all the videotapes and articles and notes scattered around, though admittedly my project was nowhere near as high-minded as any of his. Luckily, Lyle wasn't around to witness my obsession.

Then one day I looked around and something just switched off—whatever signal the brain sends itself to switch you from manic to depressed, I got it loud and clear. So I had all this stuff, so I knew my enemy...so what? What the fuck was I going to do about it? There wasn't anything I'd found that I could wave at Lyle, saying, *He's a dirty bird, a cockie doodie.*

It's pretty obvious when I'm depressed. I stop ordering from

FreshDirect and pay cabbies to hit Krispy Kreme for me. I don't get dressed. I let the phone ring. And instead of listening to music, I watch TV—a lot of TV. I watched CNN's coverage of Milosevic's trial until I realized that (a) I was only watching to get a glimpse of Lyle and (b) I was starting to understand what I was seeing and hearing. Talk about something to send you into a depression.

I was just about to turn it off one day when lightning struck. Actively bipolar brains are perpetually, restlessly hungry for data, for input. It ain't no thang for me to read a book, watch the news, and read the ticker on the bottom of the screen at the same time. And there on the ticker, a gift from God:

NEW REALITY TV SHOW TO LOOK FOR AMERICA'S BEST SINGER-SONGWRITER

I was up and out of bed and Googling in seconds.

Did I think I was America's best singer-songwriter? Did I think twice about how likely I'd be to vomit if I were ever on TV? Did I think about the extreme unlikelihood of my even getting on this show? Hell, no. I was leaping, sparking, I was a Guild Navigator chock full o' spice and folding space at a frantic speed. I just knew, I just *knew* this was it, the thing I needed, the ticket to a new (Ronny-free) career, the ticket to respectability in my profession, and most important a way to beat Sam Sparks at his own game. He'd be on the show, I had no doubt. I read as much as I could find about it—I was a little behind the curve, thanks to my not-answering-the-phone thing. Madison Square Garden, two days from now, line up and audition for the Young Broadcasting Corporation's new series, *The Bottom Line Showcase.*

What was I thinking? Crowds of people would be there, and even if I were to get on, television would make me a public person, prone to comments from strangers. It was dumb, it was stupid, it was…crazy.

Nothing is more appealing to the bipolar mind than the idea of changing *everything, overnight.* I could have it all—wealth, respect, and my husband out of Sam's imminent clutches. It could be. It could. It just had to be.

FOUR

When I saw the line, I nearly vomited. I tried to tell myself they were all lined up outside Madison Square Garden to buy tickets to some mega-act, but I knew better—it was a Monday, and nothing went on sale on Monday. News crews were filming the line, interviewing young guitar-wielding people who'd already been there one night and were cheerfully anticipating another night of waiting. There were straight-haired girls canoodling on Casios, mop-topped boys idly sticking screwdrivers into electric guitars hooked up to street performer–quality amps, and persons of indeterminate gender wrapped in Mylar playing the harmonica. One significant stretch of the line could have been excised and turned into a John Mayer look-alike contest. I went around the corner—and around the corner again. I suddenly realized that if I were going to get into the auditions for *The Bottom Line Showcase,* I was going to have to actually get in this line, now.

YBC might have generated more publicity and excitement for the show by holding nationwide auditions, but holding them only in Manhattan had a certain elitist cachet, as well as being economical, the network being based in the city. It also meant people were coming from across the land for this one shot at the show.

I'd only gone down there to make sure I knew which door to go in the following day. Now I wanted to kick myself. How easy I'd had it; I'd totally forgotten that New York City is chockablock (literally, as the line around MSG proved) with struggling, ambitious performers who would seize any opportunity and run with it. I was overwhelmed, awed even, by how much deeper their desire to succeed was than my own. All I'd really wanted was to show up Sam Sparks and let Lyle know that I could still do something unpredictable and crazy (in a good way); I knew I had no chance of winning—hell, when I thought about it realistically, confronted by the sheer numbers of the competition, I knew I probably couldn't even get through the first round. I was *old*—too old for a show on YBC, anyway—and the whole Christie thing was bound to come out and get me laughed off the show. I would do for the *Showcase* what William Hung had done for *American Idol:* mortify the masses with how completely clueless so many people could be about their own incompetence (only not deliciously bad enough to be celebrated like Hung).

When I first walked away, I was acting on instinct. When I see a line, a crowd, an endless wait amidst so many people, nothing on the other side of the door is worth braving it. Wait for the video of the movie, download the live album of the concert off iTunes, buy the original cast album later—much later. And yet—as I got further away, as the exuberant geysering energy of those kids was absorbed back into the general percolation of the city, I started feeling low. Guilty too. Yeah, and sad. Then angry. That's when I got scared.

When you're fully in the grip of my condition, there's no sweating the small stuff, because there's no such thing as small stuff. Sure, the slightest whiff of possible future success translates into carillon bells and flights of angels, but also the slightest bump in the road causes whiplash and soon you're screaming in pain, rage, frustration. Do one thing wrong and you'll find your own fist in your guts, punching you like nobody else ever could. The fish oil had leveled the road and kept me between the lines, but it had its limits. It couldn't keep me from feeling some magnitude of pain in genuinely dramatic circumstances. This was my barometer—if I felt myself screaming in emotional pain despite the fish oil, it was probably because I had a good reason.

In other words, something told me I shouldn't, couldn't, mustn't leave. In my mind's eye I could see Sam articulately navigating the channels of international factoids, and the glow on Lyle's face. Sam Sparks was a Serious Person, and SPs don't flinch from The Work (whereas flinching from The Work was, I had to admit, just what I'd had in mind). I don't understand how they do it, I really don't. Maybe they have some marvelous upbringing throughout which their parents continually watered and fertilized them. Maybe it's just genetic, that confidence and self-assurance. Maybe they had better educations, which implanted all those morals and work ethics and ideals. Maybe in their past lives they were as fucked-up as I am in this one, and this life is compensation. All I knew is that somehow I had to pretend to be one of them, even if the only way was for me to pray to God to grab my strings and manipulate me, turn me around, and plant my ass in that line.

But first, I'd have to do some shopping.

Okay, so I went a little overboard with the shopping. And I know why: Looking at that line around Madison Square Garden, I'd felt totally powerless. And shopping was a way of reasserting myself, reassuring myself that I still had buying power if nothing else. Did I really need a sleeping bag suitable for twenty degrees below zero? A PowerCat portable heater? A North Face Denali jacket? A Camelbak bladder and an REI thermos? I definitely needed the Arctic Zone cooler for the food from Zabar's that I was laying in. And of course I needed the Coleman lantern for the stack of books and mags I'd need to get through the night.

Several hours later, when I got back to the Garden in a hired car, I felt a bit like Edina Monsoon, unpacking so much stuff onto the sidewalk behind these kids, some of whom didn't have anything more than a scarf and a beanie to keep them warm through the night. I deliberately didn't look around me as I set everything up, stacking cardboard boxes and plastic wrappers for the driver to take away. I didn't look up because I thought I'd see them laughing at me, and I needed to build my fortress before I confirmed this. I know what I looked like: an eccentric dilettante with more time and money than talent or sense. But the storm was whipped up in me now, the manic rage that substituted for will power. I was here, I was *staying,* I would *do* this, I *would.*

"Need a hand with that?" a young female voice asked as I was struggling with the heater. I looked up to see a pretty girl with straight blond hair and an expression in which I could find no mockery of my thorough preparedness.

"Yeah, please. I'll hold if you pull." Not the sort of thing to say to a strange girl, I suppose, but she willingly pulled on the heater while I held the box, and the damn thing finally came free of its Styrofoam prison. "Thanks, I owe you one."

"Pay me with one of those sandwiches and point the heater at both of us, and we're even." She was smiling as she said it, and I relaxed. I always feel more comfortable with people when I know my role, and plainly my role here was to share the wealth, which was no problem. We quickly got huddled up against the wall, the heater banishing the October chill.

"Jean," she said, shifting her sandwich to her gloved hand and wiping the ungloved hand on her pants before shaking mine. "Adam."

"Thanks for the heat and the sandwich. I only came down here today to scout out the place, and if I leave now I'm fucked."

"Me too! I saw the line, turned around, bought all this shit—charged it, actually—and came right back. I still lost half a block's place in line." Why did I have to say I charged it? Why pretend I couldn't just as easily have paid cash? Well, actually I couldn't *just* as easily—Lyle had sat me down and we'd gone over our finances, and while he hadn't said anything in particular about *where* to economize, I'd promised in general to try, and now I'd broken the promise, albeit for a good cause.

"I would have done the same if I hadn't had a panic attack and had to sit down anyway." She leaned close and whispered in my ear. "My plastic's in my pocket; I'll pay for the booze and Chinese food later."

We looked at each other and laughed, two little kids who'd sneaked out of the house to camp out on the sidewalk. "I don't know what I'm doing here," she said, flipping her hair casually and naturally and staring into the distance with her cornflower blues—the kind of girl Ralph Lauren would want to model for him, the kind of girl who never would. "I could...I don't need to do this," she said, cutting herself off before revealing something. "I mean, there are easier ways open to me, not to boast."

I thought of Ronny Wycoff. "I hear you." I had some inkling what she meant—she was a rich girl, I knew them on sight. She could get gigs, she could get a record deal, Daddy knew someone who knew someone, no doubt.

"But look at the Strokes," she said, frowning. "I mean, they rock, but who wants to put up with all that shit about being a rich kid and how that made it so easy? You know? If I win this, or at least do *okay,* then nobody can say..." Again she stopped.

"If I win this, nobody can say I didn't do it on my own."

I nodded. "You want to be Taken Seriously."

She heard the capital letters in my voice and laughed. "It would be nice."

I believe that the two foremost Young Patrician enclaves in America at this moment in time are the Lower East Side of Manhattan and Williamsburg in Brooklyn. Anyone who doubts that breeding will tell should check it out, carefully. They can grow the scruffiest beards, sport the most animé hairdos, comb the thrift stores for the most pathetically ugly (and therefore sexiest and coolest) clothes, but they can't hide It, the result of countless generations of well-fed, stress-free, country sport–invigorated lifestyles. Their porcelain skin remains unstained by liquor, cigarettes, and heroin; their hair may look slept-on at all times, but catch one of them in sunlight and you'll see that nothing really sticks to its natural high gloss. And try as they might to move aggressively downscale, you can see their ancestors reaching through their DNA and narrowing their cold Puritan eyes, pursing their thin, carved lips in disapproval of what their patrimony hath wrought. They magically disappear from the scene at 30, teleported back to gracious lawns, floral prints, and rabidly conservative politics. Jean, I got the feeling, was *from* them but not *of* them. If she won this show, she wouldn't have to go back. Genetics might claim her later, but you could see her fighting it now.

I was grateful for Jean's acquaintance, not only because I liked her but because she quickly became my buffer between myself and the rest of the line. The others around us were young, enthusiastic, gregarious, and chatty, and fortunately for me, so was Jean. She fielded any comments directed our way, be they friendly requests for some coffee or snide references to my British-officer-living-civilized-among-the-savages setup. Some smart-ass asked if he could have my gear when we left base camp to scale Everest and Jean retorted, "Try it and you'll lose your fingertips, and not to frostbite." My hero.

Disconcertingly, our little kingdom soon became the center of an impromptu party. And how could it not—we had heat, music (no lack of people willing to perform), food, and (we're talking about musicians here) lots of booze. Nobody showed any sign of wanting to go to sleep, which meant I wouldn't get to either. Like I said, it takes so little to be sucked into the social whirl—usually just a little willingness, but in this case all it took was proximity. Normally, nothing fills me with dread like the phrase "a festival atmosphere," but there was no other way to describe this—and to my great surprise, I was enjoying myself. There was no leaving this party I'd accidentally thrown, so I might as well enjoy it. It would all be over in the morning, when I'd be rejected for the show and could go home knowing I'd tried. With that comforting thought, I let myself smile and nod and occasionally dare to say something to someone besides Jean.

I was, unexpectedly, as proud of myself as a Little Leaguer who'd just hit his first home run, bursting to tell Dad. So I called Lyle. "You will never guess where I am."

"You never fail to surprise me, Adam," and I could hear the warm smile in his voice.

"I'm sitting on the sidewalk with about a thousand people, outside Madison Square Garden, waiting to audition for a YBC show to find the best singer-songwriter in America."

There was a beat of silence. "You know, it's only your own surprise—which I can hear in your voice—that convinces me you're not having an Episode."

I laughed. "I can't believe it myself. I just…" Just what? I thought. What on earth was the news ticker version of what I was doing?

"Not that I don't think it's a wonderful idea," Lyle said hastily.

"I'm not at all saying you're crazy for doing it. It's just, well, not like you to, you know..."

"Join a crowd of screaming youth for the chance to be made a fool of?" I laughed. "No, I just...I want options, not some mandate that I go to work for Ronny. I want to know if I have what it takes. I want to know..." I want to know if I can keep little Crystal Allen from my Stephen, I thought, having seen *The Women* on TMC the previous night. "Well, I want to see what happens."

"I love you, you know. Whatever you do."

Well, if you think I'm going to describe the lurchings of my bipolar bivalves at that particular moment, forget it. Suffice it to say that Lyle not only had a woman's brain, he had a woman's intuition sometimes too—that particular ability to read right through your words and reply to what you didn't say. No heater, no thermos, no sleeping bag was going to keep me as warm through the night as this call would.

"I know. I love you too. Wish me luck."

I ended the call and returned my attention to the carnival around me. A Warholian panoply of YBC cameras were already out in force, battalions of cameras getting a bite of almost everyone in line. After all, who knew which of us would end up the winner? I could already see this footage being used in the final episodes to show the winner standing in line with the mere cattle for the last time in his or her young career—and so could the rest of the media-savvy youth around me. They made the most of it, hastily rearranging hair or clothing, aggressively shouldering guitars moments before staring abstractedly into space as if their thoughts were on Higher Things. Others prattled about the Journey being the Reward, and the friendships they were making being the most important thing. Still others, more earthbound, simply elected to sing a bit or show off a dance move. I hid behind Jean, and no one with a camera made any attempt to circumvent her—lucky for me, Jean had decided to do an awesome Marilyn Monroe impression, complete with cleavage, some of the plastic wrap from my purchases making a hastily improvised skirt she could pretend to try to hold down as she stood over the subway grate, as an obligingly leering cameraman waited for a good gust from below to give him the money shot.

This was prime YBC stuff, even after the channel's makeover. The Young Broadcasting Channel had originally made its cable debut as the Young Bastard Channel about a year or so prior. *Young Bastard* had come out of nowhere to become one of the most successful magazine launches in history, taking advantage of one of those particular moments in which underground becomes mainstream, and the demonized become the demographic. It happens all the time these days; performance artists specializing in hanging from the ceiling from hooks in their skin, disco dollies in shiny silver shirts who lived for E, K, and the Crystal Method, skate punks who'd cheerfully resigned themselves to permanent bankruptcy in order to ride all day—all were suddenly raised to the purple, usually via a music video, and their whole scene and style (at least its exterior shell) was suddenly taken up by Dartmouth boys, frat rats, and other, well, young bastards. Sleeve tattoos and septum piercings were sported by future sales and marketing executives, investment bankers, and other scum of the earth as they stage-dived to chaotically loud guitars and hoarsely shouted lyrics about anger, usually nonpolitical and generalized enough to ensure mass appeal. Each generation rebels against the strictures of its elders, and this generation had been force-fed Tolerance like Ipecac, with much the same result. Told to hold hands and sing and love everyone and sublimate their nasty macho urges and ask women "Can I touch you there?" before making any kind of move, they had gleefully shocked their elders by becoming as intolerant and crude and un-PC as they could be. *Young Bastard* celebrated the demeaning of women on every cover, rejoiced in members-only locker room gay bashing (in the form of articles like "How Not to Look Queer"), and ran fashion layouts featuring trucker hats with Confederate flags on them, wallets on chains tucked into jeans falling off hips, and girls reclined in the iconic pose known to most of us only from mud flaps.

It was a natural to turn into a TV channel—hell, if people will watch a Golf Channel, there' s a market for anything. And the demographic tuned in, in droves. Unfortunately, the editor and publisher of YB, who was also the creative director of the TV channel, had an unfortunate predilection for peeping. Photos taken in women's dressing rooms at unnamed department stores had been big in the magazine, the big black bars over the women's faces masking their identity. But take what makes a magazine and put it on TV, and watch as it gets the Hayes Code reintroduced (see under: Janet Jackson). Feminists decried it loudly when they saw it in the magazine, dehumanizing and objectifying women, but only when there was salacious footage to accompany their protests did network and cable news give them airtime. The Public Burning still being our president's offering to his core voters, YBC was heavily fined by the FCC, denounced in committee hearings, and gained 2.7 ratings points.

YBC's reaction to being fined was to try to outrage even more of the country. Now, it's one thing to staple your scrotum to your leg and quite another to make a girl run a gauntlet of young yahoos throwing eggs at her and then hosing her off. The magazine had answered to nobody, but television is the province of large corporations, and faced with a boycott of their products by both the religious right and the PC left, YBC's corporate masters decreed an overhaul, magically transforming the Young Bastard Channel into the Young Broadcasting Channel, its new president of programming handed a clear mandate to retain the channel's core demographic, without offending anyone, while simultaneously increasing market share among girls 14 to 29. Good morning, Mr. Phelps.

Someone in YBC's programming department woke up one morning and realized that all the girls who had formerly been pining for smooth, creamy vanilla boy-band boys were suddenly pretending to be too cool to have, like, oh, my God, a total crush on Conor Oberst or John Mayer or Chris Carrabba. Clearly this was the golden ticket—guys who were too short, skinny, sensitive, and soulful to threaten other guys. However, MTV had hog-tied all the already-famous singer-songwriter dudes and dudettes. Thus, YBC decided to create their own, with *The Bottom Line Showcase.*

Time has a strange way of passing more quickly in Manhattan than it does elsewhere. When I first moved here, I met people who were breathless, boasting that they didn't have a free moment—which sounded to me like either a slice of hell or total bullshit. But if you even partly participate in life here, time *does* get away from you. My night in line was a perfect example of it: Before I knew it dawn was there, and the doors were opening.

I just had time to call the car service to come break camp for me before the line started moving, surprisingly fast. "Hold my hand, I'm scared," Jean cracked, and as always with her generation there was both irony and truth in her words. Inside the Garden we discovered why the line was moving so fast. The whole thing had been set up with martial efficiency. Each of us was handed an application and a clipboard and motioned to one of the many seats while we filled it out. Then we got in another line and were directed to the next available teller, er, table, where you handed over your application, showed ID, paid your forty-dollar "registration fee" (the thousands of hopefuls thus ensuring the show was profitable from day one), and waited while they did a cursory Web scan on your name to see if you already had an album out on a major label and were therefore disqualified. The age of burn-it-yourself meant everyone who ever wrote a song had put out a CD, so the rules of the show had only excluded professional solo artists—mercifully, my failed album had come out on a label that was anything but major, and its dismal sales meant I still qualified as an amateur.

A more thorough background check than an Internet search would of course be done later; deep background checks had finally become staples of reality shows after the last Bachelor and Bachelorette had been revealed to be, respectively, a gay porn star and a semi-professional stalker. Although disqualifying any musician with an arrest record would be sure to produce a handful of finalists with all the fire inside of Debbie Boone.

Then, another line to another set of rooms, where you had thirty seconds on guitar or piano to prove that you could actually play (this part seemed to weed out about one in five hopefuls, whose tearful grief at not being included was well-documented by the cameras, unlike their subsequent rage at discovering they couldn't get back their registration fee). There was no attempt to verify that any of the singer-songwriters could actually sing, and why should there be, what with caterwauling being so commercial these days.

If you'd gotten this far, it was time for your digital head shot. I would've begged off on this till some other date, not feeling terribly pretty after a sleepless night on the sidewalk, but I saw people ahead of me trying to substitute their eight-by-ten glossies to no avail, so I smiled for the camera, hoping nobody would ever see the photo.

Suddenly it was 3 in the afternoon and we were done, disgorged onto the sidewalks in a sort of giddy exhaustion. Information began circulating like hooch—one thousand of us had made it all the way through, to the first show if nothing else; only one in ten would make it through that round. But it was official—I'd made the show! They weren't the worst odds, I thought, suddenly happy.

Impulsively, I hugged Jean, surprised to find myself having bonded to a stranger so quickly. Harrowing experiences have a way of doing that to people, and I was relieved that we'd both made it, at least this far.

"Home is the sailor, home from the sea," I heard Jean say, as she pointed over my shoulder. "Look." Camera crews were gathering around one of the other contestants (now, officially, that's what we were).

"I'm not some blow-up dolly, you know." I immediately identified the familiar voice of Christie Squires. In disbelief, I peered over the press heads at her. "I can read, and write, and even tie my own shoelaces. Though you'd never know that from all the people ChrisCo hired to tie them for me." The reporters laughed, but suddenly a lawyer appeared out of nowhere to shake his head in warning.

"Christie, why are you trying out for this show? Why don't you just…"

"Coast on my name value?" She cut him off. "Put out a record everyone will say sucks before it even comes out because I'm just some fembot who couldn't write her way out of a paper bag? No way. I wanted to be a performer, not a puppet, and I'm going to be, even if I have to start at the bottom of the ladder and work my way up to prove it."

She looked right at me, suddenly realizing that I too, had just been through the mill inside. She sort of snorted as she smiled at me, as if to say, "Et tu?" I saluted her smartly, to her surprise. She examined my face for sarcasm and, finding none, saluted back. Whoever we'd been before, we'd both been inducted as buck privates in a new army; we might end up facing off against each other later, but for now we were comrades—knocked down, laughed at, and determined to be Taken Seriously.

Jean grabbed me. "They've announced the name of one of the judges. You ever hear of some guy named Ronny Wycoff?"

It was just after Christie had broken big but before I'd met Lyle, and I was in London as part of the ChrisCo entourage. People go on about the romance of train travel, but let me tell you, for sheer pleasure there's nothing like a chartered jet that's been custom-remodeled for that rock and/or roll lifestyle. We were hardly the most decadent bunch—Christie holed up in the bedroom to watch *Scary Movie* while the rest of us sipped champagne and bullshitted in the giant living room that was the main cabin. Success was still new to us, and we weren't yet jaded about the impossibly obscene amounts of money that seemed to come to us from all directions.

"We should be snorting coke, or boffing models, or breaking something," Robin suggested. All of us were familiar with that most notorious flying fuckfest, the Led Zeppelin tour plane; however, all of us being over 30, we settled for drinking Veuve Clicquot and watching the hard-to-find DVD of *Liquid Sky,* which was part of the plane's collection and a movie so full of decadent behavior that just watching it could corrupt you.

In London, I went on my own to see a play nobody else wanted to see, which ended up being a rather heavy-handed political satire sending up the Blair regime. Not exactly my standard fare, especially pre-Lyle, but on short notice it was either that or some prefabricated musical (the rest of the ChrisCo team might have been interested in seeing yet another staging of *Phantom,* but I've got serious Andrew Lloyd Weber issues). The play had been raved about in *The Guardian* and *Time Out London,* and the house was full. There was one empty seat to my left; naturally I was praying no one would take it, but of course that was not to be.

In the theater I'm one of those people who, when alone, digs into the *Playbill,* even if ninety-five percent of it is the same as the

Playbill I've read the night before, just to keep from being chatted up by strangers. Although I was well aware that the body that finally sat next to mine was that of what Brits used to call a "man of parts." I glanced over to give him a tight, pleasant smile, the universal signal that acknowledges our status as seatmates and my desire to be left alone. (It works on airplanes, in theaters, on buses—try it!) However, I was startled out of my shell by two things. One, the man next to me was shockingly good-looking, with these electric sea-green eyes and my favorite look in the whole world: black hair and pale skin. (My first crush was a Black Irish classmate, and that's a very pleasant memory.) Two, he was Ronny Wycoff.

As mentioned above, Ronny was a superstar—here, anyway. Londoners being even more deliberately blind to famous people than New Yorkers, the buzz in the theater hadn't changed a whit with his entrance. "Evening," he said politely.

"Evening," I replied, returning to the *Playbill* I wasn't reading anymore. I knew who he was, and I knew the rumors, which could be summed up by saying that Ronny had, let's say, a lust for life. I was single, alone in a strange city, still in possession of my hair and most of my hormones, and suddenly desperately hoping at least some of the rumors were true.

It was a warm evening in London, and I was in a short-sleeve shirt. Ronny was in a tight black T-shirt, and as he leaned over to pull something out of his left rear pocket, his right shoulder pressed into my left and the bare skin of his forearm brushed against mine. Either it had been too long since I'd had sex or Ronny was possessed of pheromones of unsurpassed quality, because this one quick contact nearly blew the top of my head off. His skin was unbelievably soft and warm and smooth, the muscle below taut and bulging. "Sorry," he said, smiling at me and winking, so I'd know he'd done it on purpose.

"No problem," I croaked, and thank God the curtain came

up then. I tried to follow the play and made a hash job of it. It wasn't that I didn't understand the politics; I read *The Guardian* online every day and watched BBC World News. Rather, it was just increasingly difficult for me to ignore the soft, steady heat coming off Ronny, along with a smell that was definitely not cologne and that put me in mind of what ancient writers said of Alexander, that he gave off a pleasant and alluring natural scent. Until this moment I'd thought that was one of the typical embellishments ancient historians used to describe kings and heroes, but now I wasn't so sure.

At the intermission, Ronnie stood up and stretched, giving me a fine view of his broad but firm buttocks. Then he sat down and said, "So what do you think of it so far?"

"It's a little over the top. I really can't see the head of the Labour Party having reporters killed. Now, if they'd had Margaret Thatcher doing it, I could believe it."

Ronny laughed. "Tony's got thick skin, it won't bother him." Now, in New York a reference to a famous person by his first name usually implies a personal relationship, but not in London. For all the clichés about being stiff and emotionless, the English are the most gregarious people you've ever seen. There's a reason E is London's biggest drug, and don't forget it was the British who invented the word "clubbable" to describe someone you'd always like to see around. Read *NME* and you can sometimes feel like the entire U.K. music scene is a midsize village in which everyone knows one another. So for a Londoner to call the prime minister "Tony" as casually as Ronny did wouldn't mean much, if you didn't know that Ronny had been one of the "Cool Britannia" crowd and had performed at Blair's victory party when he first became P.M.

"A good quality in a politician," I said, kicking myself for being unable to come up with something witty on the spot.

"Or an artist," he winked at me again. I smiled, acknowledging that we both knew who he was. At least, that's what I thought he meant, until he picked up his program and started humming a song off my solo album—"The Ballad of Frances Bean, 2023," which I wrote shortly after Courtney took her last stage dive.

What have you done with Frances Bean?
The girl who was born to rule the scene
You fostered her into preppy enslavement
She grew up never having heard of Pavement

They shipped her off to a private school
Denuded her of every gram of cool
She experimented with being gay
Grew a ponytail, drove a Cabriolet

What have they done to you, Frances Bean?
You jet around in your Gulfstream
At shopping you're a success *d'estime*
Nothing illegal in your bloodstream

Then one day you stopped to pee in a bar
Just after sound check; you picked up a guitar
It was like you'd been born with one in your hand
At last Frances Bean finally had her own band

Oh, Frances Bean, in your Pulitzer dress
They'll tell you nothing exceeds like duress
You don't need to shoot up, get drunk, crash your car
You've nothing to prove, you were born a star

What an odd choice, I thought, then realized it wasn't really. It was a song about musical fame and fortune, which was Ronny's favorite subject—his own fame and fortune, that is. I suppose, looking back, that in his eyes, having written about some other famous person qualified me to write about him.

I didn't take my eyes off the *Playbill*, but I was smiling. After the play, he asked me if I wanted to go have a drink, which in London has as little romantic or sexual weight as meeting for coffee does back home. He'd either done his homework on me or gotten lucky, because we somehow ended up in a nice quiet West End pub that was totally deserted even just after all the theaters got out. Knowing what I know now, I wouldn't put it past him to have paid the management to have the "Closed" sign put up after our entrance. (For that matter, he could have afforded to buy the place outright and never miss the cash.)

"So," he smiled, "I guess you've figured out this was a setup." I smiled back, dimly, as it slowly came over me what "this" really was. How could I have been so naive? I'd honestly thought we'd met by accident, thought it was just one of those collisions of talent that happen all the time in the world's cultural capitals. And more to the point, I'd thought he'd been flirting with me. He had been, of course, but it wasn't because he wanted my body—my body of work, maybe, but that wasn't going to keep me warm tonight.

"I have now," I said stiffly, vanity wounded.

He reached over and took my hand. His skin! My rage was immediately canceled out by what I'm guessing a female orgasm feels like—a warmth in the groin that jumps from there to the top of your head, then back down to your cheeks. "I love your work, Adam. You've got a depth I lack. And that's something I need very badly right now."

I had to laugh. Ronny Wycoff was Taking me Seriously, and I wasn't sure if that was a compliment or not. But I knew what he was talking about—like I said, the U.K. music scene is a chummy place, but the Brits have this weird need to pull down pretty much everyone they've raised up, after a period of time that may or may not be long enough to establish yourself permanently. If you really want to thrive in Britain, it's best to keep pulling yourself down—say, develop a crack and/or heroin habit and go to jail just as your adulation seems imminent—which will keep you an underdog in the public eye and therefore to be rooted for. Otherwise, be prepared to be knocked off your pedestal and spend a few years, or decades, licking your wounds until the nation's music-buying public, who can often be as fickle as Japanese schoolgirls about their icons, suddenly decides it's time to love you again. Ronny had been so big for so long that his comeuppance was overdue, and he'd only sold half as many millions of units of his last album in his home country as he had of the one before.

I shook my head no to Ronny's offer for a lot of reasons. First and foremost, while I had the time to write more, I didn't need the money, and to be honest I didn't have the strongest work ethic. Second, I have to admit, my pride was hurt—he'd only flirted with me to soften me up for the hard sell! I knew he boffed Italian (female) models two at a time, but I also knew he had a huge gay following he took rigorous care to string along, never acknowledging having slept with a man but always holding the door open to the possibility that he had, or would. (Pop stars can do that in countries that are not the United States and not forfeit their careers.)

And the final and most importantly reason I refused him then was the reason I refused the opportunity again when Callie offered: I had—okay, *have*—the most irrational, powerful, hormonal attraction to Ronny Wycoff. If he'd taken me to his hotel room that night and had his way with me, I would have been his scribe-slave for much longer than would have been good for me. I wanted to hear his lovely, golden, buttered-honey voice a quarter-inch from my ear for hours at a time, and not through a pair of headphones. I wanted to overdose on whatever chemical permeated that 360-thread-count skin of his.

And now, just my luck, the man who'd asked me to help save his flagging career—the man I'd turned down—was going to pass judgment on me. I had a snowball's chance, I thought darkly. Again, what if...what if Ronny *did* vote for me? What if he still wanted me, in *that* way? It suddenly occurred to me what a Serious Person would do in these circumstances, especially since my former writing partner had just gone to work for Ronny. A Serious Person would recuse himself from the whole competition—conflict of interest, the high and noble road... yeah, to ignominy, and singleton status, and poverty, I thought. I remembered the *American Idol* contestants who'd slipped through to the later rounds despite various flavors of scandal, and I was willing to take my chances that I'd at least make a decent showing before TheSmokingGun.com took me down. I could be just Serious enough not to run away from this, but not Serious enough to walk away from it.

I debated whether to tell Jean the Ronny story, which would involve telling her the Christie story, but fortunately the matter rested where it was when Jean waved at someone. "Oh, you've got to meet this guy, I should have known he'd be here. Sam! Sam!"

Clearly, musical London isn't the only small town in the world. Jean and Sam hugged and—I couldn't believe it—air-kissed. "Adam, this is my friend Sam!"

"We've met," I said as coolly as I could.

Sam looked at me, cocked his head, and smiled a sweet, sunny smile. "Really?" Either he was a most excellent actor or he honestly didn't remember me, which I knew was possible; social animals meet so many people, and I'd made the most momentary appearance on his horizon—whereas I had good reason to remember him. Regardless, he really took the wind out of my Joan Collins moment.

"Damn, I need a drink," Jean said. "Come on, let's go." What was I going to say? "Sorry, but this kid's trying to steal my husband and"—my inner Joan Collins still wanting to have her say—"I might have to throw my drink in his face"? What if I was wrong and his encounter with Lyle was one of those very harmless flirtations I'd been so sure *my* first encounter with Lyle had been? Besides, I'd need a friend on this show, and Jean was including me in her expedition, which was awfully nice of her, I thought.

I regretted my decision when we arrived at Webster's. This was one of those places you knew about even if you never went out. Webster's had formerly been a black glass and chrome gay bar with chain-link fence accents (convenient for leverage during the orgies that took place there after closing time) but had been remodeled to resemble an "authentic" dive. The checkered black and white linoleum floor tiles and the oak bar remained, though style queens had muddied the floor with various disagreeable solvents and meticulously applied permanent stain rings to the bar, which were then covered up with a layer of kitchen grease. The track lighting had been stripped out and the whole place was illuminated only by the bleary orange bulbs behind the booze bottles and the fluorescent light (courtesy of some vanished brand of beer) hanging over the pool table. The shiny red vinyl seats on the brand-new barstools had been strategically ripped and their edges sanded down as if from the wear of a thousand fat asses, and someone had been paid $25,000 to stain the toilets, graffiti the stall walls, dirty up the revolving towel, and otherwise make the bathroom inviting to drug addicts and other varieties of stall lurkers. Let us never speak of what was on the jukebox. Hipsters loved the place because it looked so "authentic" but they didn't have to worry about running into any actual authentic blue-collar types who would harsh their buzz by breaking a pool stick over their empty, deserving heads.

Now, I understand the need for bars and clubs that are

essentially fashion runways—after all, a critical segment of our economy depends on places to see and be seen. But for some reason, trust-fund kids struggling to look like they're living on a Wal-Mart employee's salary makes me think of Alex and the Droogs beating bums for fun; aren't poor people amusing! I was still wearing what I'd left the house in the day before for my scouting expedition—white sneakers, jeans, a generic pullover, black leather jacket. In context, I looked like Jerry Seinfeld. I'd have felt less out of place in a real blue-collar bar. Jean, however, was good to go in a stylized baseball jersey (white front, pink sleeves, FOXY spelled out in pink sequins; dry-clean only), kicky capri pants, and mules; Sam sported an authentic Lee denim jacket (surely purchased on eBay from a Japanese collector for much too much money) over a reproduction of an antique Foghat tee, semi-tucked into his Diesel jeans. Smashing!

"So how the hell did this Ronny Wycoff get to be a judge?" Jean asked through a cloud of smoke. Smoking had recently been outlawed in bars and restaurants in New York, which only served to make it an effortless way to Rebel. We were sitting on a bench up against the wall, leaning against reproductions of Xeroxed flyers for punk gigs from the early '70s.

"He's this old queen from England," Sam said dismissively. "He's their Phil Collins." I didn't bother to say that Phil Collins was their Phil Collins, God help them, or that however little love (lust being another matter) I had for Ronny, that insult was clearly beyond the pale. "Aural wallpaper for suburbanites. A little leer and a wink for the ladies, like some old Brighton vaude-villian in a straw hat and striped jacket."

"Hmm. Doesn't sound like I'm missing anything."

"You're not," Sam said, trying to casually put his feet up on the corner of the pool table and missing, I noted with childish satisfaction, because he was too short. He smoothly turned the move into a leg stretch that showed off this week's model of vintage sneaker to the surprising number of people in a dark bar so early on a weekday. "For God's sake, he just hired Christie Squires's old songwriter, so that tells you where *his* ambitions lie."

My blood froze with dread but I didn't say anything. "Poor Christie," Jean sighed. "Forced to subsist on a few hundred thousand dollars a year while her corporate masters drank VSOP shots out of her metaphorical navel."

"She's singing the 'Song of Bernadette' now to make herself look the victim, but I read on Gawker that she's doing Toad Elkins."

"Eww!" Jean squealed. "He's disgusting." She did a little hip-hop hand thing without even setting down her Stella Artois. "Yo, yo, I'm keeping it real 'cause I'm down with Christie, yo. Peace out, mothafuckas!"

"Well, her material's so awful, even one of old Toad's rants would be an improvement," Sam said coolly, looking off into a distance somewhere beyond the opposite wall.

Okay, so I'm not a social person. So I don't have a wealth of experience to draw upon in social situations. But I'm not stupid. And I know when someone's deliberately avoiding looking at me as they make their point.

"Well, I'm off," I said, standing up. "Good luck to both of you, see you at the first round."

"Laters," Sam said casually, while Jean gave me a hug and a promise to hook up soon. We were already on the Lower East Side, close to the Brooklyn Bridge, so I decided to walk home. I had a lot of rage to burn off and a lot to think about, and the walk would let me do both. To hell with Joan Collins—my paranoid streak wanted to ascribe downright *Jackie* Collins motives to Sam. But once I walked and calmed down a little, it occurred to me that his lust for Lyle and his loathing of me would likely have existed independently. Unlike many people as they get older, I could remember my younger self, even the bad parts, especially when I saw that self in people who were still young. How arrogant I had been in my loathing of Whitney Houston and Journey and Def White Scorpion and all the other musical earwax of my youth...how rarely I'd restrained myself from laughing at some old crocodile dressed too youthfully...how little patience I'd had for station wagons and yuppies and Republicans. (Well, some things never change.) I'd *wanted* them all to know how much I despised them, flipping my floppy Robert Smith black hair and turning on a dime in my Doc Martens so that my black trench coat swirled dramatically as I flounced away, turning up the volume on the Clash mix tape in my Walkman as I exited. It was *important* to me that they know that however much they tried to live in a world where they were all like one another, there was still a whole world out there that wasn't like them and didn't want to be, wouldn't ever be, no, never ever ever. Sam despised me because he despised Christie Squires, her music, the vacuousness of a world that ate her up with a spoon and grinned.

I stopped at "our" bench and leaned on the railing to look out at the Statue of Liberty and beyond. I was thinking with that giddy clarity you can sometimes get after a sleepless night, and I suddenly realized I was having an Ayn Rand moment. Now, this is going to dynamite any chance I'll ever have of being Taken Seriously, because all Serious People not only dismiss Rand and her books but consider doing otherwise to be a severe moral failing. Yeah, she was nutty as a fruitcake (I'd guess bipolar if I wasn't afraid of her estate suing me); yeah, her "rhymes with mine" philosophy has been used to justify countless atrocities in the realms of environmental protection, worker safety, et cetera. No argument from me. But have you ever read *The Fountainhead*? It's definitely one of those books that makes a bigger impact on you if you read it when you're young and impressionable, but the fact remains it's a pretty damn good novel. And at that moment I felt just like Peter Keating. Remember Peter? The hack architect who tries to go back to his first love, painting—at which he hadn't been half bad—after he realizes he's a wash as a builder? Then he asks Howard Roark (who must be the most Serious Person in all of literature) if he still has it, if the paintings are any good? And Howard, ruthless upholder of Standards, says, no, Peter, they suck.

I was wondering if I was Peter Keating, if even a few brief years of compromise and sellout had ensured I'd never be anything but a shopkeeper among creative gentlemen. I of all people was well aware that there was a fine line between intellectual rigor and intellectual snobbery; the latter, if you ask me, is the worst form of laziness. But when you go to crowded parties full of people you need to impress to get ahead, it helps to draw your outline in their minds in broad strokes, with brushes like "I don't own a television" or "Gore was just saying the other day" or "John Currin is a misogynist and I denounce him." Even the most brilliant people can be insecure, can go looking for someone to knock down and stand on to make themselves look taller. To laugh at a Peter Keating like me was to say, I too uphold Standards, I too despise mediocrity.

Could I, unlike Peter, turn around now, go back to trying to *say* something, the way I'd tried on my failed album? I had to try, didn't I? I suddenly realized with stomach-churning terror that I *really was* going to be on this show, at least for one episode, and that meant I was going to have to—*gulp*—come up with and perform at least one song. Words *and* music. On my own. And this was a hipster-oriented show; even if I'd been a barely twenty-something girl, I'd still have to come up with something "artistic." Hell, *Christie* was going to have to come up with something artistic, wasn't she? There was some consolation in the fact that the longest knives would be out for her, so the rest of us could take cover behind that.

But what to write? I'd always believed in a spoonful of sugar with my medicine, always tried to write about even the blackest subjects with some humor. I remember how I found out that Lyle knew me better than I knew myself the day he gave me a book to read. "I think you'll enjoy this," he said. I looked at the title and laughed.

"Karl Marx? You're giving a biography of an economic theorist to someone who can't balance his own checkbook?"

Lyle smiled. "Give it a shot."

So I did, and Francis Wheen's bio of Marx read like one of the best novels ever. Sometimes I even found myself laughing out loud. The Brits have an edge on us in this department, as anyone who's ever read *The Economist* knows—they've never been afraid to leaven their serious matters with a little humor. After that, I even tried (and failed, admittedly, but I tried) to read a "translation" of Thomas Hobbes's *Leviathan* into modern English. The author, who was a friend of Lyle's, felt strongly that it was an important book that was only being read, at gunpoint, by a small slice of college students, and that modifying the tangled syntax of the book's seventeenth-century English would be no more blasphemous than "translating" *Beowulf*. Of course, he had to defend his decision against people who accused him of watering down a classic, people who fulminated about the decline of Rigor in academic study, people who despised him for picking Hobbes of all people to transport to the modern world. And he did it all with a grace and humor that actually got the book into the Amazon.com top 100 for a few weeks.

Obviously I wasn't going to dig deep into economic antiquity for source material for songs, but somehow that was the idea that floated to the surface of the liquid in my brain pan—was there something I could write about, something Serious that I could make my own, a "concept album" approach, if you will? Something that people didn't know about, not because it wasn't interesting but because the material was dense, inaccessible, humorless...? But honestly, I was a dilettante—I mean, what had I ever studied seriously, what education or experience did I have that I could possibly turn into a song cycle...and there it was, right in front of me—well, right inside of me—all along.

You know that movie *The Matrix*? The first one, the really good one? They invented a special effect for that movie called "bullet time," which was really cool. In the midst of all this frenzied action, suddenly everything stopped; the camera rotated around the scene, capturing the frozen moment from every angle—and then, boom, the action began again.

Another of my theories: That effect really affected people because it *felt true*. We've all had "bullet time" moments in our lives, when time seems to stop, when all the pictures from all the angles we've perched at suddenly morph, suddenly link up to make a new picture, a new idea. And when the egg that's been incubating deep inside your head cracks and the shafts of sunlight surge out, it *is* as if time stops for just a moment, if only because for that moment your mind is working so fast it's like the rest of the world has had to stop and wait for you.

What had I researched rigorously, lived with, coped with through black humor? What had given me my creativity in the first place? What better musical territory than a place where serious and frivolous dwelled together in a "special relationship"? *I was a crazy person, 100% DSM-IV certified.* And while lots of musicians have been bipolar, how many of them had ever *written about it*? And how many of those had fallen prey to victimhood or romanticism and totally failed to see the great absurd joke in it?

I felt my body relax, flooding with the endorphins your brain rewards you with after a really good idea. Later on, I knew, I'd realize the potential ramifications of exposing my messiest internal parts in public, but for now the bells in my head were tolling the birth of an heir to the crown, and I let them, the *certainty* I'd missed for so long returning if only for a moment to say "Yes, that's it"—later, later would come the qualifiers and the obstacles, but for now there was only that Golden Path ahead, and the enormous sense of relief that it wasn't too late, there was still a way.

FIVE

Over the next two weeks, the field of contestants would be whittled down from a thousand to one hundred, with the judges seeing a hundred hopefuls a day over ten working days. The show took over the Bottom Line nightclub in Greenwich Village, a classic old joint that had seen the dawn of many a performer's career. It was a stroke of genius, I thought—a small, intimate venue with a lot of history that would throw a patina of Authenticity over the whole process.

I would be in the last group to be judged, which had its good and bad points. The bad news first: The judges would be burned out, and by that point everyone on stage would probably look and sound pretty much the same. I imagined the temptation to just eenie-meenie-miney-moe your way down the list would be pretty hard to resist. The good news, though, was that I had two weeks to get ready.

And let's face it, when you're going on TV, "getting ready" doesn't just mean polishing up your material; it means polishing *yourself* up. I mean, let's be honest—think about your typical famous and successful male rock star. What do they have in common besides talent? Well, as Rosie O'Donnell would say, they're all cutie patooties. Just think what success Leonard Cohen and Tom Waits could have enjoyed in the mass market had they hired personal stylists, had a little nip and tuck as time marched on, spent some of their cigarette money on Clinique and Aveda. Shallow? You know it. But I was no fool: I was thirty-something years old and I was going to be competing on a television show against people much younger, cuter, and still possessed of God-given elasticity of skin. Simon Cowell wouldn't be there tossing brilliant fat singers off the show, but his spirit, I felt sure, would hover over the proceedings. The only difference between Simon and so many others in the industry, after all, was that he wasn't afraid to say what so many of them were thinking.

Two weeks was hardly enough time to turn back the clock, but it was enough for a *Queer Eye*–level makeover. I called up Craig, who was aware that he would have had a job on Christie's next video had there been one, and he got me into Frederic Fekkai for a new hairdo. I got a facial, stepped up my gym attendance from a desultory now and then to a rigorous five times a week. I was a little too old to go to Diesel for a new wardrobe, but Old Navy was "downscale" enough—without being too tatty-looking for me to bear—to allow me to blend in with the other contestants. (One reason I'd never be groovy: I had an insurmountable, irrational abhorrence of thrift store clothes—the few times I tried to wear something from a used-clothing store, I'd always wondered, *Who died in this shirt?*)

Lyle was enormously supportive of the whole process, though (as always) a bit dismissive of my assertion that The Work was going to take second place to The Look.

"It's a *talent show*, Adam. You could be writing, rehearsing, researching with all the time you're spending on primping. Not to mention," he said with mock sternness, "the expense I know you're going to for some 'look' you think will be necessary to succeed."

"There is no expert in the field who'd deny that all my

cosmetic ablutions are necessary for the performance of my work, and therefore tax-deductible. I'm helping the economy and lowering my taxes every time I have my pores minimized."

He laughed. "It's all so..." He trailed off.

"What were you going to say?"

"Nothing, really."

"You started to say something, then you changed your mind."

"No, I just... No offense, love, but it's all so surprising. It *is* wonderful, but it's also so unlike you."

I laughed. "To do something crazy and impulsive? Hey, that used to be my stock in trade."

"You know, if you do well on the show, it's going to raise your profile. By which I mean not just in your line of work, but on the street. People will stop you, talk to you..."

"Yell at me, throw things, I know. I just...I just feel like this is my last chance. To be something, to be someone."

"You are something, you are someone!"

"I mean, a Serious Artist," I lowered my voice dramatically on the last two words. "It's this or Ronny Wycoff. Who, by the way, is one of the judges."

"Oh, no."

"Oh, yes. See, *now* I know what you're going to say," I cut him off. "You're going to say conflict of interest and all that and that I should recuse myself, blah blah. That's what a real Serious Person would do."

"No," he said thoughtfully, surprising me. "You don't have a preexisting relationship with him. You turned him down when he offered you a job—twice now. If anything, *he* should recuse himself from judging *you*."

I laughed, reassured by Lyle's learned opinion. "Thank you. I feel better." And I did! I'd laughed at the idea of Furrowing myself into a moral quandary over this, but in truth, I'd worried about what Lyle would think if no one else.

"I wish I could be there to cheer you on," he said softly, and if I were a woman I'd have had to change my underwear. But then he went and said something that flipped my stomach over. "Do you remember Sam Sparks?"

"Yes. Yes, I do."

"Well, he's in the contest. He made it through the first round too. Maybe the two of you will run into each other." Lyle seemed to find that an exciting possibility.

"How'd you know that?"

"Oh, we talked the other day, ironing out some details on this concert."

I am not a violent person. But I have been known to punch walls, pound desks, and kick doors. At this moment, I wanted to punch, pound, and kick Sam Sparks. The little rat had been there the same day I had, and he hadn't even mentioned me to my own fucking boyfriend! I thought of saying, Oh, yes, I know, he and I went out for drinks immediately afterward, didn't he tell you? But knowing Lyle, instead of arousing suspicion it would only make him think I was enjoying the professional conviviality of Sam's company, that I actually approved of the little rat.

I don't hate very many people. Dislike, despise, sure, but I reserve *hate* for people who've really made my life hell. Rick, my ex-boyfriend, who traveled back and forth from N.Y. to S.F. on business twice a week and had a whole other life (and lover) on the other coast (and who was always ragging on *me* for my various moral failures). And Jesse Helms, for all he's done for me and mine. That's about it. Now I added a third, in a long bloody stroke. Sam Sparks had ruined my day and was trying to ruin my life, and that put him on the list.

The day of my first show, I was up early and ready hours before the fashionably late noon start time (still frightfully early for most of the grooveoisie, nevertheless). But the last thing I wanted to do was arrive too early and have to either make conversation with strangers or face silent and ruthless Star Chamber examination of my shoes. So I was pleasantly surprised when my doorbell rang and there was Jean, holding a pink box.

"We can eat these now, or I can spike them with laxatives and 'share' them at the show." We ate them, lard and carbs being exactly what my nerves needed, though I didn't eat as many as I wanted because a full tummy would've messed up my diaphragm control. The sorting hat had put us both on the last day, and we'd gotten together a few times to trade gossip, speculation, Internet rumors, and mutual hopes and fears. I felt a bit guilty bonding with her so quickly—as if after Callie's exit to London I'd just gone to the store and bought a new Callie. But there was one difference neither Jean nor I entirely forgot: Whereas Callie was my collaborator, Jean was my competition.

A quick non-rush-hour subway ride and we were in Greenwich Village, where everybody looks like an artist, especially the investment bankers. We showed our Golden Tickets at the door and were admitted to what looked to me like old home week at Performing Arts High School. Kids (well, they looked like kids to me) were smoking, strumming, and sipping coffee, many of the cups enhanced with a splash from a flask. The main floor had been cleared of tables and chairs and set up with rows and rows of folding chairs, which had immediately been disordered by the contestants into pairs or circles or simply made less orderly on general principle.

Jean worked the room while I shuffled through my sheet music, which I didn't need, having done this song several hundred times, but which I'd brought along to clutch like a life preserver and bury myself behind rather than expose myself to what I was sure would be the scorn and ill will of the other contestants. (And because, superstitious, I thought if I didn't bring it I'd be like one of those *Idol* contestants who suddenly can't remember a note or a word of their song.) Yes, it was just paranoia and insecurity; I knew damn well that musicians are a collegiate and clubby lot, always eager to trade tips and news and enjoy the company of anyone who's also been crazy enough to give so much of themselves over to such an unpleasant and unprofitable enterprise. But while I've always been great with pretty much any kind of person in ones or twos, I'm completely at sea in a room full of strangers, no matter how much we have in common. (And then there was my Christiemockaphobia, which you've got to admit had some valid reasoning behind it in this crowd.)

Then Mr. Headset Clipboard came on stage and asked us all to take a seat. We all turned to the table, draped with a white tablecloth, at the bottom of stage right, along with three empty chairs. Everyone knew who the judges were now, and we all tried to look jaded, but truth be told it was exciting to be seeing them in person—even if you had no respect for their body of work, they were all what we were hoping to be: rich and famous.

Ronny was the least well-known but the richest of the lot. His $68 million contract with Omnivorous Records had already paid off for them, despite U.S. domestic sales of only 200,000 copies of his last album. He couldn't get arrested in America, but in the U.K. his tour dates had sold out within hours of going on sale. He hadn't Hammered his money away on bling and entourages; in fact, he was on his way to becoming one of the most substantial property owners in England. Even in a room full of people wearing MAKE TRADE FAIR shirts, he generated plenty of envy if not respect.

The other two judges were Nell Makepeace and Bryce Warburg. Nell was part of YBC's attempt to bring artistic credibility to the show; she'd lived in the Village since before anyone, even the 'mos, wanted to live there. She'd made her reputation in the '60s with songs full of sentimental humanism—you know, antiwar songs about flowers, anticapitalism songs about children sharing their candy, antipollution songs about loving trees so much you—basically, she'd been the inspiration for the term *tree hugger*. Nell was enjoying a revival now, partly the reward any American public figure gets after decades of sheer endurance, partly grudging tribute to her unwavering commitment to all the hippie shit that was starting to look—under a Republican legislative, executive, and judicial troika—like the only thing that might save this country from becoming a Chernobyl from sea to shining sea. Also, she'd been den mother to several generations of performers and behind those granny glasses was an eagle eye for talent.

Bryce Warburg was there to represent the commercial side of the business. Bryce had made his fortune cruising repair shops and skate parks for the kind of boys who could be photographed nude or nearly so in grimy black-and-white, and therefore transformed into the kind of softcore porn that upscale queens put on their walls and called art. One of those boys had turned out to have—in addition to interesting piercings, self-designed tattoos, and a legendary penis—a singing voice frighteningly identical to Frank Sinatra's. Bryce had realized that the same queens who bought pictures of Zeke Hawthorne would also buy his album, see him in concert, and promote him through the gaypevine, and that there was no reason someone who was not Bryce should be the boy's manager and skim the cream off the top of what could be milked from this cow. Zeke, no fool, had been the only one of Bryce's models savvy enough to negotiate a royalty on every likeness sold; he and Bryce had an honest business arrangement, and Bryce provided him with the sort of entree to the inner circle of rich and powerful queens in the record industry he never would have gotten access to (as a singer, anyway). Rumors that the two of them had been secretly married in Amsterdam were constantly renewed on the Internet and were probably untrue, though you never know.

We all applauded politely as the judges took their seats, and the lights and cameras came to life. The show's unctuous host was Neil Gates, one of those smarmy infotainment reporters who, by dint of the popularity of his whoop-whoop yuck-yuck talk show on the old *Young Bastard* channel, and various blood connections to powerful people at the parent corporation, had managed to snag this gig as our own would-be Ryan Seacrest. While he rattled on about the amazing adventure ahead, I looked around the room for someone I hoped I wouldn't see, namely Sam. There was no sign of him, to my relief. Which meant he'd already been through his first round—which meant he was already out of the show or on to the next round. I resolved to ask Jean if she'd heard anything, but that turned out not to be necessary. She sat down next to me in a huff as the first singer began, noodling out some Céline Dion–esque tune.

"We're the curve weight," she snarled. "Bastards."

"What? What do you mean?"

"At Ivy League schools, they keep a certain number of sub-par students around to weight the curve. To make the good students look even better. We're the dregs. They saved the fucking dregs for the last day. We're the ones who're supposed to fall by the wayside in the first few rounds. Dilettantes and poseurs and"—she waved her forbidden cigarette at the girl onstage—"lite-rock-less-talk wimps."

It didn't take an intuitive leap to figure out that Sam, with his already accumulating trendiness on the New York scene, had been put into an earlier round and promoted on. Nevertheless, I was elated at Jean's news and broke into a big smile. "What's so damn funny?" Jean demanded.

"Hey, if we only have to show up the bottom feeders, we're a cinch for the next round."

She looked at me for a minute, then laughed. It took me a second to realize I wasn't the only one with self-esteem issues. During our gossip fests I'd heard her sing and play, and she wasn't half bad. It dawned on me that despite their casual poses and breezy voices, there probably wasn't anyone in this room who hadn't at least come *close* to vomiting over this whole thing.

Then Céline Dion Jr. was done, and despite signs held up by production assistants that said LOUD APPLAUSE, or probably because of them, she got about the same response a mediocre lounge singer might get in a half-empty bar. "Now let's all give a warm welcome to our next performer, Adam Bede!" Neil Gates cried with the same enthusiasm he'd once mustered daily for every half-ass starlet who'd lift her top on his show, and my bowels turned to water.

Jean grabbed my hand as the cameras turned on me. I suddenly realized the digital photos they'd taken of us were to help the crew recognize us. I clutched my sheet music like a security blanket and got up on the stage. Bryce had his fingertips pyramided under his chin, Nell smiled encouragingly, and Ronny winked at me.

"I'm Adam Bede, and my song is called 'For a Walk.'" I sat down at the piano, took a breath, and started.

I have a compact with my demon
A deal that keeps us both from screaming
He's kept restrained, and yet his chain
Must betimes turn into a leash
Without his odd day of free rein
Our contract he declares in breach

I have a compact with my demon
I know I'll never be a free man

118

I've learned to live with certain pains
Despite what holy fathers preach
A saturnalia now and again
Keeps him from extending his reach

My demon loves his earthly pleasures
Not for him the next life's treasures
We take turns being the aggressor
Neither always the acquiescer
He goes out, he's the transgressor
I come home, I'm the confessor

I have a compact with my demon
I think you understand my meaning
He'll cause me some amount of pain
Yet I confess, our night walks teach
Pleasures of which I can't complain
Until he starts to overreach

This was an old song, one that almost made it onto my
album but that I pulled at the last minute—out of, I'll confess,
sheer terror. Because if you don't know this song is about drugs,
you're not paying attention. (All the best songs are about drugs:
Weezer's "Island in the Sun"? Vicodin. Depeche Mode's "Never
Let Me Down"? Heroin. Foo Fighters' "All My Life"? Drugs,
drugs, drugs.) This was, mind you, just before federal and
municipal Puritanism had made decadence so fashionable
again in our fair city, but just after John Ashcroft had become
our attorney general with the intention of turning *The
Handmaid's Tale* into a documentary, and I didn't want to be on
record as having done anything that could one day get me sent
to the Drugulag. I consoled myself over my cowardice by envi-
sioning it as a B side to my second number one single, or maybe

a song I'd only play live at my sold-out stadium shows. Naturally, that meant it had been rotting in a folder on my computer all this time.

I have to say, I wasn't nervous once I started. The first thing I had to learn as a performer—and the hardest—was to pay attention to my song and not my audience. When you're deathly afraid to look up and see boredom or disgust—well, you don't look up.

There was a moment of silence as I finished, and I waited for the desultory applause Céline Jr. had gotten. To my surprise, whoops and cheers erupted from the others. Fatalistically, I'd chosen my darkest material, which was exactly what went over with this crowd. Whether it would sway the judges or not was another matter. I went to my mark at the front of the stage to receive their verdict as the camera mercilessly recorded my reaction.

Bryce was first. "I'm reminded of Byron. If he'd had a love child with Emily Dickinson. And that love child had grown up to be David Bowie." Everyone laughed and I smiled, suspecting that this was a compliment. Like grudgingly good reviews you read in *The New York Times*, it was so artfully constructed that you couldn't extract a favorable blurb for the life of you.

Nell nodded. "Very interesting. I'd just note that at the end of the second verse you use the word 'reach,' and at the end of the fourth the word 'overreach.' You've got a nice rhyme structure going, and I don't think you intended to repeat yourself. Just fix that and you've got a...well, I can't say a lovely song, but a good one, no doubt." I nodded and thanked her, amazed that she'd caught that without having made a single note on the pad of paper in front of her.

Finally it was Ronny's turn. He stretched and said, "Well, mate, I'll tell you, I've got a demon or two in *my* menagerie," and he grinned as those who knew who he was, including his fellow judges, laughed. "And if you can manage yours, I could use some pointers." More laughter. "Good job, good job."

I thanked them all and left the stage, the cameras on me, knowing that I'd made it, that I was on to the next round. I'd be on national television, if only for a moment, and I had to laugh. It was just what I'd wanted all those crazy years, to live every moment as if it were always the last scene of the original *Star Wars,* and there was nothing but triumph and joy in my heart, and love and worship in those around Me, the Center of the Universe. And I guess I laughed because I was astonished, frankly—I'd spent so many nights alone on my bed, dreaming so vividly of how it all *should* be, and then gone to parties or clubs where, to be honest, I often forgot I *wasn't* famous, *hadn't* proved myself, and ended up acting like I already was the Great Man because I so fiercely thought I deserved to be one. And I guess maybe the reason I'd become such a hermit crab over the years was partly because I'd woken up after more than one manic evening and realized what a fool I'd made of myself, to think that anybody could possibly have thought *I* was anyone or ever would be…the flip side of manic egotism being depressive self-loathing in ruthlessly counterweighted doses. Best to stay home and make a fool of yourself where nobody can see…and now, the irony—for once I'd stood up modestly and with no expectations, and just done the as best I could, and it had been the first time they'd cheered.

I hugged Jean as I came off the stage and she went on. She did a song about love gone bad—damn, the girl could sing some blues! Sure enough, she made it through too. We were dying to go drink something other than the Starbucks coffee provided as a promotional tie-in, but we weren't allowed to leave. The cameras wanted lots of hands clapping after each song (additional clapping for some songs would be mixed in later, we found out when we watched the show on TV). As the show went on I realized

Jean was right about the dregs. Some people who never, ever should have gotten out of Madison Square Garden alive had been given delusions of adequacy so that they could be filmed making asses of themselves for the nation's amusement—and so that Ronny and Bryce could deliver catty lines about their cluelessness or lack of talent.

If you've ever seen early rounds of *American Idol,* you'll know what I'm talking about. I'm afraid generations are growing up in our fair nation with absolutely no objective, constructive criticism. "You can do anything you set your mind to," they're told by chirpy teachers and TV shows and songs and movies. "Anything at all." Unfortunately, there are some things some people can't ever do. One of those is sing; the desire to do it is not in itself enough to make you capable of doing it. And until the moment Simon Cowell tells them, "You're never ever going to be a singer," nobody has ever once, say, encouraged them to take up a musical instrument instead. They stand there like cattle who don't realize the bolt has already been shot through their heads, and then they stand in the hall outside and affirm with all their heart that they *will* be singers, they *will,* he's *wrong.*

Nell angrily defended these losers at first, until she realized she'd been set up as the Paula Abdul character, at which point she turned the tables. Each judge was allowed to pass three people into the next round regardless of the opinion of the other two, and that day Nell used hers to promote the contestants who'd taken the most abuse from Ronny and Bryce. This probably made the poor talentless bastards feel better, and definitely delighted the producers, who were getting ratings-snatching cat-scratching right from the get-go. This—and the Starbucks coffee—was pretty much the only thing that kept me awake until we finally got out of there at 11 P.M.

I was bone-tired, but Jean was just waking up. "Come on, let's go celebrate."

"If we coulda booked out of here about 10,000 hours ago, I'd say yes, but I'm burned, hon, I've got to go to bed."

She frowned. "You're going to have to start getting used to late hours, superstar."

I laughed. "I'll cross that stage when I come to it."

When I got home, the call was already on the machine—I'd made it, one of ten to go to the next round. I felt relief but little else. Except, of course, fear. I was going to be on television, and if I fell, I'd fall in front of millions of people. All my delusions from my old full-on crazy days would now have an opportunity to make themselves come true—people *would* be pointing at me on the street, laughing at me if I'd made a fool of myself the night before. The irony of it all was almost laughable: To make my dreams come true, I'd have to risk all my nightmares coming true too.

I'll tell you something—I miss being crazy sometimes, especially at times like this. Back in the day, moving on to the next round would have been the signal for the Royal Fireworks Music to play in my head, replete with the loud, colorful display it was written to accompany. Irrational exuberance has its uses—it props up economies, religions, military-industrial complexes...and people like me. If I'd still been crazy, I would have *known*, just *known* that it was my manifest destiny to make it to the finals, to be crowned the winner. Which would have made for crushing disappointment somewhere between here and there when I got breezily dismissed, but in the meantime would have kept me pumped up, enthusiastic, and most important, creatively fertile.

YBC was making a sweeps event of the show, and the results of the ten first rounds were being aired five nights a week for the first two weeks. So again I had two weeks to prepare for the first live broadcast round, during which time I could watch the show and size up the remaining ninety-nine contestants. Oh, and write some songs.

Over that time, as I watched myself and the others on the preliminary-round shows, the pattern in what I was watching became clear to me. I wouldn't call it a *setup,* but clearly some key demographic desires were being fulfilled by the contestants who moved on. There was a large swath of Keane-eyed boys with lips bigger than their hips, many of whom were of Benettonishly indeterminate ethnicity; there was the brassy fat girl who'd show 'em all; there was Everyone's Best Friend who cheered for everyone who made it and cried with everyone who didn't; and the willowy boy who everyone thought was a big closet case but wasn't really because he still didn't know himself that he was gay. There were a handful of beautiful girls—including Jean and one punkette who was so Brody Dalle–ish that I kept looking for that luscious Josh Homme every time I saw her—but most of the girls looked and sounded like proto Whitney Houstons—all technical perfection and no soul. In short, enough good-looking people to lust for, enough average or less-than good-looking people to identify with, and enough talent to keep you caring. I thought my beauty boot camp must have paid off, since I was clearly the only person over thirty who'd made it through—not part of YBC's demographic at all.

And, of course, there was Sam. I'd thought he was charming in Lyle's office—as I lay curled up on my couch with lemon water and a rice cake (the camera adds ten pounds) watching the second show, I realized I hadn't seen anything yet. He announced that his song had been written for a concert he was helping organize to draw attention to the plight of asylum-seekers in Britain. And then the humble smile as everyone applauded, then the hand through the deliberately disheveled hair, the frown of concentration, and then some song that would have made Billy Bragg proud—hell, would have made Billy Bragg famous if only he'd been as gorgeous as Sam.

I had to hand it to him. It was righteous, and heartfelt, and made him look "sensitive." Of course, it didn't denounce the British government or people directly (which Billy Bragg would've done in the first verse); it was really more one of those soft-focus pleas for compassion. If I sound cynical, it's probably because to me it felt target-marketed; if Sam were singing on the same subject in some East Village dive, I have no doubt that the song would have been a lot more incendiary. As he performed it that day, it was to protest music what Big Audio Dynamite was to the Clash—good, yeah; world-altering, no.

Of course, I thought bitterly, he must have known that with subject matter like that, and by stating his involvement with the benefit concert, he could rely on a veto vote from Nell to move him on regardless of what Bryce and Ronny thought. The camera cut to her from time to time, and it was clear that however sharp-eyed she was in the talent department, her Achilles heel was clearly anybody whose politics aligned so neatly with hers.

"That was beautiful," she said, sure enough. "Really moving. I wish you the best of luck with your concert." Sam smiled and ducked his head.

"Interesting," Bryce said. "Protest music is a very hard sell, though. Not something likely to get you signed to a label."

"Ahem," Ronny said, arms folded. "Listen, mate, if you're so concerned about the unjustly imprisoned, you got a lot of those in America you could be singing about, you know. Maybe you could throw this concert of yours down at Guantánamo Bay."

Safe in my living room, I hooted and hollered, kicking my legs in the air with joy. The look on Sam's face as Ronny took the piss out of him was priceless. Shock at first, then a narrowing of the eyes and pursing of the lips that he couldn't prevent, camera or no camera—and suddenly his shucks-a-mercy response to Nell and all the teenage hearts it had sent aflutter were all for nothing. I was astonished that Ronny had it in him, the words and the nerve to say them; then I remembered his dismal U.S. sales figures and realized he had nothing to lose. All publicity is good publicity, and being misquoted and denounced the next day on Murdoch news channels around the world couldn't hurt his career here and could only help back home.

Then of course there was the night Christie was a contestant, which turned out to be the highest rated of the first round of shows, naturally. It was going to be one of those "water cooler moments" nobody dared miss, so not only were her fans watching but millions of others who'd tuned in just for the curiosity value—could the legendary hand puppet perform without the hand?

She walked up on the stage with the poise of a seasoned performer. She nodded to the judges and didn't smile as she said simply, "Hi, my name is Christie Squires, and my song is called 'On My Own.'" She had no guitar, so I waited for her to sit down at the piano. But she just stood there and started singing a capella.

> You held my hand, you drove me around
> You pushed me higher on the swing
> You sewed my clothes, you cooked my meals
> But it's time for me to do my own thing
>
> I know you think you know what's best
> And maybe then you did
> But it's time for you to give it a rest
> I'm not a kid, I'm not a kid—anymore

I had to hand it to her—it was a brilliant idea. It sounded like a song any adolescent might sing to a parent, but she and I and everyone else knew damn well that it wasn't. Christie

Squires had just declared her independence, startling us all by proving she just might make it on her own.

The rounds were shown out of order; the round with Jean and me aired on the first Friday—the night YBC's target demo was least likely to be watching TV. I watched myself on television for the first time and tried to be as objective as I could (of course I was also TiVoing it for later reevaluation). Did my face look scrunchy when I sang with my eyes closed? If I'd relaxed more, some of the song's humor could have come through. I sounded okay, the positive response I thought I'd gotten had indeed been there, but I realized I needed to do better if I was going to stay on. I made notes as I watched, both on myself and the others—Lyle would be proud, I thought, of my meticulous research.

Said research was actually an attempt on my part to stay busy and keep my anxiety at bay, especially with my communications from Lyle having narrowed to occasional short e-mails. Several terrorist attacks had taken place on Karadzic's prison in attempts to free him, which prompted various Balkan states into elevated saber-rattling and surprise military exercises, so I saw much more of him on CNN and heard almost nothing from him on the phone.

I went to bed that night feeling pretty good, all things considered. Then I woke up Saturday and got the paper, and my heart sank. YBC was being investigated for age-discriminatory hiring practices, and as part of their official denial they noted that a 35-year-old was one of the successful contestants on their most youth-oriented show. (Setting aside my personal trauma for a moment, I had to savor the cluelessness of a network that considers a 35-year-old to be a senior citizen.) Was that it, I thought? Was I just as much a part of the setup, graduated to the next round just for PR purposes? I told myself to look at my notes, watch the TiVo, but I was afraid to. Maybe I was still suffering delusions of grandeur after all. Who the hell had ever achieved pop music success at such an advanced age? (I might have reminded myself, had the fountain of ideas had any water pressure behind it, that Kim Gordon of Sonic Youth was over 30 when they made it, and Debbie Harry was no spring chicken when Blondie's tide was high.) Add to that Lyle's absence and the inescapable memory of Sam—young, young Sam—in Lyle's office, and suddenly I was riding the cyclothymic curve downward.

Depression is made of certainty and delusion as completely as mania is; only the delusional certainties are pushing you down rather than raising you up: You're a fool, it's hopeless, I'm tired, I can't. And who in that state would ever dare to challenge a blank piece of paper and summon forth from it new life? So I didn't write any songs. I had one more in my treasure chest that could get me through the next round, but after that I'd need to be writing a new one every week. I sat at the computer and all I saw was my own reflection. The reflection of an old hack-writer of bubblegum music, meant only to be discarded casually and then cursed when it stuck to your shoe.

The secret to success in New York, the one foundation stone you can't build without, isn't the ability to socialize, isn't the drive to conquer, isn't the discipline, though you need all those as well. No: It's that very bottomless self-confidence that is fatal in the incompetent but indispensable in the talented, a bedrock of belief in yourself that can weather innumerable rejections, setbacks, tumbles, plots against you. "I know I can, I know I can," the little engine said, but I didn't.

That night I went to the bathroom to perform my evening ablutions and my hand froze midway to the bottle of omega-3. Maybe it was the Bad Idea Bears on my shoulder, but a little voice said, *What if? What if you don't take it tonight? Or tomorrow? Or the next day?* Bipolars love self-medication; we're always aware of how we feel, and often the easiest way to alter the emotional weather in our heads is to drink, or smoke, or eat, or worse. No doctor can put two fingers on a psyche, monitor its pulse, and grade it against a clinical norm—the only measurable outcome of what we put into our bodies to fix our heads is how we *feel,* how well we operate the heavy machinery that is daily life, how close we can ever get to that state that doesn't appear in the *DSM-IV* but should: functionally insane.

The textbook is full of instances of people who felt "fine" after taking lithium for a while but didn't like the side effects, stopped taking it, and ended up in the ER days later looking like extras from the movie *Quills.* But I'd never been on lithium; I was a mere Bipolar II, not some tragic Bipolar I. What would happen if I stopped the fish oil? Would I open myself up to searing pain again, to crushing disappointment? Sure. But I might also have a nice long hypomanic episode, in which I'd feel energetic, self-confident, creative...

Lyle must never know, I told myself, and that was as close as I got to rationality. I decided then and there that if that's what it would take for me to be somebody, to save my career and my marriage and my finances, if I was going to have to go a little crazy to do this thing, well, God help me, because that's what I was going to do.

SIX

Despite this flagrant neglect of my mental health, I managed to keep up my gym attendance, hoping the endorphins would help keep my humors stable. As two more weeks passed, I kept taking my emotional temperature, all too well aware how my brain fever would present itself—in stores, I tested my patience by choosing the longest line, more often than not finding myself behind some superstitious old person who wouldn't surrender their checkbook for an ATM card and who tripled the wait time with such questions as "What's the date today?" (this after the total was announced) and "Now who do I make this out to?" And since I didn't find myself screaming offers to pay for their groceries if they'd just get a move on, obviously I hadn't tilted too far off balance yet.

I started feeling more creative almost immediately. Maybe that was the placebo effect, but whatever worked. Little rhymes danced across my consciousness, demanding to be written down for future insertion into more complete works. I found myself waking up earlier each day—but that might just have been a consequence of the exercise and/or my excitement. I'd dart out in the morning for a grande mocha and dart back to channel the caffeinated inspiration onto the page. The hard part was setting the words to music—I could noodle around on a piano, but basically all I was doing was plunking a few keys as background for what was really more like spoken word. It was small consolation to remember that Christie couldn't play any instrument—pop stars were expected to sing in the studio, and dance on the stage, but not even to sing *and* dance at the same time. Innumerable performers are grateful to Madonna for pioneering the headset-microphone combo. Anyone else might have looked like one of those operators standing by, but with her reputation as a control freak she looked like she was constantly receiving information from the production team, and for all we knew sending commands back between verses. But their gratitude stems not from the ability to sing and dance hands-free, but from the ability to *look* as if you were doing both at the same time. Watch carefully: The performers who lip-synch their shows always wear headsets. They're the red herring to throw you off the fact that, unless said performer really *is* Madonna, they probably don't have the fitness to sing *and* dance at the same time.

The one thing that made me think maybe I *was* losing it a bit was that people on the street started looking at me in a funny way—or were they? Was I going crazy again? Normally I'd say yes, Adam, you're being paranoid, but the fact remained that I *had* been on national television, which made it a real possibility that I wasn't hallucinating.

Then one morning I was at Starbucks when a fight broke out between two dogs whose owners had left them tied up outside. As they bolted out the door to break it up, the guy behind the counter looked at me and said, "Guess they didn't get their odd day of free rein," and winked at me. I blushed, smiled, and took my coffee. It was real! I had made an impression on someone! It's every artist's twisted pair of desires: to make a deep, private, personal impact on an individual, and to hear as many of them as possible acclaim him at once.

It was interesting to me to see the kind of people who remembered me from the show—the kind of people I'd never have imagined watching it. First and foremost, they were almost all my age or older. The fiftyish woman with the black hair, bobbed and laced with gray, a smart overcoat, no makeup save just the right lipstick for her coloring. The Wittgenstein look-alike behind the counter of the used bookstore. The traffic cop who looked like a budding opera singer, who dropped the whistle from his mouth to yell, "Hey, how ya doing, buddy! Good luck, okay?"

So many of us harbor rock-star dreams, no matter how far we've aged out of pop music's core demographic, no matter that for most of us the only stage we'll ever sing from will be in a karaoke bar. Amidst all the fresh-faced youth on *The Bottom Line Showcase,* there I was, a senior citizen as far as the bell curve went. That guy who won on the reality version of *Fame* turned out to be about my age, but he'd only revealed his true age after winning. I had to suspect that the discrimination suit against YBC had been a godsend to me, the only reason I'd gotten into the first round.

God, how many nights back in my crazy days I'd dreamed of mass adulation, instinctively sure it would make everything better. And now here I was: a socially inept and isolated person, and yet all I had to do was walk around Manhattan for a while and I'd get little smiles and nods from people (not for New Yorkers any uncool overt public display of recognition). I'd come home pleasantly amazed and refreshed and ready for another day of work. I could see how fame could be a drug, or at least an irresistibly warm bubble bath. (Of course there's a dark side—think of Courtney Love rampaging through Manhattan around the tenth anniversary of Cobain's death, hurling mike stands and flashing titties, desperately trying to get someone to turn the spotlight back on her.)

The show was an immediate hit, its ratings sky-high—no doubt largely due to the combined viewing power of Christie fans and those who hated her enough to want to see her fail. There were now 100 contestants left, and ten a night would duel it out onstage for two weeks of live weeknight shows. The judges were still there to criticize or praise, but their power to add or remove contestants was gone; now it was all up to the votes of the home audience.

YBC had come up with a brilliant idea. Each viewer who wanted to vote had to register with YBC, either online or through text messaging via their cell phone. Ostensibly this was to keep people from voting again and again, but it also meant that if you weren't young and groovy enough to have Internet or a cell, you couldn't vote. This gave the show a huge cachet with young people who despised anyone who wasn't on the cutting edge of communication. In addition, someone at YBC had clearly seen *Max Headroom,* because they came up with the idea of allowing the audience to start voting on the night's contestants *right from the beginning of the show.* In other words, Christie's fans could stuff the ballot box starting at 8:01 Eastern Time, and her competition would have to per-form underneath a giant tote board that displayed a bar chart showing each contestant's votes as the hour went on—thus dispensing with the fiction that any talent show was only about talent.

Even more savage, YBC had also set up the user accounts so that you could log in again during the show and change your vote, ensuring maximum instability in the performers and max-imum interest in the viewers. To cap it off, the ten contestants' scores and their fluctuating place in the pecking order ran across the top of the screen like a NASCAR ticker. Moreover, the ticker ran onscreen *even during commercials,* which made the commercial time on the show all the more valuable because advertisers knew that for once viewers would be glued to the set even during the orations of the Obnoxi-Clean guy. All this quickly made *The Bottom Line Showcase* the must-see show of the year.

You had to pity anyone who was seeded in Christie's part of the draw; they didn't have a chance against her legions of adoring fans, none of whom would have been caught dead without a text-messaging cell phone. But as the weeks rolled on, I started to wonder if that seeding had been as deliberate as it would have been at a tennis tournament. From the opening minute of Sam's night, his bar on the chart was an obelisk towering over the plinths of the other contestants. He'd already been written up in all the weekly gossip rags—photoed up would be more like it, as his beautiful, sullen face and artfully disarranged hair occupied more room in *Us* than any mere words about him— and his appearance on the cover of *Slim Teen* indicated that he'd already been anointed King of the Screaming Teenage Girls. The competition they threw up against him was good enough to keep viewers from tuning out, but none of them were nearly as hot.

To my relief, Jean squeaked through her performance, although something strange happened just after she finished. Neil always chatted up the contestants backstage after their performances. "So, Jean," he asked her after what had clearly been an emotionally wringing performance in the Alanis Morissette vein, "how are you feeling tonight?"

She flipped her hair in a way that would have been obnoxious if she didn't do it so naturally. "Not too bad, I think I did okay."

"So is this as stressful as, say, talent night at the Turner School?"

She froze—you could see it on camera. "Something like that," she said stiffly, walking off stage against all governing etiquette of live interviewing, which dictated that only the interviewer could end the conversation. I'd known Jean was rich, but the Turner School! If you've never heard if it, it's a school in Atherton, California, where San Francisco Bay area hippies-turned-yuppies sent their children to learn drum banging, protest chanting, face painting, love, tolerance, and Marxism—but the reason it was still around despite all that was that those subjects were only ancillary to one of the most rigorous performing arts curricula in the nation. There were plenty of scholarship students there (part of the Founding Persons' earnest desire to expose their wealthy offspring to "real people"), so there was no reason for Jean to be mortified at being found out as a former student...unless, that is, there was something she didn't want people to know...

"Okay!" Neil Gates shouted cheerfully, as if being snubbed was all part of the job. "A big hand for Jean Ploughford!" The camera caught her as she whipped around and sent eye daggers Gates's way, before stomping off the set.

Then it hit me. Jean Ploughford! Her parents were Ned and Sally Ploughford, famous tunesmiths from the '60s. They'd made their first million singing saccharine love songs to each other and their successive separate millions singing bitter, vengeful songs about how they'd done each other wrong. It was a guaranteed eternal market, as lovebirds would purchase their duet work in the first flush of joy, and then, after the split and the wrangling over the record collection, go to the solo work for consolation and justification.

Suddenly everything fell into place. When she'd been talking outside the Garden about her other avenues to success, that's what she'd meant—not her wealth, but her parents' connections in the music biz. She'd had to register for the show under her real

135

name, but she'd been performing as Jean Ford—until now. There was no doubt in my mind that the producers had chosen the most dramatic moment to unmask her. She'd wanted to do this with no connection to her parents, but in the information age there was no realistic hope of ever getting away with any such secrets.

I felt a moment of sadness for her until I was distracted by the realization of what this meant for me. The second Friday night, the last night of the first live rounds, would be my next round—was the same kind of ambush in store for me? I didn't want my history as Christie's songwriter exposed; that would mean all the hipsters voting against me because of my association with her as well as all her fans voting against me because of my part in the evil empire that she'd painted as having controlled her every move. But there was no doubt it would come out, and I'd be screwed.

If I were a Serious Person, clearly I'd have hunkered down and done The Work regardless of imminent doom; it would have been my duty to go down with the ship, to die trying. I would have taken consolation in the companionship and esteem of my fellow Serious People after a job well done, no matter what material failure resulted. Instead I felt the tingling of my first manic flush since stopping the fish oil. Suddenly the rules were irrelevant, the competition was insignificant; I could get up there and sing a song full of cussing and yelping and howling and rapping and Nina Hagen–esque arias and in the end I'd just be remembered as that guy who wrote "AWOL at the Mall."

Certainty settled on me like a familiar, warm old coat. Doomed, damned, and dumb for thinking otherwise... I remember once having a fit of rage when I heard some novelist at one of Lyle's (early) parties talking about how fascinated he was by the subject of "failure." I thought it was absurd: No matter how spectacularly his novels failed commercially (and they did), whatever talent he lacked as a novelist he made up for as a master of foundation-kissing, seminar-licking, and conference-schmoozing. All his luminous and promptly remaindered prose had been dedicated to the various colonies, endowments, and centers who'd ensured that his failure was a softer feather bed than most people's success. And in the end, "failure" was his subject only because it was one of those words that make too many Serious Persons do that Bill Clinton face—the solemnly bowed head, the pursed lips, the tightly squeezed eyes—meant to communicate how Seriously he took whatever he was doing.

Well, here I was, about to fail big time: critically, commercially, and publicly, with nothing to fall back on but my ass. I was about to watch Sam Sparks's star eclipse mine not only on my living room television but in my bedroom as well. All the surprised, kind smiles I'd gotten from strangers on the street were about to be replaced with mocking laughter. If that motherfucker wanted to know what failure was *really* like, he should tune in Friday, because I was about to teach a master class.

My night came. I'd never been calmer. I was resolved that if I was to go to the headsman's block, I would go like Anne Boleyn, regal and poised. And yet I also planned, in the words of Patsy Stone, to "go out with a bang." You had to give YBC credit: This was no *American Idol* sort of search, looking for someone who could adequately perform in genres they had no love for; we were given free rein in our material and not expected to submit it beforehand—the only rule being no words declared naughty by the FCC.

I was to be the third contestant that night. None of us had been written up in the press yet, and any flack could tell you that tonight's planned sound bite for the morning shows would be my exposure as one of the Great Satans behind ChrisCo. Right before I performed, this bitchy girl Nola, whom I'd hated from day one, went out and sang a song dedicated to her sick grandma. Her bar on the chart went up and up as the camera cut to Nell Makepeace wiping away a tear (she was a sucker for sap, as the contestants were quickly learning) and Ronny lifting one crossed arm, in Bush Sr. fashion, to look at his watch. Ronny knew what I and the rest of the contestants knew, which was that Nola was the meanest, most spiteful old cat you'd ever been stuck in a room with, but put a camera on her and goddamn if she wasn't immediately possessed by the spirit of Little Nell. But the audience didn't know this, and they didn't like Ronny, so his disdain only jacked up her tally. I could see her two years from now, thanking God at the Grammys even as her concert T-shirts were cranked out by slave labor in China with her full knowledge.

I was called out on stage, but the ordinary process was disrupted as Neil Gates accosted me before I could get to the piano. "Adam, how's it going?"

"You tell me," I said warily. "Doesn't this part usually come after the performance?"

He chuckled nervously. "Yes, it does. But we've just gotten the most interesting piece of information about you."

"No, you haven't. You've known all along. And you've waited until tonight so that there'll be an interesting piece of news tomorrow to keep the show in the headlines on *Entertainment Tonight*."

I heard a hoot from Ronny but didn't dare look that way. Neil's bland oatmeal face was rapidly turning colors. "Okay, Adam, then what *is* this interesting piece of information?"

I smiled, putting on a game show voice. "Gee, Neil, there are a lot of interesting facts about me. Why don't you tell me which one you've got for the folks at home tonight?"

Neil glared at me. "I'm sure the *folks at home* will be interested to hear that you're recently unemployed, thanks to the end of your job as Christie Squires's lyricist."

"Yes, Neil, Christie's recently decided to go her own way, on this very show, in fact. And I'm glad I could be part of the organization that gave her her big start, and I wish her all the luck in the world in her future career."

"Adam, what do you think about these allegations that Christie was exploited and abused by you and your co-owners of the corporation that…"

"Well, Neil, it's like this. Christie was a performer. You can be the biggest diva in a Broadway show, but someone has to write the show-stopping song for you. *You* could be the best host a reality television show ever had, but that isn't ever going to give you a piece of the syndication pie." There was scattered laughter at Neil's expense. "May I play my song now?" And without waiting for his reply, I sat down at the piano.

Okay, I thought. Okay. Calm down. I was swirling with rage, with satisfaction, with wild manic energy. Channel it! This is the last time you'll ever sit at this piano, on this stage, the last time the American public will ever see you on television. You're Anne Boleyn, you're Anne Boleyn, commend your soul to God and die like a queen. I started to bang out a bluesy riff.

> Well, I was born broken and my head hurts
> Spent my life looking for something that works
> Therapy, sex, chemistry, I don't care
> Just get me out of here, put me any elsewhere
>
> Deliverance is bliss, sugarcoat my nerves
> Eighty migs of OC or the like will serve

Or you can promise me your lifelong love
Till you meet one younger, cuter, and I get the shove

Or I could go shopping, run up my charge cards
To the limit on bling and caviar
Bid on eBay for the real Excalibur
Or a coat made of endangered fur

Buy a couple pounds of chronic hydroponic
End up with delusions Napoleonic
Hit the clubs in search of something erotic
Hit the floor when my drink's dosed with autohypnotic

'Cause I was born broken and my head hurts
I'm in need of some serious social work
Fixing my head, now there's a major project
Unless I win this contest, which would defy all logic

That'll fix it all, the roar of the crowd
Spending one spin cycle as the sacred cow
The worship of strangers in the here and now
Is the only joy for me heaven might allow

It's funny. You spend years perfecting your craft, working
on technique, finding an individual voice, shaping, honing,
struggling. Then one day, you don't give a shit. It doesn't matter. You do what you feel like, because all your serious effort
has been for naught. What did Johnny Depp have to lose when
he took on *Pirates of the Caribbean*? What did Johnny Cash
have to lose when he covered Nine Inch Nails? Sometimes it's
when you stop being so serious, when you stop caring about
what everyone thinks you're "supposed" to do next, that you
can do what your gut tells you is next for you, impulsively,

recklessly...sometimes that's when you do something that lasts, that matters.

I'm not saying I'd done anything that would last, but what I did know is that after I finished belting out my Muddy (or Ethel) Waters imitation, the crowd—ordinary people now and not just my fellow performers—was clapping. People were pointing to the tote board, which I hadn't looked at once during the song—my rating was out of the basement at last. I didn't know how much of it was my song, and how much was my arrogant attitude about this charade, but for the first time in my life I'd struck a nerve with a mass audience without the filtration system of some other performer between me and them.

Bryce was applauding politely, Ronny grinned and gave me the thumbs up, and Nell wiped another of what seemed to be an inexhaustible stock of single-serving tears. I bowed to the audience with a bit of a flourish (I couldn't help myself) and walked off before remembering that I was supposed to talk to Neil Gates again. Fuck him, I thought, feeling like an honest-to-God rock rebel and loving it.

Backstage, I accepted the congratulations of the other contestants, most of whom had already developed a healthy dislike of Gates and had also figured out that these first rounds were pretty rigged. My cell phone rang and, recognizing Lyle's cell number, I stepped into a bathroom.

"You stopped taking your fish oil," he said calmly.

I froze. "What makes you say that?"

"I'm at the American ambassador's residence. He was kind enough to allow me to watch your show on satellite."

"Oh. That was nice of him."

"Yes, it was. Adam, what are you doing?"

"I'm trying to win this fucking farce of a competition," I said irritably, more at what I knew was to come than anything yet

141

said. I wondered if he'd been watching trash TV on satellite at the American ambassador's house the night Sam performed. "I needed inspiration."

"So you stopped the omega-3s."

"What makes you say that?" I repeated myself.

"Because I know you. Because what I saw on that stage was...a wild thing. There was this light in your eyes that...Adam, I'm worried."

"You made an intuitive leap," I said lightly, but Lyle was not to be deterred.

"Adam, you told me what it was like before for you, how awful the pain was. Do you really want to risk that?"

"Yes, I do."

"Why?" It was almost a cry of pain, and it startled and upset me. It was the kind of noise someone makes when told a horrible piece of news.

"To keep what little I've got left. To have a career. To have an income. To keep your respect."

"Adam, do you really think my respect is based on your worldly success?"

"To keep your love," I blurted. "To keep you from leaving me for Sam Sparks."

There was a pause that told me I hadn't been entirely wrong, that there was an allure to Sam for Lyle. "That's preposterous," he said, a second too late. "I'm not leaving you for anyone." But I knew Lyle's voice the way he knew my face—he was abstracted as he said it, as if it was just dawning on him how he might really feel about this wonderful, politically committed, talented, gorgeous young man who'd been taking up his time in a captivating manner lately.

"Lyle, you have to trust me. I know what I'm doing. Yes, I stopped taking the omegas. I need to feel *fertile*, I need *energy*, I need...I need to do this. If I can't win, I need to...to make a showing. To leave this thing officially considered a Serious Person."

"Serious People don't try and get an edge by stopping their psych meds!"

"Serious People don't fucking *need* psych meds. They've never been fucked-up in the head enough about themselves to think they're nothing, they're nobody, it's all for nothing— they've never had to walk around this city as a living fucking *joke*. Lyle, I *won* tonight, I won, I just know it. I'm in the final ten. Please, please, believe me, I'll go back to normal after this is over. I know it's a terrible mistake, it's the kind of act that would cost a professor tenure or a doctor his license, but Lyle, I'm not a professional, I can afford to take a risk, I can't afford *not* to..."

He sighed. "Oh, Adam. I'm coming home. If you're going to do this, you're not doing it alone."

I cried then. I sobbed. It was okay: I was alone in the bathroom backstage where it was safe to cry, where no camera could milk it as a long solemn synthesizer note signaled the fade to commercial. "I'm sorry, Lyle, I'm so sorry."

"Don't be sorry. Adam?"

"Yeah?"

"You were magnificent tonight. You sent shivers up my spine. But no matter how great you might become, it wouldn't be worth it to me to lose you in the process. I'd love to be the only person who knows how great you are, if that's what it cost to keep you sane. But if that's not enough for you..."

"I'll quit. I'll quit the show. It is enough, I don't care, I don't want to lose you..."

"I'm coming home. Everything will be all right. I...this decision, it's not... You don't have to be crazy to be gifted, Adam."

"No? That album you loved? The one that you were so wild about that morning we met at the *Today* show? I was as

143

crazy as a bedbug when I wrote it, you know that."

He laughed. "If you won't take a mood stabilizer, I'll be your mood stabilizer. I'm coming home."

"Thank you. Oh, God, Lyle I've missed you so much."

"You only needed to tell me and I'd have been on the first plane."

"I know that. That's why I never said it. You have a real career, and I'll be goddamned if I was going to be the wifey who can't open a jar of pickles without hubby's help."

"CNN has all kinds of people who can sit in The Hague all day and then spin it down into two minutes of airtime. But I'm the only one who knows how to handle you." I could hear the grin in his voice and my sobs turned half to laughs.

"I'll see you soon. You have no idea how glad I am that I'm going to see you soon."

I was getting ready to go home, content to see my results the next morning (pretty sure I'd win unless West Coast reactions to my little rebellion were radically different than East Coast sensibilities) and, honestly, happiest about the fact that Lyle was coming home. It had been five weeks, the longest we'd ever been apart, and a reunion was overdue.

But just as I was about to leave, one of the staff grabbed my arm. "We need you to stay till after the news."

"What for?"

"All the finalists are going on live at the end of the 11 o'clock news. Don't you watch it?"

I tried to think of something tactful to say. The best I could come up with was, "I don't get my news from YBC."

YBC's on-screen ticker had done wonders for the shows that followed *The Bottom Line Showcase,* since the votes still pouring in were displayed on the ticker like urgent National Weather Service bulletins, right through the last minute of

the 11 o'clock news—which, this being YBC, was an amal-
gam of Fox News, *You Gotta See This!* and *The Man Show.*
Titties, spectacular Agony of Defeat clips, more titties, a joke
from one of those services that cull wacky news clippings for
the benefit of drive-time DJs, a girl with big titties doing the
weather, and about ten minutes of "Yellin' 'Bout Football," a
segment consisting of four guys (two ex-pros and two former
coaches) yelling at the top of their lungs about football—
anyone caught merely talking would be shouted down. The
news ticker ran along the bottom of the screen, and, equally
as important, the vote tally from the *Bottom Line* ran across
the top—an effect that a few people called and complained
was causing them vertigo. The very last minutes of the news
(after numerous teasers throughout the broadcast) were dedicated to a review of that evening's *Showcase,* with the winner announced only after one last commercial break. This
was often anticlimactic, like the night Christie wiped the
floor with the other contestants, but other nights it was a
ratings boon.

I sighed. "I need some reading material, I'll be back."

He frowned. "You're not supposed to leave."

"I'll be right back."

He shook his head. "Producer says you're not supposed to
leave."

"Bye bye," I said, and was out the door. I could see the reason for the order; we were all musicians and therefore liable to
disappear at critical moments, only to be found hospitalized and
incoherent days later. And I could see why the young staffer
wouldn't want to jeopardize his career by being the one to let me
run wild. Still, I didn't care—I'd started the evening defiant and
had no plans to change my ways. Besides, since I didn't smoke,
what the hell was I going to do for the next three hours without
a magazine?

New York is a media town; you can't walk two blocks without finding a news stand. I had loaded up with the new *Us* and *In Touch* and was reaching for the latest *NME* when another hand reached for it at the same time. "Oh, sorry, go ahead..." I started, then stopped. It was Sam Sparks.

He bowed sweepingly. "After you. To the victor belongs the spoils."

I smiled tightly and nodded. *Asshole,* I thought, picking up the last copy with satisfaction.

"Seriously," he added, and I looked at him again. His eyes were shining feverishly and I realized he'd been either drinking or smoking something or both. "What you did tonight—somebody had to fucking do it. I—" He stopped himself, but I could imagine what he was going to say—*I couldn't believe it was you.* "This whole thing, it's...it's such a setup. Every night, they've set someone up to win. And you weren't supposed to win tonight. It was supposed to be that bitch Nola."

Whether he was my enemy or not, I was relieved that I wasn't the only one who was seeing things this way. "That's what I thought. Christie up against a bunch of losers, you up against a bunch of ugmos..."

He smiled. "So I'm not an ugmo, gee, thanks."

"My life would be a lot less complicated right now if you were."

He *examined* me, for the first time. What little time I'd spent around him, he'd stayed studiously aloof, never looking at me when he cut me to ribbons. It's what young people do, especially young gay men. Christopher Rice nailed it when he wrote in *The Snow Garden* about "gay eyes"—the way gay men are so aware of everything and everyone around them, until they become aware that you're aware of *them,* then suddenly you're the only thing they don't see. Now he was *looking* at me—the ultimate compliment, my promotion to his caste.

"You're going to hold it against me that I want to fuck your boyfriend?"

"Not that you want to, but that you're actively trying to. You've read him, you know how he works, you know just what it takes to turn him on."

"Do I? He's been with you for years, so maybe I don't." He thought for a moment. "Then again, after tonight, maybe I do."

I bowed as cavalierly to him as he had to me, and we laughed. It occurred to me that he'd thought Lyle fair game because I wasn't worthy, back when I was just Christie's hack writer. Now it seemed he was announcing the end of the siege. I still thought he was a stuck-up little shit; he probably still thought I was a sad old sellout. And yet, here he was, making a gesture.

"I got a call," he said. "Be at the set by 10. What's up?"

"We're all going on the 11 o'clock news, right at the end. Guess they want to line up all the finalists for some kind of promo thing for next week."

"Sure, all the winners from the last nine nights and then they announce who gets through tonight, makes sense. Will our own little Bert Parks be there?" he smiled, knowing from tonight's show that I had no love for Neil Gates.

"Could Miss America be crowned by any other?"

We walked back to the club in silence. One of those Henry James silences, I guess—where both characters have just given each other enough to chew on that conversation would only diminish what had gone before. I mean, what was there to say? Gee, you're swell? Good luck, you deserve to win? You're my new best friend, I love you? He offered me a stick of gum and I accepted; as far as I was concerned this confirmed our truce.

Jean was standing outside the club, smoking and looking skittish. "All my hot Friday night plans canceled," she complained without introduction.

"Who knew fame would be so bad for your social life," Sam quipped, taking her cigarette.

She lit another and sighed. "I guess I should practice my Miss America face." Her features went blank, then an astonished look overcame her; she covered her open mouth with her hand (the one without the cigarette so as not to spoil the wholesome effect), hunched her shoulders, and began to "cry."

"So," Sam said casually, "Miss Ploughford, how does it feel to wear the crown?"

Jean frowned at her real name. "Those assholes, those fucking assholes, those motherfucking assholes!"

"Nice; you could practically set that to music," I suggested.

"I stood in line like everyone else," she complained, and I could see she was hurt as much as angry. "I didn't call anyone for a favor. I didn't use my parents' name. I wanted to be judged on my own fucking merits! And now I'm wondering if this whole thing isn't a setup. If the deck was stacked so I'd make it this far, because being the child of my famous fucking hippie parents makes such good PR." That made three of us who smelled a setup. She looked at Sam. "The way you're here because you're so cute." She looked at me. "The way you're here because of the Christie thing." The natural progression of this line of thought was clear; the winner was probably already being engineered in a YBC board room.

Glumly, we watched the police take away the crowd control barriers, only a handful of teenagers still loitering around, hoping to see someone famous or be miraculously discovered themselves. Suddenly I felt dumb—all my talk about being Taken Seriously, and when it came down to it my fate was, at best odds, in the hands of a bunch of screaming teenage girls. Silly us, forgetting that this was a profit-making enterprise, that we were just the lumber for the mill, to be clear-cut at will.

We filed inside, where a fair percentage of the audience had been persuaded to stay with the lure of a big announcement and, more important, an open bar. There were a few girlish *eeks!* in Sam's wake, not all of them from girls. At the bar, we were informed that contestants weren't to be served alcohol, so we took turns swigging from Jean's flask. We drifted onto the stage as slowly as possible despite—or because of—frantic announcements that we were going *live, right now!*

The audience dutifully cheered as the cameras went live and Neil Gates stood in front of the ten of us. "Let's have a big hand for all the finalists!" The nine already through, including Jean and Sam, smiled as if for their class photo. Then, as the last minute of voting ticked away, I repressed my urge to vomit as I watched the tote board. I was neck and neck with Nola for that tenth slot; I had a pretty good idea people were voting for the *idea* of me and what I'd done, versus what Nola represented in pop music, more than who they actually thought was the best performer. I mean, anyone who thought my outburst rocked would instinctively hate Nola and her America's Sweetheart routine. Finally, the bell rang and there I was, just barely a winner. Fortunately for me, Nola's nicey-nice schtick meant she couldn't do anything as unsportsmanlike as demand a recount; she was forced to hug and congratulate me (though she did dig those press-on nails into my shoulder with more force than enthusiasm required).

"I want all of you at home to stayed tuned now, because we've got a big surprise in store for you...and for our finalists!" And then he walked offstage, motioning us to follow. What choice did we have?

The cameras tracked us outside, where a minibus was waiting for us. We were all herded inside and the door shut behind us. I sat near the window farthest from the cameras. Christie was the last one on the bus, and as she looked for a seat, we locked eyes. I thought, why not—if I can make peace with the man who wants my husband, why not with the girl who wants my money?

She sat down next to me as the bus pulled away. "You did good tonight."

"Thanks," I said neutrally, then decided to ask, "Are you referring to my song or my little speech?"

She laughed. "I liked the speech better. Listen." She turned to face me. "I'm not out to get you, or Aquanetta, or any of you guys. But I had to break free, and I had to break big. You know what I'm saying?"

I nodded—I did know. She couldn't just leave us; how much press was in that? But to sue us, to denounce us! Only that way would everybody would be waiting to see what happened next. I realized then that she was almost certainly bound to win this competition, not because she was the best, or the prettiest, or even the most popular going in, but because she knew how to work this system we'd found ourselves in.

"I know what you're saying. Nothing personal, just business. Like *The Sopranos*."

"Pretty much, yeah." Like most of the others on the bus had already done, she lit a cigarette. "I always liked your songs. For, you know, what they were."

"Well, I'll be interested to see what you come up with on your own," I said, repaying her for that last comment.

She darted her eyes at me for a moment, then softened, realizing what I'd said was only fair. "I'll be interested to see that myself," she said.

A few minutes later, we were at one of the recent follies built in the East Village, condos that looked from the outside more like movieplexes, sold to groovy millionaires who wanted to say they lived in the East Village but didn't want to live in a building that couldn't accommodate their needs for T1

Internet lines or guarantee the safety of Fresh Direct delivery people.

Then the ten of us, and Neil, and a cameraman of course, got in a freight elevator to the top floor. (It was actually the regular elevator, which had been built to look and work like a freight because that felt loft-ier to prospective buyers.) The cameraman was positioned in the back of the herd, so he caught the effect as the elevator doors opened onto the penthouse.

We walked into one of the largest and most obnoxiously decorated units I'd ever seen. A sinking feeling came over me as I realized how much it looked like a *Real World* set. In the background I could hear Neil prattling to the camera about how, in their youth, great artists of faded golden ages had lived and struggled together in quaint poverty, how their great artistic movements had been born in frigid lofts and cozy cafés... Obviously whoever wrote and approved that speech was unaware of the irony of talking about artists in slum garrets as we walked into this showroom of an apartment.

"And now, for the next two weeks, our contestants are going to be living here, sharing their creative vibe, making music and magic happen right before your eyes. That's right, folks—*The Bottom Line Showcase* is moving to 9 P.M., so that every night at eight we can bring you *this* show, a full hour of what goes on behind the scenes as our contestants..."

"Fuck you!" Sam said on national television, only YBC's eight-second delay button saving them from another FCC fine. "We don't have to put up with this shit. This is bullshit. You don't own my fucking private life. You're not going to show me brushing my fucking teeth on TV. I didn't sign up for this, and I'm not going to do it. None of us are? Are we!"

"Actually," Christie said coolly, "if you read the release we all signed when we auditioned, it says we're obligated to 'perform promotional duties as requested through the duration of the Show's First Run.' And being on this show could definitely be considered promotional duty."

I suppose I wasn't entirely surprised at how closely Christie could read—and remember—a contract, including its capitalized and therefore officially defined terms. What did surprise me was the look on Sam's face: I'd have sworn it was terror. Some of the others were grabbing for the mike, dishing up how great it would be to be around such inspirational, creative people and how the memorabilia generously on loan from the folks at the Hard Rock Café would inspire more creative inspiration, blah blah blah.

Then I remembered. If I had to live here, that would be two more weeks without Lyle. He'd be coming home for nothing. Even if we could meet, there'd be a camera monkey on my back at all times. Fortunately, I doubted Lyle and the American Ambassador to the Netherlands were up watching YBC news.

And then there was the other part—my daily life vivisected for two weeks on national television. People hanging around the water cooler the next day discussing how I looked when I woke up, how I brushed my teeth, anything I said or didn't say… My music, my work—that I could now handle seeing mocked and dismissed; but to be a soap opera character, a rat in a maze with scientists noting my every wrong turn with a clipboard…I freaked just thinking about it.

So that was it. I was done. I was leaving the show. Bipolar absolutism, extremism, jumping to conclusions? You bet. I swung my fag bag up over my shoulder. "I'm off," I announced to Christie, Jean, and Sam, the four of us having unconsciously made a little clique off to the side. "My boyfriend is coming home, and I'm not losing him."

"You'd rather lose this?" Christie asked me, surprised.

"Well, to be honest, I'd probably be in more danger of losing my mind here than my boyfriend, but then I wouldn't be much good to him, would I?"

"Oh, God, please stay," Jean said. "I just know this is going to be bullshit. Don't make me do it alone."

"You don't have to," I said, desperately trying to abdicate. "Sam is here, and…" Then I thought about Sam and his look of fright when the arrangement had been announced. "Listen, I'm about as useful a flotation device as a top hat on the *Titanic*. I'd just end up needing *you,* and trust me, it wouldn't be pretty."

"We need you, you've got to stay," Jean insisted, and to be honest, there was something about that "we." I wasn't a quick bonder; I made precious few friends and had little use for the rituals necessary to maintain acquaintances. But outside of Lyle (and a lover is no substitute for friends), since Callie had moved to London this *had* become the "we" in my life.

I looked at Sam. He was pale, trembling even. Jean had already been burned in public once by the show, and it still meant enough to her to prove something that she was willing to risk being burned again. I looked at Christie and thought, *I should know this girl.* All this time she'd been both the willing puppet and the shrewd time-bider, the blinking tee-hee girl for Diane Sawyer and the media manipulator outside ChrisCo the day she sued our asses. And only in the last couple of weeks had I met her eyes and seen someone…interesting. And where would I have been without her? I never would have made all that money, I never would have met Lyle, I never would have ended up here…

I'd lived by myself in the city ever since I could afford to, worked only by myself or with Callie, and this—nine room-mates and a production crew—was a hell of a lot more people than I'd ever been around on a regular basis. It wasn't what I'd prepared myself for, God knows, when I signed up for the show, but I shouldn't have been surprised when all the rules changed—more and more often, reality show producers dreaded waking up to discover that their audience had lost interest in the single novel premise that drove a series, so more and more often they were bending "reality" again and again through the duration of each show, tossing people off the show only to see the losers' unexpectedly high Q ratings and snatch them back into the fold.

And it occurred to me that as the "finals" would last for the next two weeks, who could anticipate how the producers might twist us up yet again, get us voting each other out of the house or having to eat large quantities of live icky things before each performance. Here's another little bipolar secret—yes, we get *so sure* about things, so certain how they are and ought to be, but when things change abruptly, we're already in motion, already impatient at any rate for what comes next, secretly glad that for once the world is moving at our pace and not its own. I could manage it, emotionally, if I went back on the fish oil—which I was going to do anyway with Lyle coming home.

What would Lyle do in the same circumstances? If there was something truly and indisputably Wrong about the whole thing, he'd elect to end his participation. But if it was just that the going was about to get rough, that suddenly there were obstacles popping up like Bop-a-Moles, would he quit? And I knew damn well that if a true friend asked Lyle to do something, there'd be no doubt in his mind. These were not my true friends, not yet; I was far more frugal with that currency than the paper stuff, but they were my...what? My buddies? That was an odd concept for me, as any halfway point is for the all-or-nothing mind. Jean was asking me for help not because I was qualified to give it but because I'd been with her through what had probably been the most embarrassing episode of her life.

And Sam? Strange, the weird kind of bond you sometimes develop with someone who wants what you want, and what you have. I mean, the fact of being attracted to the same special qualities in another person sort of gives you something in common right there, a shared sensibility if nothing else.

I was too tired to argue anymore. I dropped my bag on the floor and Jean hugged me in thanks.

I would call Lyle, and he would understand, and, I hoped, he would approve. It would hurt, I'd be so sorry I did the right thing, I'd miss him so much for a while longer—a while like a thousand years to my fucked-up sense of time—but here I was, here I'd put myself, and here I'd stay.

SEVEN

We had until noon the next day to pack our suitcases for the next two weeks and remand ourselves into custody…I mean, move into *The Pad,* as YBC was calling the residence and the reality show, with astonishing cluelessness—how '60s, and not at all in a hip ironic way. I'd just have time to meet Lyle at the airport before kissing him goodbye again, but there was no way I was going to let that opportunity slip by.

Now, I'd always thought that those secret passenger lounges were the kind of thing you only got into by being rich or famous, or semi-rich, or semi-famous and making a scene. But I hadn't stood in the passenger greeting area at La Guardia for more than a few minutes before a nice young man in an airline uniform offered to whisk me into a more private area, to which Lyle would be shepherded upon arrival. None of the others patiently waiting had looked twice at me, but to at least one airline employee, I was enough of a somebody that I shouldn't be exposed to even the *possibility* of harassment. The lounge had plush couches, free champagne, and tasty snacks—now *this* was a perk of celebrity I could get used to.

And so Lyle and I got a relatively private reunion. "I don't know if you heard..." I began.

"I heard. You're joining a commune."

"A work farm, actually. Job Corps for musicians."

"What can I do to hype your whuffie?"

This was one of our little jokes. Cory Doctorow wrote a novel called *Down and Out in the Magic Kingdom*, which posited a future when all your material needs were taken care of and the only currency that counted was "whuffie," essentially points you garnered through your social interactions by gaining the esteem of others. You'd never starve or be homeless without it, but your ability to enjoy the finer things in life depended on your maintaining the good opinion of others. Since my social interactions were extremely limited, I regarded the possibility of such a world with perfect horror, as I'd be the poorest person in it.

"That's closer to a necessity than you might think," I said, and explained what was about to happen for the next two weeks. *The Pad* would air for an hour each night, followed by the *Showcase*, but as of tonight, we'd be competing for votes from the minute *The Pad* went on the air. In other words, from now on in addition to our musical talents we'd be graded on our ability to play well with others—or on our ability to stage bitch fights, depending on the fickle nature of the voters' tastes.

Lyle Furrowed. "Is *The Pad* a live show?"

"No."

"Then you're all at the mercy of the producers. They can take a day's footage and cut it any which way they want." This was one of Lyle's pet peeves—early in his career, he'd been naive enough to allow print journalists to interview him without tape recorders, and he'd been startled to see how a lazy writer could take a couple steno pages of notes and turn what were allegedly his words into statements he'd have to phone everyone he knew to disown. The fact that this couldn't happen to you on live TV was why he loved CNN.

"One of your philosophical friends could write a book on the nature of reality when 'reality' is what comes out of an Avid."

"By the time you've finished your tenure on this show, you could write it yourself."

I sighed theatrically. "Oh, Lyle, you're always telling me that I should follow through on my little brainstorms. Don't you realize by now that I'm the idea guy, that—like taxes—details are for the little people?"

He laughed at me, as I'd intended. "You're following through on *this,* aren't you?"

I sighed. "Yeah, I am. Thank God it's a short-term commitment. I'm sorry you hauled your ass all the way back here when I'll hardly be able to see you for two more weeks."

"Why not?"

"Because there'll be a fucking camera monkey on my back everywhere I go! Because I may or may not get a moment of privacy when I have to take a shit. You don't want to be under the microscope like that…"

"Yes, I do. If you're under it, I'll be right there with you. We're a team, Adam. We're a couple. All for one and one for all."

Of course I cried. Damn, that was twice in two days—more emotion than I was used to letting out. I tried not to listen to myself when I said it was the lack of omega-3s that was making me more susceptible to these waves of emotion, and since I was sobbing kinda loud, it wasn't hard not to hear.

We took a cab home, I packed, and Lyle accompanied me to the East Village in another cab. Outside the building, he hugged and kissed me for the benefit of the cameras hanging around waiting to record everyone's arrival. "I'm very proud of you," he said.

"I love you," I said, and there it was—now everyone would

know that I was a big old 'mo, and I could only hope that the Fab Five had paved the way for tolerance, at least as far as America's living-room TV screens. And if not, well, fuck 'em all, I wasn't about to leave my boyfriend for two weeks without giving him a kiss and the three magic words.

As we separated, Sam pulled up theatrically on the back of a scooter, a backpack and guitar slung over his shoulders. He hopped off and exchanged a lascivious kiss with the girl who'd driven him; she smiled at the cameras (which had come in for a closeup of the whole thing), flipped them off, and spun away.

"Hey," Sam said to us, and I nodded. Lyle shook his hand, they traded pleasantries, and Lyle left. It certainly didn't bother me to have Lyle see Sam kiss a girl, but it did bother me that, for the audience at home at least, Sam would be thought heterosexual based on that must-see clip—which would be better for his score, without doubt.

In the seconds we had in the elevator, that privacy airlock between the front door and the penthouse, I asked him, "So, who's your girlfriend?"

"She's a friend. We fuck sometimes. Why?"

"Just wondering. Thought you were on the team, that's all."

"I'm bi. You know, just because I think Lyle's hot doesn't mean he's the only person in the world I want to fuck."

I laughed, deciding to say no more. For people my age, the word "bisexuality" still carried loads of political baggage, as well as distasteful mental pictures of unattractive '70s "swingers" having it off. We'd grown up in a world more bipolar than I'd ever been myself: America versus Commies, Black versus White, Women versus Men, Gay versus Straight, Christians versus Heretics. Doctrinaire extremism was for most of us the natural response to any social or political or religious idea; we swung immediately to Us/Them, Either/Or, For/Against. And in the era of the Moral Majority, that had been especially true about sexuality. If you were heterosexual, necking in public would be applauded; if you were homosexual, even holding hands in public was cause for public burning followed by the eternal kind (God's punishment in the afterlife somehow never being quite grisly enough for some on Earth). For radical gays, you were either gay or straight; bisexuals were people who were "really" gay but who kept one foot on the other side of the fence, so that when the shit came down and we were rounded up, the bisexuals would be able to call on at least one female to testify to their "normal" sexuality and be spared. Any attempt to see a third way was considered cowardice and folly.

Kids these days, however, growing up in a far less bipolar world, weren't so obligated to line up on one side or the other, especially when it came to sex. Yes, 9/11 may have reignited that bipolarity politically ("You're either with us or against us"), but it also made feeling good now even more crucial. On any given night in a Manhattan gay bar's back room, you'd find more than one *Vice*-reading, Wall Street–employed, dateless young Orc stopping by to get a blow job rather than going home without release—and more than one hot young gay boy going home with the girl from work he came with, just to see. Sex wasn't a political act anymore—it was just sex.

Besides, even if I'd felt like raising the subject of the whuffie Sam had just accumulated with a certain demographic, just to see how he'd respond I noticed that the slight tremor that had manifested last night was still with him. It was hard to put a finger on; he was just *vibrating* like a tuning fork. Something was scaring him, but what could it possibly be? Before I could ask him, the doors opened and we were on camera again.

The penthouse had been decorated in what you might call Contemporary Target Dorm Room. The sunken living room had red carpet, a purple couch covered with green and orange cushions, a terrarium–cum–coffee table full of Hard Rock memorabilia, halogen lamps with royal-blue sconces, and giant posters of NYC's hottest underground bands (or at least the ones who'd recently signed with record companies willing to pay YBC to promote them).

All heads and lenses turned to us, the last arrivals of the day. Goody gumdrops, it was time to bond with our roomies.

In addition to the four of us you know, there were four girls and two guys. Nick was your typical Byronic rock type, with tumultuously lavish wavy black hair and the tight Chelsea Scowl that was the natural relaxed setting of his sculpted porcelain features. Nick played the guitar, but his instrument of choice was that hair, through which he ran his long slender fingers the way others might caress a harp. Like many performers in Manhattan, he'd gotten the reputation around town as a poetic type, based more on his choices in wardrobe and watering holes than any lyrics he'd written. Like Chance the gardener, I suspected Nick had gotten this far because the less he said, the more gay men and teenage girls could project onto him.

Then there was LaQuinta (named, we would later discover, after the motor inn in which she was conceived), a decent, career-minded girl taking a ride on her Whitney Houston–esque voice—i.e., technically perfect and ideal for studio recording but eerily lacking in what you might call soul. LaQuinta had probably made it through because she gave good interview, having perfected the "nice" things to say in years of beauty contests, and because she had mastered Smile on Demand technology.

Jean, Sam, and I all traded glances at our first in-person viewing of Kat. "She" had a deep, husky, Sheryl Crow–ish voice, and no wonder, since "her" Adam's apple was apparent to anyone who'd spent time on the streets of New York late at night and had dodged the great screeching tumbleweeds of feathers and hair that were the packs of drag queens who roamed in the most unexpected places. I had to hand it to her: She could almost pass. Very little makeup, clear nail polish, long hair only slightly fluffed up and out—in short, none of the accoutrements that scream DRAG QUEEN. Today Kat had made the mistake of wearing a cowl neck, which was probably enough to dupe the casual observer but not us. (She'd go to a turtleneck the next day and stay there.)

Connie was—well, remember Debbie Boone? 'Nuff said. Smile, dear!

Then there was Trey. Poor Trey. Someone from one of the gay mags had already accosted him on the street and asked when he'd come out of the closet, to which he'd responded with a hurt and angry glare. The South is full of boys like Trey, who may or may not be gay—and if they are, they're in no position to tell you because they don't know it yet themselves. Preferring the company of women, they're raised churchy, their social lives taking place within the context of Sunday social dinners, Wednesday prayer meetings, and Saturday choir rehearsals— perfect venues for ignoring the whole idea of sex. Shy and self-abnegating, Trey had been pushed into the competition by his fellow choristers, who insisted that he "sang like an angel." His creative efforts were run-of-the-mill Jesus Rocks Christian pop, but he'd gotten to the finals because he sang them with such fervor and conviction that now and then they could raise a couple hairs on the back of even the most secular neck.

And then came the nasty surprise. We knew Muddie Mae Suggs would not be here. Muddie Mae had appeared on the 11 o'clock news last night with the rest of us, and before you could say "Hold the presses!" the 'bloids were blaring that she was a runaway child bride from Arkansas, who'd been naive enough to think that a fake ID and a bottle of hair dye would conceal her from her abusive old crocodile of a husband, even on national TV. His dramatic trashing of the hotel lobby where she was staying and subsequent revelations to the crime beat reporter that Muddie Mae was 15 years old and therefore not qualified for the show ensured that her next televised appearance would be on Court TV, suing her aged husband and her con-artist relatives for all they didn't have. We knew she'd be replaced but had thought it would be with her runner-up.

Silly us. There, in all her iguanic glory, was Nola, soaking up the klieg lights and smiling as placidly as the cat, post-canary. We were introduced to our "new friend" by a hard-looking old broad who introduced herself as Shelly—one look at Shelly and you could hear her shouting, "Broadway doesn't go for booze and dope!"

"I'm going to be your den mother!" she said cheerily, cracking her makeup with her insane smile. "And chaperone, if need be," she added with that "just kidding" tone people use when they're not kidding but don't dare say their shit with a straight face.

"We're all sorry Muddie Mae can't be here," she said, "but this morning we conducted a poll on the *Showcase* Web site, asking which contestant our viewers would most like to see get another chance—and here's Nola!" She started clapping and Trey, LaQuinta, and Connie dutifully followed suit. Christie lit a cigarette.

"Cut!" Shelly barked, and the cameras went off. So, I thought, she was going to be the second unit director on this charade. "Christie, this is a nonsmoking house."

"There's no sign."

"We didn't think you'd need a sign to know that. There are city regulations, you know."

She took a drag and exhaled, taking her time about it. "This isn't a public space."

"Well, it's against the rules of the show, and if you want to stay on here, that's all you need to know."

"I didn't read that anywhere in the rules. Or the contract." I had to hand it to her; if her solo career failed, Christie had a bright future as a courtroom lawyer. Or an actress, I thought, remembering her tearful "I didn't know what I was getting into" performance the day she sued us.

Shelly made a sour face and grabbed for the cigarette; Christie, a veteran of years of complicated choreography, stepped aside and allowed Shelly to swipe at air. I don't know if anyone but me noticed that Jean was recording the scene with her cell phone camera.

"You listen to me," Shelly hissed. "I don't care how famous you are. This is my set, and if you don't follow my rules, you're off of it."

Christie shrugged and called her bluff. "Make the call." She and Shelly stared at each other for a moment. We all held our breath.

Ever had cats? I mean, more than one? More than two? They've got a very interesting hierarchical system. They'll each try and find the highest perch in a room, giving them temporary dominance over the others, but in any household there's only one cat who's truly Kitty Number 1 at any given time. Every now and then the other kitties will take a swipe at her, out of inbuilt Darwinian reflex—an attempt to see if they can unseat her. Shelly and Christie were deciding who was going to be Kitty Number 1 in this house.

"We'll deal with this later," Shelly said, looking away and therefore losing the kitty staring contest. "Action," she said briskly, and the cameras rolled. "Room assignments. Sam, you and Nick will share the Ikea Pad. Adam, you and Trey are in the AOL Room. LaQuinta, you and Kat are in the Coca-Cola Suite. Christie and Nola are in the *Slim Teen* Room, and Jean and Connie are in the Palazzo de MAC."

"Oh, MAC!" Connie enthused. "Do we get free makeup?"

Kat hugged LaQuinta. "I just know we'll be best friends!"

While the cameras captured what I hoped was phony enthu-siasm, the rest of us looked at one another. Trey was plainly terri-fied of rooming with me, having been well inculcated with the "common-sense truth" that (a) all gay men are sexually insatiable, and (b) we found all men equally irresistible. Nick and Sam looked at each other and then simultaneously cut their eyes away to some distant point—barspeak for "no way." I suppose someone thought it was a good idea to put the hipsters together, but the hipsters clearly weren't happy (since it presented the terrifying possibility that in close quarters, one of them would be revealed to the other as Not Hip).

"Trey," I said, my words like headlights on the poor deer. "What say we switch? Sam and I are old friends; I'd like to room with him." The look of surprise on Sam's face was nothing com-pared to the relief on Trey's.

"Gee, that would be great," Trey sighed.

"No switching," Shelly said firmly. "These have been set—"

"By the marketing department," I interrupted. "For what they think will provide maximum drama and conflict. Which is not exactly conducive to creativity, frankly. Sam?"

"Sounds good to me."

Then I whispered in Shelly's ear. "If you really want drama, don't you think Nick and Trey would make an interesting room pairing?" I watched her pupils dilate and she nodded.

"Okay, this one exception. And *that's it*." She stormed off to yell at a crew member for nothing in particular.

I turned to Christie. "Sorry, guess I hogged the moment. Didn't give you a chance to get out of rooming with Nola."

Christie dropped her cigarette into a complimentary can of Coke. "On the contrary. I think it'll be a very interesting chal-lenge." And she smiled at me, and I had to laugh.

"As for Connie," Jean said, "I can push her around if I have to, I'm sure."

"Well," I said, miming the emperor from *Amadeus*, "there it is then."

The cameras didn't capture much that day; mostly just backstory bio clips, a mélange of head shots, old tape, and footage of us unpacking. As much as I would have liked to sit in my room and read a book, socializing was mandatory—unless I wanted to watch myself reading a book on TV while the rest of the "household" talked about my lack of school spirit out in the conversation–slash–snake pit in the living room. Fortunately, LaQuinta and Nola did most of the talking, and when I discovered that we were expected to cook our own meals, I slipped off to the kitchen.

Realizing I'd found a space safe from the ever-tracking cameras, Jean soon joined me there, at which point a camera crew followed. This was good to know: As a general rule, if you were alone, they wouldn't follow you; only when you were with someone else was there action worth shooting. We deboned chicken and chopped chives (the refrigerator's contents would have satisfied Julia Child) and talked in a low murmur about chefs who were hot (Eric Ripert, Anthony Bourdain, Todd English—oh, God, Todd English). Soon we'd discover the floor below ours was the control room, where Shelly (or the Eye of Sauron, as Sam started calling her) watched the various feeds and decided where crews would go—fortunately for us, like many reality TV shows this one had a slim budget, and there wasn't enough money to guarantee a full-blown Andy Warhol Experience with every moment captured for posterity. So our boring chef talk (how many young bastards watched enough Food TV to know what we were talking about?) ensured our privacy for a real conversation, as the crew was sent off in search of greener pastures.

"What's your room like?" Jean asked. "I can't sleep in mine. The walls are orange and pink."

"Ikea," I shrugged. "It's very dorm room. I shudder to think about the AOL Room."

"I'm sure Trey will love it. Every time one person came in, the other could say, 'Welcome!' and you could both dissolve into gales of wholesome laughter."

"Ha. So did Connie bring a teddy bear? Or a stuffed unicorn?"

"Hello Kitty. And lots of it. Enough to stock an eBay store."

I shuddered. "Do the windows open?"

"I thought of that," she said, handing me some freshly scrubbed Yukon Golds. "And no, they don't. Want to know what's worse? *You can't get the batteries out of the smoke alarms.*"

"My God. You'll have to smoke on the huge balcony with its commanding view of, um, well, nothing really, is it."

"So, you and Sam," she said, drying her hands. "What's the deal?"

"What do you mean?"

"There's something going on there. I don't mean sexually, just…something."

"Yeah," I nodded. "It's weird. A few days ago, as you may not know, he was the number 1 threat to my domestic bliss, and therefore some little shit who had to be destroyed. Now, well, I don't know. He still wants my man, but in an abstract, art-appreciation kind of way. I think. I hope. And I…I don't know. I like him. Pisses me off, that."

"Sam's cool. He's got, you know, issues, but you…"

She stopped as the doors opened. LaQuinta and Nola waltzed in, entouraged by cameras. "You should have told us you needed help!" LaQuinta scolded us. Before we knew it, Jean and I had been shouldered aside as LaQuinta prattled about good times in her grandmother's kitchen and our roasted chicken with tarragon potatoes about-faced into fried chicken and mashed potatoes. Jean and I shrugged and made our exit.

At the end of dinner, Shelly manifested to make an

announcement. "I just wanted to let you all know that there are going to be some very exciting changes on the *Showcase*. I'm sure we'll all be inspired by them." She clapped her hands like Sister Bertrille. "Each night, the show's going to have a theme, and you'll be writing a song around that theme. And even better, you'll be writing that song…with your roomie!"

I hate that corporate-speak, where they can never say "change" or "challenge" without handing me the emotional modifier I'm supposed to accept as my own reaction. I've rarely found top-down excitement to be infectious, and this was no exception. "Monday's theme is…Love!"

Gawd, I thought; it's bad enough they had to steal from *American Idol,* but talk about a vague topic! I stole a look at Sam, who was as blasé as I was about this challenging opportunity. Then, I couldn't help stealing a glance at Trey, whose iron-willed refusal to look at Nick rusted through just long enough for the longing in his eyes to come through before his gaze was reaffixed to the table. "You'll all have tomorrow and Monday to work on this one, but I'm giving you a heads-up now: There's going to be a new theme every day, so we'll all be working very hard from now on!"

"Who's *we?*" Christie mouthed to me from behind a hand concealing her lips from any cameras. I smiled. I had to wonder how different everything might have been if I'd gotten to know this girl before, instead of just having been content to put words in her mouth.

"And to inspire you all, we have a special treat. Please give a big welcome to our visitors, famous songwriters Ned and Sally Ploughford!"

All of us—and the cameras—watched Jean turn pale in shock, then purple with rage. She stood up, but the drama of the gesture was lost since the rest of the cast was already standing up to applaud the smiling, nodding pair. Well, "pair" in the abstract—I couldn't imagine these two fighting fish into the same bowl without any bloodshed. They shook hands with the cast as Jean stood there. When they looked at her and both extended their open arms to her, she burst into tears, even though they'd probably been prompted into that loving gesture by Shelly. Her rebel parents had finally tumbled into the great maw of television, whether for love of publicity or for love of Jean it didn't matter—now and forever on this show and any career to follow, she'd be the "daughter of," under their shadow despite her best efforts. She accepted their hug, but then bolted for her room, where I followed her.

"I'm out," she said. "I'm gone. I'm not doing this."

"Jean," I said, watching her trying to stuff everything into a suitcase. "It's not your fault. It has nothing to do with you. Nobody's parents are their fault."

"That's not it! I came on this fucking show to make it on my own. Now that's fucked."

"Okay. Fine. So the cat's out of the bag. Your mommy and daddy are a pair of old hippies who nobody but adult contemporary listeners still recognize. Big fucking deal. Why don't you get a job as a maid somewhere, because then nobody can say your parents had anything to do with that? Jean, *people are hateful*. They will talk shit about you just because they can—some people will hate you just to spice things up, just to be contrary. It's the salt they toss on their dinner conversation. That's how it works! Well, I say fuck them! People suck! Fuck people if they think you only succeeded because of your parents!"

She laughed. I'd definitely gone over the deep end, and it *was* funny—here I was on this show where my success depended on my whuffie, and I'd just told all my potential voters that they sucked and should be fucked. "Fuck you," she said, smiling.

"No, fuck *you*," I laughed. Then I finally noticed the cameras, which had scented drama and tailed me. "*Scarface* auditions, take one!" I said to the Eye.

Jean had a conversation with her parents—after some negotiation, this took place on camera but outside audio range, so only the emotions on their faces could tell you that some happy ending had been reached. They left, and then, as far as I was concerned, it was bedtime. The Eye knocked off at 11, thank God, but only in the bedrooms—stay out in the living room and you were fair game 24/7.

In our room, Sam was bopping to the Postal Service, clearly getting ready for a night on the town. I moved several of his shirts from the easy chair to the floor, where they joined what must have been the majority of his wardrobe.

"Hey, don't mix those up," he chided me. "I haven't decided about those yet."

"How many shirts were you planning to wear tonight?"

"Hmm." He appeared to seriously think about this for a minute. "Like any good Victorian girl, I've got to be prepared to spend most of my day changing clothes."

"Right, I see; you're going out to drop visiting cards on countesses till tea time."

"How do you know I'm not eloping with a guardsman?"

"Because somehow, I can't see you falling for someone with furious mustaches."

He chuckled. "No, I'm going to see BRMC. All black, no red."

"Oh, I love them!"

"Then come with. Dude, they've got tickets here for *everything*, every fucking concert you'd wanna see. It's like a beautiful dream."

"No, I don't think so."

"Oh, come on, when's the last time you saw them live?"

"Well, never."

"You're kidding. Why not?"

"I don't really go to concerts."

The song stopped and Sam turned to me in the awful silence as if I'd just farted as I knelt to the Queen of England. "You what?" he said in shock.

"I don't go. To concerts." I waited for his out-of-body experience to conclude so he could respond, but he continued to stare blankly at me, so I went on. "People. Jostling. Vomiting. Stolen things. Roofied drinks. Ditz chicks at coat check handing you someone's buckskin fringe jacket."

"You are not for real," he said flatly. "You're a fucking *musician,* how can you not see live music?"

"Well, a lyricist, not really a musician; I can't really even play the piano, I just kind of fake it. My partner, Callie, she did the music. I mean, I sang the lyrics and she'd play it on the piano, change a note, we'd..." I trailed off. As I'd been talking, Sam had been busy ransacking my closet. With an efficiency he'd been incapable of when it came to his own outfit, he quickly laid out shirt, pants, and jacket for me.

"Put them on," he commanded.

"Thanks, but—"

"Hey." It was a command, not a greeting. "Listen. Live music is *life.* Playing live is how you find out whether your shit is any good. You go into a studio and sing into the man's can, he jacks around with it, you don't really know what it sounds like to *other people.* But you go on a stage on a Saturday night, in front of a bunch of drunken attitudinal twenty-somethings desperate for someone to feel superior to, and you hit it spot-on...I mean, you feel this *wave*; it's some wild primitive shit, man. And how the fuck are you going to *get* that energy if you've never been out in the crowd *giving* it, knowing what that moment is like when you've just *gotta* give it." He laughed. "It's like man-fucking. How can you top a guy unless you've been properly topped yourself?"

I laughed. It was strange—it was like I was listening to myself, full of pronouncements and theories, if only I'd been younger and cuter and had the...*ease* with which Sam seemed to operate in the outside world. "Okay, okay," I said impulsively, telling myself I did indeed have something I wanted to experience: watching Sam in what was obviously his natural environment. "Just swear you won't leave me alone."

He beamed and serenaded me as he tossed me my outfit. "Now, hush, little baby, don't you cry-y-y."

New York at night. Anyone who doubts the existence of a collective unconscious has never been swept into the stunned joy of thousands in the theater district at 11 P.M., or the tense, competitive sexuality of Chelsea at 1 A.M., or the delirious throngs spilling out of live music venues across town at all hours of the night. My New York nights had been drinks, theater, dinner, home, the chaos outside each destination merely the choppy seas between tranquil islands.

Sam's New York *was* those choppy seas; he had the astonishing ability to start conversations with strangers on the subway. This is astonishing to me not only because I'm so socially challenged, but because I thought that like me everyone on the subway would assume that if a stranger started talking to them, it would either be an appeal for money or a lecture on how gnomes in Zurich run the world economy. Sam would compliment a girl on her outfit with just enough gay to relax her and get her talking; he'd see a guy in a band T-shirt and ask him if he'd seen them live last week. After all the "real life" encounters I'd seen staged for Christie, I of all people could tell that none of this was for the cameraman attached to us—it was just Sam, his way.

172

Out on the streets again, he said, "I can't believe we have to write a fucking *love song.*"

"But think of the latitude we have. 'This is not a love song!'" I yelped, John Lydon–style. "This-is-not a love song."

"Love stinks."

"Love, love will tear us apart again."

"Love is a stranger."

"Love shack."

"That's a happy song."

"I know. I'm tired."

"You liar. I can see it in your eyes. You're having fun."

"I'm keeping my mind occupied, so I don't collapse in terror when we get to the show."

"Here," he said, fishing a pill out of his pocket and handing it to me.

"Oh, Xanax, I already took that precaution before we left."

"In for a penny, in for a pound," Sam said. "Take your vitamins." He produced a joint and lit it. Call me bourgeois, but I'm always shocked when people smoke pot on the street, even here. *The police,* I think. *They'll get you!* Sometimes I think the only reason I didn't turn to a life of crime is because I was always sure that I'd get caught my first time out.

He offered the joint to me, and I took it. I reasoned that while the weed would make me paranoid, and manic, the Xannie would shave off the rough edges. Besides, I was out to taste youth, metaphorically speaking—I'd already made one reckless decision by going off my head meds, so as Sam said, in for a penny...

The airport wasn't the only place celebrity paid off. We didn't have to stand in line at the club—funny how even the pushiest New York crowd grants leeway to a couple of guys being filmed. After all, it's the kind of situation so many of these people came to the city to get into.

Sam was true to his word and stayed close, leading me through the crowd. I don't know if it was the Xanax or the weed or the creeping enthusiasm I was starting to remember, but it felt as if most of the crowd was on my wavelength: Not once was I shouldered into spilling my drink by someone backing into my path; my feet moved at a steady pace rather than starting and stopping in the modern dance rhythm crowds had always seemed to require; and accidentally brushing firm young flesh seemed like the point of being there, instead of a call for an automatic "excuse me."

A local band was already playing, mostly ignored save by a handful of their friends, girlfriends, and hard-core fans bopping furiously in front of the stage. Sam had chosen my all-black outfit well: I blended in, no doubt. I watched as his little body somehow squirmed to the front of the crowd at the packed bar, where he almost immediately magnetized a bartender into taking his order. Some other would-be patrons glared at his nerve, others pretended not to notice they'd been deemed less important, and a few others stared openly at Someone From TV.

He wriggled back out just as expertly, somehow carrying two beers and two shot glasses. He handed me one of the beers and a shot of something. "Bottoms up."

I did the shot and shuddered. "Cactus Juice! God, I can't believe they still make this."

"Yee-hah!" Sam hollered, mimicking the cowgirl on the DeKuyper label. "The evening isn't on till the first tequila's down."

Somehow I caught a rhythm in his sentence and sang back, "So do a shot and suck a lime and please try not to frown!"

He was right with me. "Then drink your beer, do not fall down, and do not break your crown!"

"Because we're all counting on you to buy the next round!"

"Bzz! Extra syllable, you lose."

"Think seventeenth-century English poetry, then. Substitute "'cause' as a single syllable conjugation for 'because.'"

"That's some ill communication. No fake words allowed."

"Why not?" I said with authorial arrogance. "I make up words all the time. They're only 'fake words' until someone else starts using them."

"And they tell two friends, and they tell two friends. So what are some of these alleged words?"

"Hmm. Well, suddenly living in the East Village has been an education. I thought everything scary and unattractive had been Giulianied out of town. So wrong. There are still so many skeezyflies and jackamuggers."

"Define."

"'Skeezyflies': people buzzing around the streets late at night, clearly undernourished and poorly clothed, with indeterminate motive and destination, who nevertheless radiate some malevolent intention, motivated criminally, psychotically, or both."

Sam frowned, concentrating. "Nice. 'Skeezyflies.' I'm hearing a reference to tsetse flies there. And I suppose 'skeezy' is a word now, isn't it."

"Very good!"

"Let me guess the other one. 'Jackamuggers': muggers, carjackers, jacklegs, carpetbaggers."

"Carpetbaggers, I didn't think of that. And 'jacklegs'—I thought my mother was the only one who ever used that old word."

And on we went. If it hadn't been for the mellowing effects of my chemical cocktail, it might have seemed an intuitive leap to realize that Sam was one of my kind. Instead, that knowledge just sort of seeped through my consciousness over the course of the evening, like a contact high. Funny: Our verbal gymnastics, cooperative and competitive at the same time, led me to this obvious conclusion the same way queens of yore used certain cultural references as secret handshakes, ways of flagging one another without anyone else catching on.

Here's a secret from the kingdom of the mad: There are few pleasures on earth like the electrochemical psychogalvanic rush that two bipolars, both in hypomania, can derive from conversing. Think what it's like to be a truly great athlete, to be alone at the top of your sport. At some point, you get bored with beating the other guy by a vast margin. You long to go up against someone who's as good as you are, someone who can reignite your ambition, your fear, your joy, your pride. Honestly, it's not nearly as fun to say something clever only to be told how clever you are as it is to say something clever to someone who hears you as if you were singing Handel, who dares to walk into your church and not only sing back but add a counterpoint, rewrite the chorus, and call you to respond. You take what they throw down and you run with it, because it's like *Chariots of Fire*—if you don't run, you don't win.

BRMC put on a great show, or maybe it was just me. Thank God *Spy* magazine isn't still around, publishing pictures of pathetic tycoons trying to boogie, always getting them with their pates shining and their eyes closed. I'm sure I looked as much a fool that night as I danced to my favorite songs, and cared less.

It's weird. For all my dread of people, all my terror of being judged and laughed at, I was actually okay with the Eye following me around all day. To be honest, once you've been paranoid, all whacked-out sure that everyone's looking at you and talking about you—well, once they certifiably *are*, it's oddly comforting. When the invisible fears that drive you crazy turn to visible facts, what's to fear?

It was Sunday, and we were supposed to be spending the day writing our songs, so we could polish and rehearse all day Monday. But I didn't wake up until 11, and when I did the clock inspired in me the shock, guilt, and disorientation of the early riser. We'd gotten out of the club at 3 and wandered around until 5 in the morning, stubbornly refusing to go home without fresh Krispy Kremes. I'd gone to bed wired on sugar and conversation and lay there listening to Sam snuffle and snark in his sleep while I turned the night over in my head, stunned by the pleasure of it.

Fortunately, most of the camera guys were off (God bless union rules), and the ones who were working looked like they too had had a few the night before. So since Sunday was Shelly's day off, it was light duty for all involved.

Besides, there wasn't much to film: Nothing is less visually appealing than watching people write. The best Hollywood could ever do was to put a writer in front of a typewriter and either have him smile as he pulled out pages and added them to an ever-growing pile, or frown as he crumpled them up and threw them at an overflowing trash can. Sam was on first-name terms with some of the crew, and he helped them meet their quota with some footage of the Artist Struggling to Create—a cute young guy with a guitar slung around his neck, trying to find the right notes, was a far more appealing visual than me prone on the bed, slightly hung-over, pretending I could string six words together.

I've got to admit, there was one feature of *The Pad* I would have liked for my own home. One big room had been turned into a Starbucks, right down to the wall sconces, the blond wood, and the whole Verve catalog on shuffle—and we were the only customers. The whole north-facing wall was a window, and it was a real treat for me to sit in a window seat and see without being seen. I got on as well with the cute baristas (a hand-picked harvest from stores around town, selected for their telegenicity) as Sam did with the camera crew, and I was enormously grateful on a two-grande-mocha morning that I didn't have to go out in public in order to be properly woken up.

Christie was at a table, paper and pen in contact with each other but with no apparent friction having occurred between them. She looked up and hey'd me as I came in for my second beverage of the day, and I nodded blearily. I chatted up the aspiring actor behind the counter as he worked the machine, and as I glanced over at Christie I found her looking at me, her features composed like she'd just made a decision. After I got my drink, she said to me, "You got a minute?"

"Sure." I stood there waiting for a quick question and she laughed.

"Okay, more than a minute. Sit down, will ya?" I sat down across from her and sipped my drink, waiting. "I'm trying to get some stuff down for tomorrow, and I'm kind of stuck. I was wondering if I could get your opinion on something."

Now I was awake, and my surprise must have shown, because she laughed again. "Don't be so startled!"

"Well, I'm flattered that you'd…"

"And don't be so polite, and distant. Please. Adam, I…hey, you know, I'm not sure I've ever even called you by name before. Isn't that bizarre?"

"Well, um, Christie," I replied, and we both laughed at ourselves.

"Fuck, we sound like news anchors," she said. "Listen, first I wanna say, I took that job with you guys because I wanted to be successful in a hurry. Remember, you had me sing 'Boyfriend in a Band'?" I nodded. "You know what's so great about your lyrics? You're always letting people in on the joke. If they're bright enough to catch it. And if they're not, so what, not everybody gets to the center of a Tootsie pop, you know? I sang that song and I fucking *knew*, I knew what you were doing and I knew I was the right one to sing your songs, I could do them justice, and they wouldn't make me look like a fool, at least not to anyone who was really paying attention."

I don't know why I suddenly got all emotional. I suppose all this time I thought that Christie had been laughing at me as much as any of Lyle's Serious People. And if there was one thing I'd learned at parties, it was how to tell when someone was bullshitting me to get what they wanted. Christie wasn't bullshitting me, and for some reason what she'd said meant a lot to me.

"And here I am," she went on, "in this contest, and I'm supposed to write *whole songs,* and I can't play an instrument, and I never even wrote schoolgirl *poetry* about ponies and shit when I was younger, and…" She stuck out her lower lip and blew a hard sigh up through her bangs. "And I'm not asking you to write anything *for* me, but if—when—I have something, will you look at it? I don't want you to fix it for me. Just tell me what's wrong with it?"

"Of course," I said. "I…thank you. I'm so…I'm amazed you don't despise me, despise my songs. I always thought…"

She smiled. "Listen. You're not the only one with issues, you know. I mean, you have no idea how nice it is to be here. To know this is one-way glass." That was news to me; no wonder there weren't any gawkers below as there would be at *TRL* or any other such locus du jour. "Yeah, there's the cameras, but everywhere I go there's cameras. Here, there's no *people,* screaming 'Christie! Christie! There she is! We love you!' They'll fucking love you to death some days. But I wanted to make it, to be somebody, so every day I turned it on—tee hee hee! Whee whee! What's more fun than being me! And the day I sued you—sorry, the day I sued ChrisCo—I thought, I'm *free,* I'm free to say my own words, to sing my own words, to say nothing at all to people on the street when I don't feel like it. And…and now I'm so fucking free to speak, I don't know what to say."

I gave that a moment. I set aside her words about the crushing pressure of the mob, the need to be somebody, words that could have come out of my mouth as easily as my words had come out of hers only a short time ago. I could feel mania coming on; I felt like I was standing in a lobby and all the elevator doors dinged open at the same time, and I could ride them all at once, one to the basement, one to the penthouse, push all the buttons in another one and stop on every floor. I was trying to hold back the flood of speech, of feeling, that was coming on, which would have been all about me and how I too felt all those things, which would have eventually wound around to a digressive, showy tour through everything I could have said about writing song lyrics, almost none of which would be useful to her right now. She had given me a gift, and I would give her one back: I would keep the cataract of words from overwhelming us both, I would let *my* words through the dam with measured care.

"Okay. Your first song, the one you did to get through the first round. It was…it was *right* for you. You wrote what you felt when you did that one, right? When you sang, 'I'm not a child anymore,' I sort of thought, that's a clever PR move. But that's because you'd sued us, and I didn't like you." We both laughed. "But you wrote what you felt about the whole thing, I know that now, after what you just told me. Am I right?" She nodded quickly, openly absorbing what I was saying.

"Okay. You're a new songwriter, so keep doing it like that—write down what you feel, just the way you'd tell someone if you were saying it out loud. Hell, just say it out loud, see how it sounds."

"Right, and if someone hears me talking to myself, they'll lock me up as a crazy person."

"The difference between a crazy person and a genius is, when you're a genius, if you live long enough, one day you wake up and your crazy ideas are suddenly called 'common sense.' We're artists, we've got a special exemption that *allows* us to be crazy." She laughed and I smiled. "Seriously, you're writing songs—you need to hear how they *sound.* And you have a great voice; write to your voice. Why do you think some songs are full of words like 'oh' and 'hey' and others are full of 'I' and 'we'?"

"It depends on your range," she said.

"Right." I went on from there, and Christie made a note now and then. Sometimes you don't know how much you know until you pass it on to someone else; as I laid out the basics for Christie I found out just how Serious I'd been all this time about what I could suddenly call, without anyone laughing at me, my craft.

The rest of the day Sam and I didn't do a damn thing. Sure, sure, on *Idol* it's the grasshopper hotties who opt for the hot tub and get kicked off early, and it's the eager ants who hole up in their rooms and rehearse their songs until they collapse so that Simon won't bite their heads off. But this was a different show.

"You can't rush the Muse," Sam declared ardently when were out on the balcony enjoying the late fall afternoon, smoking a joint. I was thoroughly enjoying being stoned, had totally forgotten the way it let me take a pleasant little walk through the gardens in my head. I'd been so uptight, I thought, so afraid of anything that would tip me over. But the view from tipped over was pretty nice.

"Creativity's not a faucet you can turn on and off," Sam asserted. "I've written some of my best songs in fifteen minutes. Ha! That would be a good one! Let them film me all day tomorrow doing nothing, then, right before the show, I write a song."

"You mean we, Kemo Sabe."

"I mean we. Sorry." Sam paced up and down the balcony while I lolled dreamily over the rail.

"Well, I don't know," I said. "I mean, change it from a faucet to a pump. You gotta prime a pump. Isn't that what it's called, when you push the lever thing a bunch of times before any water comes out of the ground?"

"Like *I've* been on a farm."

"And all that Muse and 'the universe will provide' stuff, I don't know, that's so…crunchy. You know how I think of it? Like sometimes, when I'm stuck? I just *delegate*. I say to my subconscious, Here, you figure this one out. And I totally forget about it, I don't micromanage the process. And then, guess what? When I need it, there it is, on my mental desktop."

"And if it isn't, since you've willed yourself to forget about it, you wouldn't know if your subconscious was slacking off on you, would you?"

I laughed. Actually, I giggled, stoned silly. I was so entranced by my own bright shiny thoughts that I didn't really notice *how* Sam was saying what he was saying until his voice got faster, his pacing turned to stalking, his sentences getting longer and starting to lose their thread.

"Well, there's no time for unconscious simmering. A *love* song," he spat. "They'll all be up there tomorrow night, whoo-ooh ooh, whoa oh, yeah yeah baby baby. Love's the opiate of the masses; you're sold this whole fucking idea that love will fix you right up, some other person's going to come along and all your problems will disappear, hell, they'll all just fucking *drown* in your eternal bliss…"

If I hadn't been so stoned, so unsure of the evidence of my senses, not to mention my ability to process, I probably would have asked him the question that needed asking right then: Just how crazy are you? We'd never exchanged an ordinary word about our mutual friend, only sly references to Byron and Cobain. But even stoned, I knew full-on mania when I saw it.

It's the pot, I told myself. I cut him off and told him to calm down, and he did. You'd be amazed how effectively manic episodes can be terminated by someone who's rude and fearless enough to interrupt a crazy person's rant. I was even successful in convincing him to spend some time decompressing in our room. Meanwhile, I went to the kitchen, where, since the show's portrayal of down-home cookin' was apparently played out, Jean and I were left alone to make supper.

"So you and Sam," she said, just as she'd said yesterday, but with a smile in her voice that indicated all that had changed.

"Yeah, me and Sam," I agreed, and wondered why that worried me.

I didn't really know what was going on with the rest of the cast—er, contestants—until I saw the "reality" show that night, the little I could catch during my warmups for the *Showcase*. Amazingly, LaQuinta got more airtime than Christie, but then LaQuinta was really working the program. She had absolutely mastered the art of staring out the window, head cocked at just the right angle, when the light was just right; strolling the East Village thumbing through sidewalk sales; and rolling the street patois with the people she talked to. Never mind that she'd been raised in Brentwood and had attended private school; you'd never have guessed she hadn't been born down with homey. And she had totally nailed her production of the navel-gazing monologues each of us was expected to produce—curse you, *Real World!*—on the subjects of success, family, triumph, struggle, and the other housemates. Plus, her roommate the tranny spent almost all his/her airtime talking about how pretty LaQuinta was.

Trey was the polar opposite of LaQuinta when it came to handling the Eye. Where he came from, MTV was the devil's workshop, so his self-awareness around the cameras was absolute zero. I didn't like what I saw—cameras peeping through doorways and zooming across the living room, always catching Trey as he gazed with glazed fascination at Nick. It wasn't *fair,* I thought. He was starting to look less like a deer in the forest—who at least has a chance to hear you rustling in the brush and run for it—and more like a fish in a barrel.

At least on TV, Jean and Connie got on surprisingly well. If there's such a thing as a beta female, Connie was it. But Christie and Nola—I had to stop my vocal exercises in their tracks to watch, knowing how good both of them were at pulling the wool over the general public at will and wondering how they'd fare against each other.

Nola and Christie were shown at a window-side table in our Starbucks. The camera was physically distant from them, as if according due respect to girlish intimacy, but the microphone gave that lie away by picking up every coo and bill. "I just have to say," Nola gushed, "I'm so glad to be working with you, it's so good to have your years of experience on our side." *You're old and used up and I'll conquer you.*

"I'm so glad I could help you out! I've spent my whole life working, so it's good to spend time with someone totally out-side the industry." *You know nothing of stagecraft. I've got magic tricks you've never heard of, I'll pull lions out of my hat and they will eat you.*

"I've spent my whole life working too! Well, in a Wal-Mart and a McDonald's"—Nola laughs self-deprecatingly—"nothing as glamorous as you." *Here I remind our viewers what a princess you are, whereas I'm one of them.*

"Yeah, that's tough. I've worked a lot of sixteen-hour days, but I know that's nothing like having to sling burgers and hash browns all day." *I've gone weeks with my total hours of sleep in the single digits; see what the grease has done to your complexion.*

Halfway through the *Showcase,* we ran through our songs, nobody getting much applause—but no blatant derision from the judges either (their only power now being their ability to sway voters). Kat and LaQuinta did an okay Salt-N-Pepa–style song, though they'd probably get extra points for their snappy choreography. Nick and Trey's song was—well, weird. It was clearly not much of a collaboration; if you can imagine Donny Osmond writing lyrics for Bauhaus tunes, you get the idea.

Christie and Nola were second to last, before me and Sam, and the tote board showed pretty much everyone evenly behind Christie before she sang a note. Then Christie announced their song. "This is called 'Diamonds Are a Girl's Worst Friend.'" Nola rapped the first two verses, her contribution:

> Yo, listen up, this is what I gotta sing
> I'm sick-a hearing how I need the bling bling
> Started with homies shot dead on the news
> Somebody went and popped 'em for a pair of shoes
>
> You got a rock on your finger the size of Gibraltar
> But it ain't from no man who took you to the altar
> He's a gangsta thug, he's straight out of jail
> Girl, the jewels he gives you are your coffin nails

Nola was actually quite convincing as a rapper—the style enabled her to let out the thug within that her castmates knew well. Then Christie took the chorus, in a voice as crisp and clear as the one in which she'd once sung "Boyfriend in a Band," only now her tone had changed, as if she'd had said boyfriend and found him wanting:

> Nothing says love like a bright shiny pebble
> If you don't think so, you're some kind of rebel
> Auction off that ring at a charity benefit
> It'll make you crazy, living for this bling shit!

And with that she pulled off a very expensive diamond ring

(I knew how expensive because I'd once heard Robin tell an infotainment reporter) and threw it into the audience. It was impossible to tell which parts of the collective gasp were the result of which crime: the hurling away of valuable property or the naughty word from the mouth of America's sweetheart. There was a scrabble for the ring, and an old man held it up in triumph the same way he might have shown off a foul ball at the ballpark, little realizing that a crowd full of Christie stalkers, professional eBay auctioneers, and hysterical preadolescents was vastly more dangerous than any mere drunken bunch of bleacher bums. I think Security got him out in one piece, but I'm not sure.

After that, hardly anybody paid attention to me and Sam as we sang "our" song. I'd known all day that we were screwed, and the crowd confirmed it for me as Sam snarled out the chorus:

> He's a superstar with a pretty face
> And every night you dream of his embrace
> I'm sorry, honey child, it's a truth you gotta face
> You're another teenage girl in love with a closet case

Now, I'm no dummy when it comes to pleasing teenage girls—lyrically, at least. But Sam had declared that morning (as far as I could tell, not having slept a wink Sunday night) that *this* was our song. He'd been adamant, with the same sort of fury he'd shown on the balcony on Sunday—only this was Monday, I wasn't stoned anymore, I was resentful of his assumption that I'd just let him write "our" song, and I realized that while on both the occasions I'd seen him like this his fury had been righteous, it had still been fury, a free-floating aggravation that seemed only tenuously tethered to any personal passion.

"I hate these guys," he fumed. "They're *gigolos*! They take these girls for a ride, promise them anything's possible, then go off and suck [*bleep*] in some back room."

"And that offends your sense of chivalry or something?" I asked, aware that the Eye was recording our struggle.

"As a person who [*bleep*] men and women, depending on my mood and who's hottest that night, it offends me to see jerks who are basically pole dancers for teenage girls, willing to grind a little harder for the $13.95 they stuff in their jockstraps, letting them think they'll someday get to touch their [*bleep*]. I mean, these girls worship these rock stars, and the best they can really ever hope for even with the heterosexual ones is to give them a [*bleep bleep*] backstage one day."

Kapoof! That proclamation aired on *The Pad* around 8:22, and from that moment you could watch his rating plummet. And after the whole song aired on the *Showcase* (me reduced to plunking the six notes I knew on the keyboard while Sam sang and power-chorded his way to the bitter end), he was just about gone off the radar. He'd not only made teenage girls go "Eww!" with his bisexual declaration, he'd then turned around and slapped them with the absurdity of their most cherished delusion—the one he'd been the object of until that moment. And it didn't get any gay voters to play for his team; most all of them were voting either for Christie (camp value) or Nick (who was officially Hot). It would have been one of those classic rock-and-roll moments of self-immolation, almost perversely glorious to behold, if it hadn't been for the edge of spite in his voice and the fact that what might go over as passionate conviction in person was clearly insane on television. I'd lost some whuffie too, probably because, even though the viewers knew it was *his* song, they also had seen me let him walk on me. I was now in next-to-last place—saved from being the class Goat by Sam's award of that honor.

Meanwhile, Christie's ratings had also taken a temporary dive, as she lost the Nice vote. But then she trended upward, probably taking some of Sam's lost votes. By the end of the night, Christie had a clear lead.

Back at the penthouse, I tried to quell my irritation at having lost so much face (and so many points). Normally I might have worked and reworked the best words to use to open a constructive conversation with Sam about what he'd done to me as well as himself, but mania was starting to prune my dendrites with all the enthusiasm of Edward Scissorhands and none of the art. My own tides of rage were producing nothing more expressive than *Fuck you, you fucking fuck!*

Sam, meanwhile, was bouncing off the walls. "Did you see that? Did you see their faces? That was unbelievable. Fucking awesome!"

"You just lost. *We* just lost, thanks much. I don't know what you're so thrilled about."

He turned on me, nostrils flaring, smile delirious. "Lost? This farce? I couldn't win this thing. You know it, I know it. You can't win. Can't you *see* it, see the fucking *pattern?* All these fucking morons have a head full of prelabeled boxes; they have just *got* to cram you into one of them as soon as they can so they can shut the lid and not let the reasons you're so different from them trouble them ever again. They want to put me in this fucking box called HIPSTER MUSICIAN, and I'm not getting in it! *I'm* something new, *I'm* something these motherfuckers have never seen the likes of! Oh, but I'm not what they've already got in their heads is what they want and like. They want songwriters to stir shit up the way they want Dr. Phil to tell them 'You spend too much' or 'You're eating to avoid your emotions,' when what he needs to say to these fucking *idiots* is that their lives are hollow and empty, that they're selfish and greedy, that they need to get rid of their motherfucking Truckasaurus

SUVs and stop voting on the basis of the price of gas, and…"
He stopped for a split-second to light a cigarette. "I got news,
assholes, my rough edges weren't stuck on me by some fucking
photo stylist somewhere. I'm not the same old thing in brand
new drag, not the kind of shit some cynical old Simon Cowell
bitch would pick to sell to the lowest common denominator at
the highest list price…"

Let me try and give you a physical representation of what it's
like to have a "flash of intuition." I think I can do it—when you
have my condition and have made it to my age without having
been institutionalized, you have more than one of them in your
life experience file. One was hitting me right now as Sam carried on, referencing a book he rifled through his shit to find,
only to discover instead a CD that said it so much better—here,
listen, this is it.

Think of the Luxor Hotel in Las Vegas. Most big ideas are
like pyramids, which start with a wide base of "common knowledge" and angle upward to a point. Thousands of ideas float
around; most disappear or are discarded. Some, however, result
in the creation of whole fields of study, some of which will stand
(evolution) and some of which will fall (say, phrenology). Take
any field of study, and most of those working in it are only
adding footnotes to the original genius's main text; every now
and then, a new discovery (the selfish gene, the meme) will
purge that field of old, wrong ideas (the earth is flat, and the
universe revolves around it). All of it is *reaching* for a "theory of
everything," all of it is trying to get to the point. Almost all
human progress is pyramidal, in my uneducated opinion. The
thing is, in the semi-orderly march of human progress, that
pyramid is built in a kind of half-ass way, its sides totally uneven,
as people figure out things faster in this department and slower
in that one (Earth is millions of years old, and God created it in
seven days).

But imagine if you could look at this incomplete lopsided structure—which doesn't even *look* like a pyramid yet to most people, because they don't know what you know: that all this knowledge is pointing toward the same destination, that some day it will all hook up, that the great theories will someday prove one another—imagine if you stood before this half-built thing without a blueprint, but you still *knew* what joist would join what beam, and which arch was the key supporting one, and why that wall couldn't be built any higher until...you put all those pieces into place, the whole thing AutoCAD-drawn in your head as fast as one of those *Modern Marvels* clips of a massive edifice going up in thirty seconds.

But nobody else can *see* what you see, they can't do the geometry you've done, because the symbols are all Greek to them. Nevertheless, you've finished the pyramid in your head, and that 42.3-billion-candlepower beam of light at the top of the Luxor is *there,* in place and hooked up to all that's below it. Its light is on for all who can see—people can see that there is a light, all right, hanging there in space, but they can't imagine how it could sit right there, can't imagine what you've had to imagine in order to be able to place, and power, that light... But they know you're right: That light is right where it should be. And a thousand careers are built putting into place the proof that all the joists and beams and arches you theorized belong right where you said they did.

It's like all those times you thought, about a book or a song or a painting, *This is completely perfect. Damn if I could do it, damn if I know why it's perfect, but it is.*

And here were some of the elements of the superstructure rising in my head right now. I'd used my illness as a tool, a sharper tool than most possessed, and it was a tool that felt right in my hand. But where I held a hammer, Sam held a jackhammer; where I moved levers up and down, using a crane to build,

Sam pushed the same levers and sent a wrecking ball in random directions. He knew he had no business operating heavy equipment, but the vibration of the jackhammer made his bones sing, and the wrecking ball made such smashtacular sights. He could create big things, but once they were made he couldn't restrain himself from jumping off the top, just to see if he could fly.

Being bipolar is exhilarating—the giddy joy of unification, synthesis, light speed. But for every blessing it brings, there's a Greek-tragic price to be paid. To be able to feel so much euphoria and raise great towers in your head is also to be able to feel a horror and sorrow most people only see others experiencing in war zone footage. It's to *know* what the throne will feel like at your coronation, and what the coffin will feel like as you lie in your grave.

Think what it would feel like to be a great surfer: You're inside the pipe, it's a living thing, you're calculating every possible future direction and shape of that moving wall of water, where you need to be and how to get there; like a chess grand master you're sixteen moves ahead. For a moment you're sure, *so sure,* how that wave is curling, what nature's going to do next; it's going to make everything go your way, you're the power behind all the ocean's tides, you're going to ride this wave forever, you're goddamn Poseidon, dude…and then the ocean continues to operate on its own schedule, by its own laws, and that wall you can't draw or reinforce or control comes down on you, and you're left beached, half drowned, and the wave that broke you is now just a tickling little lapping on the feet of the people staring down at you. If you're to become a better surfer, you learn from this. If you're bipolar, the temptation is to go out there and feel that way again—and on some level perhaps you even believe that next time you *will* have control of the whole fucking ocean.

That was the part I hated, the reason I went on the fish

oil: The wave that had crashed down on me when my motley record failed to put me on the cover of *Rolling Stone*. My theory is, when people like me make an intuitive leap about objective constructs and problems, the result is quite often genius. When we make the same intuitive leap about our subjective desires, trying to will them true, the result is quite often madness. It's one thing to try and fill in the blanks in the world around us with likely outcomes, natural next steps, and empirical evidence. It's quite another to try and apply that same process to yourself, because when it comes to how very rich or how very adored or how very *something* most of my kind burn to be, there is no empirical evidence, few probabilities even, no way to be sure what comes next in life. And too often we fill in the space between us and the perfect moment we *just know* awaits us with delusions of affect; we can't ride the story's arc to our heart's desire as fast or as well as we want; we pound our hands and heads in rage against the walls that keep us from what we *should* have, and that blazing beacon seen from space is just a hallucination, a fucking cosmic joke.

Sam was mad. The people-seeking on the subway, the delusions of affect he was pronouncing even now, his near-sleepless nights even though all he ingested was Xanax, alcohol, and weed...I thought of how well I'd held myself back with Christie in our Starbucks, how *natural* it was for people like Sam and me to lift the floodgates behind our mouths and *rant,* how I must have learned something in all this time if I was now able to see what was happening to me and head it off. But Sam didn't have all that experience behind him, didn't have as many years of regrets and embarrassments to guide his behavior. I could see the future right now: Plain as day I saw him falling off his board and the tide sucking him under. And it was hard not to feel as if it was happening to me all over again—the intensely vivid nature of bipolar emotion means not only perfectly visualized perfect futures but also equally accessible and unforgettable past pains.

I had made up my mind that I'd made a friend, and to me that meant I now had an obligation far more Serious than I could have to any stupid fucking TV show. I thought to myself, in ordinary time, in ordinary words, *I made a mistake, going off the fish oil.* I thought to myself, *Shut down, halt construction; his safety line's not connected. Find a way to tell him, "I can see your future and I'm afraid for you."*

EIGHT

Ever hear of client-centered counseling? Basically, it's good customer service for crazy people. Seriously: The idea is that the client/customer is always right; i.e., he knows himself better than the therapist ever can. Client-centered counseling operates on the faith that people want to evolve, and they will find their own path to a better place inside, and the therapist can help them along but can't draw the map for them.

I was a firm believer in client-centered counseling, and I expected my mental health professionals to be as well. So it would hardly be cricket of me to wrestle Sam to the ground and force him to confront the awful truth. And as I deliberated on how I could best help him, I had to also figure out what to do for myself. Fire is catching: If you put two bipolars in a room, you better stand back, baby. I could feel a spark in myself, and I was scared. Yeah, I know, I stopped my fish oil in order to go a little crazy—but as I recalled playing Sam's little song-title game and feeling the breeze firing my embers I could see clearly the fine line between a *little* crazy and a *lot* crazy.

I'd stopped the fish oil because I was scared—scared that I

was too old and too shallow to keep a man like Lyle from the allure of a beautiful disaster like Sam, too facile to make a career doing something that wouldn't cause Lyle's friends to look at me with *that face,* too set in my ways to stop filling my days by emptying my pockets. Did I actually think I could win this contest? Now, that *would* have been delusional. All I wanted to do was make a decent showing, make the world see that I wasn't just a bubble gum machine. But now, suddenly, I just wanted to go home to my boyfriend and be sane...even if it meant disappearing from the world's radar, maybe even having to *economize.* I knew I didn't want this, I didn't want to manufacture drama for TV, and I didn't want a roommate who could push me over my tipping point at any moment.

I hadn't gone to sleep by 4 A.M., a sure sign of incipient mania, although I think I had enough on my mind to justify sleeplessness regardless. Our bedroom was the nearest to the big balcony, and through the window, I heard Sam out there, singing and playing his guitar.

I bundled up against the chilly predawn air and went out there. Sam was perched precariously on the railing, rocking back and forth as he played and hummed, and since there wasn't a camera in sight I knew this wasn't for show. "You'd better get off there," I said, pretty sure this was a good time to offer some therapeutic direction.

He looked up, eyes wide, and I knew he'd done some coke. It's funny to see the fashion statements drugs can be. Coke and meth aren't much different once they're inside your head, but coke is so acceptable these days, so chic, whereas these same people with their wallets on a chain and their trucker hats and their vintage John Deere T-shirts think meth is so déclassé. Go figure.

"Hey!" he shouted. "I've got our song for tonight!" (Naturally, Nell Makepeace had told us to write a protest song.)

I was beyond going off on Sam over the "our" shit again; right now I was more concerned about his physical safety.

"Don't do anything rash, come down off the ledge. Life is worth living."

He laughed at me, waving an arm at the city, a perpetual audience for the next big thing, anytime anywhere. "I've got to teach the world to sing, in perfect harmony, about the holy rollers and their fucking sanctimony."

"You can't say 'fuck,' it's not cable. Besides, it fucks up your rhyme scheme."

"That's not the song! Here, listen." The first verse was based on the old hymn:

Jesus hates me, this I know,
Jerry Falwell tells me so
Conform if you would belong,
Love is weak and hate is strong

Then he started banging out angry chords:

Everything you think, say, wish, or do
Jesus hates but he still loves you
We're going to burn you at the stake
But don't worry, Jesus won't forsake
You in your desperate hour of need
Which makes it okay for our hate to feed
On you

Since Jesus loves you, we don't have to
We can crush, burn, shoot, or stab you
Boil you in the cauldron of our hate
All our sins Jesus will exonerate
See, we love the sinner and hate the sin

But we can't punish sin without going through the sinner
And that's you

Love is your alibi, love is your alibi
You shot me out of love, that's your alibi
You chained me out of love, that's your alibi
You did it 'cause you love me, you killed me 'cause you
    love me…

He trailed off. "It's not finished yet."

"If you play that song, they'll burn *you* at the stake."

He scowled. "They want a fucking protest song, I'll give 'em one. All these other idiots are going to get up there and cry about animals or the environment or something that won't stir up any shit, won't lose 'em any point on their precious *tote board*…" And he was off. Suddenly I had an inspiration and broke into his babbling.

"So do I have any input into this song?"

He blinked. In the grip of Certainty, other people's feelings aren't terribly relevant—I remembered the friends I'd lost with my buffalo stances on things that in the end hadn't really mattered; my insistence on being right, especially when I was wrong. "Sure, as long as you aren't going to try and tone it down."

"Just do this. Get your coat on and let's go somewhere."

"Where?"

"A place where I can think."

It turned out that calling Shelly the Eye of Sauron was more apt than we could have imagined, since, like Sauron, she never slept. Here it was 5 A.M. and she was already at work—a fact we only discovered as we attempted to leave the building without our electronic leash. "You know the rules," she scowled at us in the lobby, to which she'd beaten us by racing down the stairs. "You need someone along to get footage. You!" she shouted at a guy who was leaving the building. She hoisted a camera with surprising strength and thrust it at him. "You're with them." He nodded and took the unit and we set off.

"So are you a member of a secret society?" Sam needled me. "Are we going somewhere you can deprogram me?"

"We're going to Fort Tryon Park," I said.

"I've never been there," Sam said, and the novelty of it seemed to settle the issue.

On the subway, Sam slouched across from me, quietly fingering the strings on his guitar, lost in composition, the camera guy kitty-corner from him, picking up some B-roll. Then, after we transferred to a more crowded train, the camera guy and I had to sit next to each other. I sniffed the air—there was something familiar, something I couldn't place. Then, as he rearranged himself and his equipment, his hand brushed mine and I knew.

They say that on *An American Family*—the first reality show, which aired some thirty years ago now (and was so shocking it kept reality shows *off* the air for said thirty years)—the Loud family was at first painfully conscious of the cameras, but that at a certain point, they just...forgot that they were there, the way you don't think about a picture that's always been on the wall or the magnets that have always been on the fridge, so that if someone comments on them you have to look to remind yourself.

I can vouch for that, because surprisingly quickly, the cameramen on *The Pad* had become invisible to us. Somehow the camera *disappears* in a French theory kind of way, and it's just you and them. Now, as a general rule, camera guys are usually hard to ignore because they're almost always hotties. It's a job that requires you to be young and agile, darting through crowds to keep the eye on the ball, so to speak. You need broad shoulders to hold the camera and big biceps to get it there. And you have to be tall to get the shot. The fellow next to me had the standard camera stud physique, so in his pulled-down hat and shades (sunglasses at night are nothing worth noticing in Manhattan), it had been easy not to notice until now that he was Ronny Wycoff.

"What are you doing?" I asked him. He looked back at me and, realizing the jig was up, gave me the grin that launched a thousand teenage orgasms.

He took off the glasses. "Hoping to make sweet, sweet love to you, doll."

"Ha. You were sneaking out of the house, what were you doing there?"

"I had business."

"So why take the camera, why the hat and glasses?"

He made a steeple of his fingertips and put them to his chin thoughtfully. "Yes, Adam, it's bigger than a breadbox. Next question?"

Sam seemed to notice him for the first time. "Hey, you're...you. I know you from somewhere."

Ronny raised his arms and asked the heavens, "Do you think a billboard of me in Times Square, in my skivvies, might finally tip the punters off to who the fuck I am?"

"Probably not," I replied for both of them. "If I were you, I'd find out who laid the gypsy curse on you that makes you invisible." Sam, even though he new understood that he was in the company of an international star—or perhaps because he knew—continued to project obliviousness.

"If this were the Tube..." Ronny proclaimed.

"I know, I know," I said, "even at this ungodly hour you'd be crushed to death by your fans, they'd have to saw a hole in the roof to get you out of the car, blah." Sam rolled his eyes.

Ronny laughed. Self-deprecation is such an integral part of

being a good Englishman that you can rag on them mercilessly and they'll just join in. He turned to me. "So what's this fort of yours we're off to play in?"

"We're almost there, you'll see soon enough."

It's quite a long ride to Fort Tryon Park, almost at the very tippy top of Manhattan. I think some Rockefeller bought all the land and left it undeveloped, not only there but on the other side of the Hudson, so you can look in any direction and see nothing but the original wilderness. Even the subway station was a step back in time, with its elevator that still had an operator and the moss-covered, nineteenth-century-looking stone building that housed it. Ronny left the camera on the subway; when I pointed it out, he shrugged. "It's not mine, is it? Some lucky fellow up here will make good use of it, don't you think?"

When you walked up the steps and across the street to the park, you were stepping back in time at least a century. This morning it was foggy and chill, which was fine with me since it meant even more privacy.

When you travel down the park's curvy cliffside paths, you *feel* like you're going even further back in time, and even the sound of the buses on the parkway below can't diminish the feeling, especially as you turn a corner and see the old castle that is the Cloisters museum. I love the Cloisters—the only tourists you see there are handfuls of French tour groups and schoolchildren bused in for a day of Edification. For those who need to pack as many sights into one day as possible, the Cloisters never makes the itinerary, because it takes half a day just to ride the subway, walk through the park, see the museum, and get back to Midtown. Only medieval buffs and hard-core joggers go up there, and needless to say that made it my favorite place in all of New York City.

Even Sam calmed down as we walked the twists of the

fog-enshrouded, up-and-down paths, through the flowers and trees and overripe greenery. Ronny seemed perfectly at home, this being the sort of place England is full of.

We sat on one of the stone walls, silent. Ronny lit a cigarette and Sam bummed one off him. After a few puffs, Sam said, "So here we are."

"Sam," I asked, "just how bipolar are you?"

He laughed. "So you noticed I stopped my lithium."

Another part of client-centered counseling? Active listening. You don't fill every silence, you don't reply to every statement. You're paying attention, but it's your demeanor that shows it, not a constant stream of "uh-huh, uh-huh." I just waited to see what else he'd say, and when I said nothing he shrugged and said, "I had to."

"Why?" I asked, knowing the answer.

"Do you know what that shit does to you? Do you think I could write a fucking *song a day* on lithium? When I take as much as they tell me to take, I can't remember my own fucking *name* some days." He laughed. "That, and I was afraid of what would happen if they found my pills. My mom would love that, all the neighbors seeing one of the Eyes zooming in on the medicine cabinet. And then Shelly would make me sit in the fucking chair and cough up some fucking hairball of a monologue about My Illness. And then the people on the street...*you know*," he said to me, and I certainly did. Not what they thought, but what you were *sure* they thought.

"You know, mate," Ronny said, "if you're that paranoid maybe you're not taking *enough* lithium."

"And they'd say I was sick, their liability insurance wouldn't cover what might happen to me, I'd be off the show. Fuck it. I can go two weeks without it. Fact is, to do this fucking thing I needed to go..."

"A little bit crazy," I finished with him, and he looked at me. "I take the omega-3s, I don't know if you..."

"Tried it. They said I was too far gone for that."

"Sam, you've been off it for how long? Just a few days? And this morning you're hanging over the balcony singing a song that will make you as beloved in this country tomorrow morning as Sinéad O'Connor the day after she tore up the pope."

"He did have it coming," Ronny noted, pulling a joint out of his cigarette pack and lighting it off his cigarette.

"I just..." How to explain it to him, in plain English? "I've *been* crazy. I've been so fucking crazy I walked the streets all night, and it was like, like the city was *singing* to me. The lights were all alive, and the cars and the people, it was all a body and I was the soul, the brain, I was the One. I was going to be on the cover of every magazine. *60 Minutes* was dying to interview me and I had to choose between them and Barbara Walters. I was..."

"You were crazy," Sam said. "And you know what? So am I. Don't think I don't know it. I'm not one of those dummies who thinks he can stop his meds and be okay because he feels fine the day he stops. I know what I'm doing."

He took the proffered joint from Ronny and took a hit. "Listen. You say they're going to hate me tomorrow. Do you know what the world hates? The world hates a sane musician. Unless you play the cello, or crank out smooth jazz, you'd better be fucking models and wrecking hotel rooms and shooting up with a gold-needled syringe with a jade barrel. You'd better be shouting at audience members who ask you to sing songs written by someone whose name sounds like yours, you'd better date Winona Ryder, you'd better be making damn sure VH1's got plenty of material for your *Behind the Music* episode, you'd better spend at least as much time generating your legend for your biographer as you spend writing *music*, you'd better stay skinny and get tattooed and keep your hair looking fucked-up. You'd better be crazy, if you want them to love you."

"But the rage when it doesn't come out the way you want it to, the depression, that awful feeling..."

"No offense? You failed. I'll give it to you, Adam, you tried. And your shit's not bad. And if you were ten years younger and twenty pounds skinnier, you'd probably make it. And you know what? When you make it, you don't *get* depressed about failing, do you? And I'm going to make it." He stared off into the future. "I just know it."

He offered me the joint and I declined. Ronny took it back and took a hit that was as sound a testament to the man's lung capacity as any note he'd ever held. "Young man," he said, after finally letting out his significant contribution to the fog around us, "the geezer has a few words for you. Believe me, I know all about building a mystery. But then there's the days you've got to make sure your manager isn't stealing your money, and the days you have to audition your touring bandmates, and the days you have to spend doing press junkets, saying the same thing over and over in sixty different 'exclusive interviews.' And that's what drives you crazy, the tedium of all that shit you've *got* to manage yourself if you're going to hold onto what you've got. And you can't be crazy for that."

"I know," Sam said, but I knew he didn't. He was in the grip of the Rapture, the certainty that this good feeling would never end, that the future was a yellow-brick road, but all poppies, no witches. "Thanks," he said to Ronny, taking the joint again, and it was clear to me—and to Ronny, his shrug indicated—that the thanks were more for the weed than for the advice. Sam got up. "Time to get back. You coming?" he asked me.

"I'll be along later," I said absently. I had come up here to think, and I wasn't done yet.

Sam shook my hand as if saying goodbye. "Good luck."

I took it because I could see he meant it. "Thanks, you too."

And I watched him wander back to the station, humming

and strumming, and I was glad I wasn't him, glad I wasn't in his shoes, glad that everything ahead of him was behind me, the conquests and the disasters both, because they're the two poles you get with this thing, and you don't get to pick which one of them ends your day.

I walked Ronny back to the entrance. "Well," Ronny said, pulling out his cell phone, "I'm calling a car. Want a ride?"

"No, thanks, I'm going to stay here a while."

We sat there for an astonishingly short amount of time before a Town Car whisked around the circle and the driver opened the door for Ronny. "You know, the offer's still open for you to work for me. I think you're fucking mad talented."

"Thank you, I appreciate that, I do. But…I don't know what comes next, but whatever it is, it's going to be…not what I've been doing."

"All right. Cheers then. You'll come next time I'm at Knebworth? I'll pay your tickets, you and the hubby, first-class all the way."

"I'd love that."

He waved as the car sped off. I sat there for a minute, wondering if it was worth the admission price to the Cloisters just to go to the café and get a decent sandwich. I didn't realize Ronny had left his cell phone behind until it rang, next to me on the bench. I picked it up and saw it was one of his preprogrammed numbers—the caller ID only said "Sunshine."

I don't know why, but I picked it up and answered it with a Ronny-ish "'Ello?"

"So you got out this morning safe and sound. Well, I double dare you to do it again tonight, lover boy."

I hung up, shocked. Then I started laughing as I realized who it was. After all, who better than the man who'd put so many words in her mouth to recognize the inimitable voice of Christie Squires?

Sam's saying goodbye hadn't been off base; I was seriously considering leaving the show. It *felt* like the right decision: I knew Sam's madness might be catching, and plus I was starting to see the pyramid's shape—and the architects of that shape were not the voting audience but the executives at YBC and the producers of both shows. Still, since I was afraid to trust my intuition, I decided to call Lyle.

"I just don't want to make another 'crazy' decision, you know?" I asked him. "The problem is, I'm not quite sure what 'crazy' would be for me right now. I mean, this whole situation is crazy, strictly defined. Think about it: The definition of *reality* is being rewritten on the show every time we turn around. It's getting absurd, it's like, what's wrong with this picture, and what's wrong with my head…"

"Funny you should pick the word *absurd*," Lyle said. "I was just reading Camus."

"And is there a connection you'd like to make there, are you changing the subject, or is my navel-gazing getting to you?" I laughed.

"No, there's a connection. Camus gave us the modern definition of *absurdity,* you know, and I was reading *The Myth of Sisyphus,* and there's a passage where he talks about reality breaking down, and he uses the phrase 'stage sets collapse.' Which, for some reason, made me think of *The Pad.* And when you talked about Sam just now, I thought about Camus's concept of 'revolt.' Which is probably not quite kosher of me, since Camus was…"

It wasn't even so much Lyle's words as it was the *fact* of them, the fact that he was off and rolling on a philosophical topic, assuming I could keep up, knowing I would stop him and ask him a question if I had one. Lyle was a solid, steady light, one that shone brightly without burning itself out; could I be anything like that? And would it be enough?

"And basically, he chose Sisyphus because it's an absurd task, rolling that boulder up the mountain when it's only going to roll back down again. And yet to stop trying is to lose, whereas to keep trying is to win, even though you can't win. You see?"

I sighed glumly. "So if Camus were directing this decision, I'd basically have to stay on the show and keep pushing the fucking rock uphill."

"That depends on what you see as the rock, Adam. Is the show the rock, or is the rock your desire to make something more of yourself?"

Well, now, that stopped me cold. From the time I'd parked my ass outside MSG, at least subconsciously I'd decided the show was the beginning, not the end of my attempt at reinvention. If I'd thought losing would be the end, I would have taken Ronny's offer.

"Can you meet me? At home?"

"You've made your decision."

"Yes. One of them, at least."

Curled up on our couch that night with Lyle, watching *The Pad,* I practiced my metaphysics by considering whether it was more "absurd" or "surreal" that I was watching a show on which my absence was being so ardently discussed. LaQuinta and Nola and Trey expressed their concern by staring pensively out various windows (get my good side, please) as if looking for me. Or for Sam, who had also spent the day away.

"Maybe they eloped," Christie suggested in the living room, through a haze of cigarette smoke, getting laughs from Bryce and Jean and harrumphs and hair tosses from the rest.

"Bigamist," Lyle muttered in my ear, nuzzling my neck. I don't suppose I'll ever forget how his face lit up when he opened the door and there I was. How stupid I'd been not to notice the difference in wattage between the light he shined on others and the light he shined on me. The first thing I did was lead him by the hand, not to the bedroom but to the bathroom, where I ceremoniously bolted down a handful of fish-oil capsules.

Sam showed up just in time to make the last five minutes of *The Pad*. In response to frenzied requests for my whereabouts, he told them only, "He joined a nunnery."

"The Cloisters was built out of parts of various monasteries, you know," Lyle told me. "So he's half right."

The show must go on, and it did. Neil Gates made one of those network anchor-brand Sad Story faces and informed the world that Adam Bede had withdrawn from the competition for "personal reasons."

"Like a hack politician caught with my hand in the cookie jar, I've resigned to 'spend more time with my family,'" I said, squeezing the arm Lyle had wrapped around me. "Besides, Sam was right," I moped slightly, "I am too old to win. It's some kind of freak accident that I got this far."

"Did it ever occur to you, Adam, that talent *might* have something to do with the outcome of a talent contest?"

"You sweet, silly man," I mocked him gently.

"Well, you haven't lost your talent. And we're not poor, you know. You won't be selling matches in the snow outside the *TRL* studio."

"I know." I sighed. "I guess now I should take all that time I used to spend shopping and, I don't know, apply myself or something."

He laughed. "Adam, the only person who doesn't take you seriously is you."

I didn't say anything, just squeezed him good as we watched the *Showcase*. Sam, flying solo, sang his idea of a protest song, and the shit hit the fan. The boos started before the first verse had ended, and before he'd gotten through the fourth he'd ended up in a fistfight with someone from the audience. The last we saw of him that night was as he was led off for stitches.

Then LaQuinta and Kat sang some song about hate being bad, and after polite (and presumably relieved) applause, Neil began the aftersong interview. "So, Kat—or should I call you Kit?"

"I beg your pardon?" she said, the camera lunging in for the close-up kill.

"Kit, as in Christopher? Christopher Mays, your real name?"

I don't know if the same sort of people go to all live TV shows, or if Sam had just put the fire in their belly, but at this revelation the crowd suddenly descended into hoots and hollers befitting the *Jerry Springer* show. As Neil introduced picture-in-picture B-roll of Kit/Kat's early performances at Trannyshack et al, I saw Christie and Jean come from offstage to comfort the now-sobbing performer. Then I saw the two of them get all the performers into a huddle, which might have looked like a group hug to anyone but me, who couldn't imagine a *hug* as the sort of action those two girls would take.

As the footage ended, and Neil moved to grill Kat again, Christie seized the microphone from his hands. "Okay, people," she said to the world in general. "That's it. We've all had enough. Either there are going to be some big changes around here—or there's not going to be a show. Jean?"

Jean took the mike. "First off, this whole reality show thing is B.S. We're supposed to be here to *create,* and you can't do that when the only place you've got solitude is the toilet. Then there's the onsite production staff constantly trying to create drama, making everyone too friggin' anxious to do anything worthwhile. So: No more reality show or no more *Showcase* either."

The rest of the contestants cheered their approval. "Damn, Lyle, you're a psychic. Just a few hours ago you were preaching 'revolt.'"

"I guess Camus's Sisyphus never had the kind of leverage on his boulder Christie Squires has on this one."

It was something to see, live TV at its finest and most...well, unscripted. A YBC exec was hauled in, but with his negotiations with Christie being transmitted live, what else could he say but yes to the end of *The Pad,* yes to the end of the tote board, yes even to the end of the *Showcase* as a contest and its immediate reformatting as a...showcase. "For all of us to show off our talents," Christie said. "Not to fight one another for number one."

I was thrilled and disappointed at the same time. Damn, what shitty timing! If only I'd stuck it out another day, if only...

Lyle ruffled my hair. "You made the right decision. You knew it was the right decision at the time."

I sighed. "I know." Living with regret was another of those Serious things one has to do, I suppose.

Starting the next day, Lyle took a leave of absence from work. He *had* been gone a lot, and I was mighty grateful for this honeymoon. I cooked breakfast, then we bundled up well and walked across the bridge into Manhattan. We picked up a couple of (used) books at the Strand, then sat undisturbed and drank mochas in an out-of-the-way café. God bless New Yorkers, for whom your degree of fame is in direct proportion to the degree of effort they expend pretending not to know who you are.

Outside the café, I turned my cell back on and checked my messages. One was from Christie; I called her back.

"So now you know," she answered the phone. I'd FedExed Ronny's cell back to him; Christie had apparently figured out that it had been me who'd answered it the day before.

"Knowing and caring are worlds apart," I replied.

She laughed. "It's bound to come out sooner or later. I'm surprised it didn't when I had a camera on me 24/7."

"You could have stayed apart for two whole weeks, you know."

"Two weeks? Ha. Have you ever touched his skin?"

"Accidentally, yes. It's quite addictive."

"I want to thank you for...everything. Starting my career and all that. I'm dropping the suit tomorrow. It was Ronny's idea, just for the publicity, a way to go out on my own with a bang. I was never going to follow through on it."

My heart soared. "So you're not going to fight us for the money?"

"Nah. I just signed a thirty-million-dollar deal yesterday. Seems everyone wants a piece of the New Christie."

It's funny, I was kind of disappointed. One gift of bipolarity is the ability to adapt, to turn on a dime, to move 180 degrees from one certainty to another, as needed. I'd already gotten used to finding more economical joys in life, and now the cataract of cash would be back on again. It took all my energy to channel my frugal immigrant ancestors and remind myself that the real money would be in Christie's new stuff, not the part that I had a piece of, namely her back catalog. The cataract would dry up over time... I resolved to hire a financial manager to put me on an allowance. After all, more than anything, I had Lyle's good opinion to think about.

"There's another thing. Tonight's the last night of the *Showcase*. We all want you to come back for it."

"I..."

"It's just gonna be all of us jamming onstage, no pressure." Funny, only a month ago the idea of "jamming onstage," live, with a bunch of "us," would have filled me with horror. Funny, now, how the very idea warmed my cockles.

"I'd be delighted," I said.

I showed up at the studio in time for the last rehearsal of our opening number. I had to laugh when I saw the name of the song. I asked who wrote it.

"I started it," Sam said, battered but smiling. "But they wouldn't let me finish."

"Those bruises are not from last night," Jean said. "We roughed him up a bit this morning ourselves, to put him in his place."

Sam rolled his eyes, temporarily subdued by his pain meds. When we found ourselves alone for a moment he said, "Thanks."

"For what?"

"For giving a shit. For the Cassandra thing. Et cetera."

"You're welcome. I hope—" I cut myself off. "You're welcome."

He nodded. Then we were swept up in the group again; it was showtime.

All ten of us walked in a row toward the lip of the stage, hand in hand. The audience had made up its mind that getting surprised beat having any say in the outcome, and they cheered us wildly.

The music had been selected to deceive a bit; it was inspiring and uplifting, implying that we were about to cover an "Up With People" favorite. Then Christie stepped forward and sang the first verse:

There comes a time just before the curtain's fall
When we sing together as one
Our music was dying, so we lent ourselves a hand,
Together we'll stand together or fall

Then we all went into the chorus, which made it clear what song we were satirizing:

We are the weird, we are the nut jobs,
We're the dark ones who brighten up your day, so let's
    start singing

211

We're all dysfunctional here, each in our special way
And we can't make the songs you love unless you set us
    free!

I was named after one George Eliot character, but in that moment I felt I had more in common with another: Silas Marner, cranky shut-in, lured out into the light of fellowship by circumstance and the essential decency of those around him. (I wondered with a smile how Christie would react if I compared her to little Eppie—if she even knew who Eppie was. I wondered if they even taught that book in high school anymore; sentiment lightly dusted with symbolism probably hadn't survived the culture wars.) I wasn't going to become a social butterfly, it wasn't my nature, but for once I could see future social interactions as opportunities for cross-pollination, as opposed to nets in which I'd be caught and categorized.

The rest of the show featured solos and duets by the rest of the cast, with Kat getting the most applause. New York adores underdogs and drag queens; I had every confidence a bright future awaited her.

As Jean and I leaned against each other offstage, she asked me the question I hadn't dared ask myself out loud. "So what are you going to do now?"

So what was I going to do? Lyle would go back to work and I would have to find a way of "staying busy" unlike that practiced by rich housewives on the Upper East Side. The first thing I was going to do was get that "background" I needed, by learning how to actually read music and play an instrument. Maybe hire a voice coach, just to see if my pleasant voice could be tuned into something more.

But what after that? I wasn't worried, to be honest. I *just knew* that something was coming together, something would happen—both because I could feel it and because I was ready to work toward it. Thing is, when you're the creative type, working toward something is rarely a straight line—it's more like a wobbly spiral, as you circle erratically around...something. You know you're getting closer, but to what?

I know this might be a nice place to say something swirly about the Journey, but the fact is, no matter how well I medicate my condition I'll always have some delusions of affect. The Journey is all well and good, but it's the Reward at the end I have my eye on—I still need that whiff of glory to keep me plugging on.

I'm going to make it to the white-hot core of this new spiral, no matter how furiously I have to work to accommodate my internal spin. I'm serious.

Acknowledgments

I'd like to thank the following people for their support during the writing of this book: Michael Daines, MD; Mikey and Meshelle Shannon; my mother, Anna; my coworkers at Northern Nevada Hopes; and all the 431 Bros. All of the above have patiently and helpfully sat through many of my "flights of ideas," a number of which ended up in this book. I'd also like to thank someone I've never met, Kay Redfield Jamison, MD. Like Adam, I picked up her book *Touched With Fire* out of curiosity and found to my surprise that it answered many questions I had about my nature that I'd never thought would be answered. Any factual errors in this book are mine.